THE WOMAN IN THE WATER

Also by Charles Finch

The Last Enchantments

The Charles Lenox Series

A Beautiful Blue Death

The September Society

The Fleet Street Murders

A Stranger in Mayfair

A Burial at Sea

A Death in the Small Hours

An Old Betrayal

The Laws of Murder

Home by Nightfall

The Inheritance

THE WOMAN
IN THE WATER

Charles Finch

Minotaur Books ✻ New York

THE WOMAN IN THE WATER. Copyright © 2018 by Charles Finch. All rights reserved. Printed in the United States of America. For information, address St. Martin's Press, 175 Fifth Avenue, New York, N.Y. 10010.

www.minotaurbooks.com

The Library of Congress has cataloged the hardcover edition as follows:

Names: Finch, Charles (Charles B.), author.
Title: The woman in the water / Charles Finch.
Description: First edition. | New York : Minotaur Books, 2018. | Series:
    Charles Lenox mysteries ; 11
Identifiers: LCCN 2017050902 | ISBN 9781250139467 (hardcover) |
    ISBN 9781250139481 (ebook)
Subjects: LCSH: Lenox, Charles (Fictitious character)—Fiction. | Private
    investigators—England—London—Fiction. | Serial murder investigation—
    Fiction. | GSAFD: Mystery fiction. | Historical fiction.
Classification: LCC PS3606.I526 W66 2018 | DDC 813/.6—dc23
LC record available at https://lccn.loc.gov/2017050902

ISBN 978-1-250-13947-4 (trade paperback)

Our books may be purchased in bulk for promotional, educational, or business use. Please contact your local bookseller or the Macmillan Corporate and Premium Sales Department at 1-800-221-7945, extension 5442, or by email at MacmillanSpecialMarkets@macmillan.com.

First Minotaur Books Paperback Edition: January 2019

10 9 8 7 6 5 4 3

This book is dedicated to

Kate Lee,
Ben Sevier,
Charles Spicer,
and
Elisabeth Weed

with enormous gratitude

ACKNOWLEDGMENTS

This book exists because of the support, insight, and careful guidance of Charles Spicer and Andrew Martin, who inspired me to write a prequel to the Lenox books and then helped me make the idea a reality.

They're the tip of the spear, but so many of the amazing people in the Flatiron were instrumental in the existence of the book, from Sally Richardson to April Osborn to Martin Quinn to Sarah Melnyk to Hector DeJean to Paul Hochman to Kelley Ragland to Dori Weintraub to David Rotstein. All of them have my eternal affection.

Elisabeth Weed, Hallie Schaeffer, Dana Murphy, the Book Group: I know how lucky I am. That's all there is to say.

I had invaluable editorial insight from my mother for this book—besides which she is my mom, and just the best. Tim and Jenny Popp, along with their wonderful encouragement, gave me a place to work. So did the Ragdale Foundation, to which I am immensely indebted.

John Phillips named *The Woman in the Water*, and since I know he'll be reading it in roughly 2021: Hi! What is the future like? Say what's up to the gang for me. Thank you!

This has been a strange year. I have never been more thankful for the friends I've found on my Facebook page (who thought I would ever write that sentence!), facebook.com/charlesfinchauthor. Come and join us there if you want the best book recommendations, plus pictures of dogs and cats. Lots of dogs and cats.

Emily, Annabel, Lucy: really, nothing is for anybody but you.

THE WOMAN IN THE WATER

CHAPTER ONE

For a little more than an hour on that May morning in 1850, the only sound in the flat in St. James's Square was the rustling of newspapers, punctuated occasionally by the crisp shear of a pair of sharpened scissors through newsprint.

There were two men at the highly polished breakfast table by the window, three stories above street level. One was in an impeccable gray suit, the other in a ratty brown smoking jacket. Both were too intent upon their work to glance out from this high vantage at their panoramic view of the soft spring day: the shy sunlight; the irregular outlines of the two nearby parks, lying serene within the smoke and stone of the city; the new leaves upon the trees, making their innocent green way into life, on branches still so skinny that they quivered like the legs of a foal.

Finally Charles Lenox—the one in the smoking jacket—threw down the last of his newspapers.

"Ha! Done," he said. "You're as slow as a milk train, Graham."

There was a teapot on the table, and Lenox poured himself another cup from it, adding a spoonful of sugar from a small silver bowl. He took a satisfied bite from a piece of cinnamon toast whose existence he had previously forgotten, and which had been prepared by the discreetly well-dressed man sitting opposite him, his valet.

"It's not speed but quality of attention that matters, sir," Graham said. He didn't look up from his own newspaper, the second-to-last of a towering pile.

"What a lot of nonsense," replied Lenox, rising and stretching his arms out. "Anyway, I'll get dressed while you finish. How many have you got so far?"

"Nine, sir."

"Ten for me."

Graham's pile of clipped articles was much tidier than Lenox's. But he did look up now—as if tempted to say something less than entirely respectful—and then gave his familiar slight smile, shook his head, and resumed his study. He was a compact, sandy-haired person, with a face that was gentle and temperate but looked as if it could keep a secret.

There were few people Lenox cared for or trusted more.

When the young master of the house emerged again, he was changed out of his shabby jacket and into a handsome suit of his own, a heather gray two shades lighter than Graham's and perhaps thirty times as expensive. Such was life in England: Lenox had been born to a family of aristocrats, Graham to a family of tenant farmers. Yet they were true friends. Graham had been Lenox's scout throughout his three years at Balliol College, Oxford, and following Lenox's graduation seven months before had moved to London with him as his manservant—seven months, for Lenox, of exhilaration, missteps, uncertainty, and novelty.

Why? Because as his peers from Oxford were settling into the usual pursuits, Lenox was trying, against the better advice of nearly every soul he encountered, and so far with absolutely no success at all, to become something that did not exist: a private detective.

He was also, most unhappily, in love.

Graham was done now. "How many did you finish with?"

Lenox asked this question as he peered into an oval mirror and straightened his tie. He had a bright face, with a very short-clipped beard and light brown hair and eyes. He still did not quite believe himself to be an adult. But evidently he was, for he was the possessor of these airy and spacious rooms in the heart of Mayfair.

This one, large and central, had the atmosphere of a gentlemen's club. There were books scattered about it, comfortable armchairs, and handsome oil paintings on the wall, though the brightness of the sunlight in the windows made it feel less confined than most gentlemen's clubs. It also contained (to his knowledge) no slumbering gentlemen, whereas gentlemen's clubs generally did, in Lenox's experience. There were tokens here and there of his two great interests, besides detection, that was. These were travel and the world of Ancient Rome. There was a small—but authentic—bust of Marcus Aurelius tilted window-ward on one bookshelf, and everywhere were numerous stacks of maps, many of them much-marked and over-crossed with penciled itineraries, fantasies of adventure. Russia was his current preoccupation.

It was this room in which he spent all but his sleeping hours.

"Ten articles, sir," said Graham, who also spent a great deal of time here.

"Evens, then. Shall we go over them this afternoon?"

"By all means, sir."

Normally they would have compared their findings immediately. Graham—sharper than all but a few of the fellow students that Lenox had known at England's greatest university—had become his most valuable sounding board as he embarked on his new career. Every morning they each read the same set of papers and cut out the articles they thought were of any relevance, however oblique, to the matter of crime in London.

They rarely matched more than seven or eight of their selections. (Ten was about an average total.) Half the fun was in seeing where they hadn't overlapped. The other half was in the immense chronology of crime-related articles that Lenox, who was by nature a perfectionist, a completist, had managed so far to accumulate.

This morning he had an engagement, however, so they would have to wait to add to their archive.

Lenox donned a light overcoat. Graham saw him to the door. "A very happy birthday, Mr. Lenox, sir."

"Ah!" Lenox grinned. "I reckoned you'd forgot. Thank you, Graham, thank you very much. Are my gloves at hand?"

"In the pocket of your coat, sir."

Lenox patted his pockets and felt them. "So they are." Then he smiled. "At hand? Did you catch that?"

"Very good, sir."

"It was a pun. Gloves, hands."

Graham nodded seriously. "One of these retroactive puns you hear so much about, sir, conceived only during its accidental commission."

"On the contrary, very carefully plotted, and then executed flawlessly, which is what really counts."

He checked his tie in the mirror once more, and then left, bounding downstairs with the energy of a man who had youth, money, and the prospect before him that day of breakfast with an amiable party.

On the sidewalk, however, he hesitated. Something had stuck in his mind. Worth bothering about? Reluctantly, he decided that it was, yes.

He took the stairs back up two at a time. Graham was tidying away their breakfast, and looked up expectantly when Lenox entered. "Sir?"

"The one about the month 'anniversary'?" Lenox said. "You saw that?"

"Of course, sir."

Lenox nodded. "I assumed—but it was in that dishrag, the *Challenger*." This was one of the least reputable newspapers in England. "Still, if today's May second—pull out the clippings from April eighth to the thirteenth, say, would you? Perhaps even the seventh and the fourteenth, to be careful."

"By all means, sir."

Lenox felt better for having come back upstairs. The letter had bothered him. He touched his hat. "Obliged, Graham. Good luck with Mrs. Huggins. Just steer clear of her, I say."

Graham frowned. Mrs. Huggins was Lenox's housekeeper. Lenox neither wished to have nor enjoyed having a housekeeper, but his mother had insisted immovably upon her employment when he moved to London, and both Lenox and Graham were in the midst of dealing with the consequences of that rigidity. "Well—"

"No, I know. Close quarters. Anyhow I shall be back before long. Keep heart till then."

This time Lenox went downstairs and strode into the streets without turning back.

From St. James's Square he walked up Pall Mall, with its imposing row of private clubs. There was a scent of tobacco on the breeze. The sky was smoothing from white into a pure blue. No clouds.

He had been twenty-three for nine hours.

Rum, he thought. It felt a very advanced age. Yesterday, or thereabouts, he had been fourteen; then in a flash nineteen; tomorrow, no doubt, he would be white haired, his grandchildren (or the younger members of a gentlemen's club) ignoring him as he sat in his comfortable spot by the fire.

Ah, well, such was life.

The clip they had both taken from the *Challenger* that morning, May 2, remained on his mind as he walked. He had always had a very good recall, and the piece had been short. He was therefore able to run over it exactly in his mind, probing for points of softness, susceptibility.

Sirs,

It has been roughly a week shy of one month since I committed the perfect crime.

Perhaps in doing so I should have foreseen how little remark the press would make upon it, and how little progress the police make in solving it. Nevertheless it has been an anti-climax— especially as murder is a crime generally taken quite seriously (too seriously, if we are honest with ourselves about the numer- ousness and average intellectual capacity of our population) in our society—to witness how little comment my own small effort has aroused.

I therefore give you advance warning that I shall commit another perfect crime to mark this "anniversary." A second woman. It seems only just to my mind. Perhaps this declaration will excite the generally sluggish energies of England's press and police into action; though I place no great faith in the notion.

With regards,
A correspondent

Far and away the likeliest thing was that this letter was a fraud. An editor at the *Challenger* who needed to fill three inches of column. The second likeliest was that it was a hoax; the third likeliest was that it was a harmless delusion; far down the list, four or five spots, was the chance that someone had in fact committed a perfect crime a little less than a month earlier, and written to boast of it.

Four or five spots, though—not so far down the list, really, as to make it impossible. Lenox cast his mind back to the period three weeks or so before, which was populated with several crimes of interest.

Most of them solved, however. None of them perfect, either, that he could recall. But Graham would pull the clippings. And hadn't there been—?

But now Lenox found that he was turning up Singletary Street, which put him in sight of Rules. Soon he would be sitting next to Elizabeth. His heart began to beat a little more quickly, and as he opened the door of the restaurant where his elder brother had arranged a birthday breakfast for him, the letter slipped out of his mind.

CHAPTER TWO

Charles's brother, Edmund, who would one (hopefully distant) day be Sir Edmund Lenox, 11th Baronet of Markethouse, was his only sibling. They greeted each other with an affectionate handshake at the door of a comfortable paneled room. Beside Edmund was his young wife, Molly (Emily in more formal settings), who was pretty and countryish, not most at home in London.

"Happiest of birthdays, my dear fellow," Edmund said.

"Well, thank you."

"I remember when I was twenty-three."

"I would be worried if you couldn't remember three years ago."

"Halcyon days," said Edmund with mock rue.

Molly kissed him, laughing. "Happy birthday, Charles."

He kissed her back. "Thank you, my dear sister."

The two brothers looked similar, but Edmund was fuller in the shoulders than Charles, who was more naturally willowy, of good height but always reckoned taller than he was because of his slenderness.

They had grown up in the Sussex countryside—and those were, in truth, halcyon days; each of them a horse for his tenth birthday, swimming in the pond next to Lenox House during summers, long-standing family traditions at Christmas, two happy parents, on to Harrow (one of the nation's pair of great public schools) at thirteen, and then, like toppling dominoes, to the University of Oxford.

Lenox was at an age when his childhood felt at once very near and very far. So much had intervened between that tenth birthday and this twenty-third one, as if the former had happened either that morning or a hundred years ago. (His horse at Lenox House, Cinder, was fourteen now. Imagine that!)

In this room, coming across to greet him one by one with hearty handshakes as they noticed him, were representatives from the various phases of his life. Their amiable fat-jowled older cousin Homer Lenox was sipping a glass of warm negus by the fire, speaking to their aunt Martha, whom they had both loathed as children and now both rather liked. Lenox's particular friend from Harrow, Hugh Smith, strode over. There were Oxford friends, too, a part of Lenox's little set in London here. A happy small gathering, whose constituents, one would have said, bespoke a celebrant of exceptional good fortune. And the Lord knew it was true his life had been fluid, untroubled by larger worries, essentially without difficulties. He was deeply conscious of it.

Except that now he had made this queer decision to become a consulting detective.

Lenox knew, though he was determined to ignore the fact, that during these first seven months in London, he had become a joke. To think of it too much would have pained him, however. And among these twelve or so people, at any rate, he was yet loved.

Soon they were all seated, and he found himself next to Elizabeth. They had said a brief hello earlier, but now she turned to him with a face ready to be pleased, fingers running idly along a silver necklace she often wore.

"Well—tell me, Charles," she said, "are you going to see Obaysch?"

He gave her a look of consternation. "Not you, too."

She looked at him with reproach. "Don't be a curmudgeon."

"I?"

"Yes, you!"

He smiled. She was a pale-cheeked young woman of nineteen, in a blue dress, with lively dark eyes and white, even teeth. They were very close friends, perhaps even what you would call best friends.

She had been married for just more than three months now. In love, days into her first London season.

"I take it you've been, then?" he asked.

"Of course. He was quite a sight, the dear. Still just a baby."

Unconsciously she touched the spot where a gray ribbon encircled her dress; she must, Lenox thought, his reflex for observation never switched wholly off, have thought every day since her marriage of the quickening that would mean she was with child.

"From what I hear, he wallows a great deal."

"There are people of whom I could say the same," she said, looking at him dryly, and turned slightly away to take a spoonful of soup.

Lenox laughed. He picked up his own spoon. "I am never entirely certain how personal your comments are."

"Good," she said.

Their conversation was the same one happening all over the city, because at the London Zoo, just then, was the greatest commotion the metropolis had witnessed in many years, perhaps even since the Queen had introduced the city to Prince Albert. This Obaysch was what these natural philosophers had chosen to call, with straight faces apparently, a *hippopotamus*: the first in Europe since the time of the Romans, the first in England itself—well, ever, inasmuch as any learned person at the Royal Academy was able to discern. Ten thousand people (an enormous number, perhaps twenty times the average) were visiting the zoo each day to lay eyes on the creature.

He was a plump potato-shaped fellow, at least according to the illustrations Lenox had seen in the papers and the descriptions that even very exalted members of the aristocracy, who wouldn't deign to look at certain foreign royals but had visited the hippopotamus with breathless excitement, had provided him.

"What tricks does he do?" Lenox asked Elizabeth.

"Tricks!"

"Yes, tricks."

She looked appalled. "I don't know if you have fully grasped the dignity of this animal."

"Haven't I?"

She gave him a disappointed shake of her head. "Tricks, indeed."

Great ceremony had preceded the hippopotamus, which had traveled up the Nile with an entire herd of cattle to provide it milk, a troop led with pride by Sir Charles Augustus Murray, Her Majesty's consul to Egypt, who had enjoyed his triumph for less than a fortnight before finding his august reputation permanently sullied by the new nickname "Hippopotamus Murray." (No matter how admiringly he was addressed in this fashion, it seemed doubtful to Lenox that Murray could feel *quite* content with it, after such a long and distinguished nonhippopotamus-based career.) Now there were vendors selling little hippopotami figurines outside the zoo. The rulers on the Continent were sick with envy. Children played nothing but hippo in the streets.

The next step was to find Obaysch a mate, and the energies of many stout Englishmen in Egypt were no doubt being squandered on that project as Charles and Elizabeth ate their soup. (Even now Lenox always thought of his mother's nursery-era lesson in manners when there was soup at table: "Like ships upon the sea, I push my spoon away from me.")

"Anyhow," Elizabeth went on, "when I'm in the country there will be few enough spectacles. I ought to enjoy those in London while I can."

She was moving to her new husband's estate in the autumn, when his military regiment returned to England, to take up her rightful position as the wife of the heir to an earldom; second or third lady of the county.

That meant there were good works in her future, visits to the vicarage. Some glamour, too, to be sure—but as their friend Nellie had put it, country glamour. Because of her personal qualities, she deserved, in Lenox's estimation, both high position and high excitement. She would have only the former in her life beginning that autumn.

"You'll return often, I hope, however," said Lenox lightly, though his heart fluttered. He had never proposed. He felt a familiar dull pain at his lack of courage; he had missed his chance. Sometimes, late in the small hours of the night, he wondered if he had missed his only chance. "Your friends here will miss you."

She pushed back against the insinuation of his question slightly— at least in her posture, in her voice, a certain formality entering them, though never anything like unfriendliness. "Oh yes, I imagine, when James finds it necessary." She leaned forward slightly to address the young gentleman on Lenox's left; a third. "Hugh, have you seen the hippopotamus?"

Hugh gave them a scornful look. "Have I seen the hippopotamus. Haven't I seen the fellow six times?"

"Six!"

"I consider him more of a brother than a friend."

"Disgraceful," said Lenox.

"You're outnumbered," said Elizabeth. "This is a table that looks favorably upon Obaysch. Hugh and I won't hear a word against him."

Across from them, deep in conversation with Eleanor Arden, another of their set, was Lenox's aunt. He appealed to her as a last resort. "Aunt Martha," he said, and the table fell silent as she looked up. "Tell me that you, at least, haven't condescended to visit the London Zoo in the past two weeks. The old ways must still mean something."

She hesitated—a gray-haired and portly older woman, resplendent in a spangled dress of gold and red—and then said, "I must admit that I paused there yesterday." Everyone at the table burst into kind laughter. She gave the room a generalized look of indignation. "One likes to keep abreast, you know, even at my age."

When the soup had been cleared and there was a lull in the conversation, even the hippopotamus parts of it, Edmund stood up. He lifted his glass.

"What about a toast?" he said.

"Yes, yes," said one or two people, and lifted their glasses too.

"Charles moved to London in the fall, as you all know," said Edmund. "So far he has not been imprisoned, lost money in a three-shell game on the Strand, or eloped to the Continent with a dancer."

There was more laughter, and Lenox called out, "Give me six weeks."

"He has also," Edmund said with stout, awkwardly footed pride, "begun his very significant work as a detective—very significant work, very."

"Hear, hear," said Hugh.

"I am proud of him for it, and I think we ought to have a double toast to him for it. Join me, please. Two cheers for Charles."

As they cheered, Lenox felt himself blush, a little hollowness of embarrassment in his throat and chest. He would have preferred no reference to his work. But he accepted the toast—said thank you—all here loved him—the moment passed—and soon the conversation again became general.

It was beneath the station of all those present here to have a profession, unless it be politics, arms, or God. It had been many generations since the families of any of them had done work with their hands, season upon season, year upon year, century upon century.

A gentleman scientist, fine, or in an eccentric case an explorer, a collector, an equerry, a horse breeder.

But even the most eccentric of these would never have dreamed of taking work as a detective. England's caste system was too inflexible to allow for it. It was this fact that had poisoned Lenox's seven months here. Only unto illness, not death, and mostly for his poor parents; but still, still.

Making it worse was how desperately little headway he had made. He was laughed off in Scotland Yard (he had tried repeatedly to make allies there) and laughed off in a different kind of way at the parties—where he was still welcome, but more often than before because of his brother, or because of Elizabeth, Eleanor, Hugh, his friends. In the fullness of these seven months, he had had two cases, precisely. And this despite charging no fee! He had solved both: one a pitiably simple matter of a missing fiancé (he had an extant family in Bournemouth, unfortunately for the young woman who had entreated Lenox to find him so that she could marry him), and one an embezzler at a midsized firm in the city.

Both cases had been referred to him by friends. Neither had led to more work.

At the end of the breakfast, some two hours later, a great deal of it spent reminiscing over old village cricket matches with his cousin Homer, he found himself momentarily in a quiet corner of the room with Elizabeth, who was donning her overcoat.

She was due at a luncheon—straight from one meal to another, she said, and sheepishly added that when she was fat, she would have to feign an illness to avoid going out—and Lenox, putting his own cloak on, took the opportunity to ask how she had been, which parties she would be going to—

But suddenly, realizing that they were by the grace of chance briefly isolated from everyone else, he said, anxiously, "Listen here, do you think I'm a fool? About the detective business. Answer me honestly, Elizabeth—be brutal. Nobody else will. Nobody whose opinion I care for."

She gave the question a look of real surprise, and then shook her head, concern in her eyes. "Never, never, never," she said. She touched his cheek. "I think you are valiant as a lion, Charles. And wondrous affable."

Before he had a chance to reply, she had turned away to say her other goodbyes. For his part, he did not move for at least ten, fifteen seconds; he could still feel her hand on his cheek.

CHAPTER THREE

Lenox walked home. His path took him through Green Park, the quiet warmth of the sunlight falling through its trees. When he arrived, Graham met him at the door—uncanny, how he did that—and opened it, taking Lenox's gloves, hat, and jacket.

"A pleasant morning, I trust, sir?" he asked.

"Very pleasant, thank you," said Lenox. "Did you pull the newspaper clippings from April, by any chance?"

"I did, sir. They're in the sitting room, along with the papers we clipped this morning. I have cleared away everything else except the *Times*."

"Thank you."

"You also have a wire from Lenox House, sir."

"A wire?" Lenox frowned. "Let me see it, please. And bring me a cup of black coffee if you would."

He needed his mind sharp, and he had consented to a festive glass of hot brandy and spice at the end of breakfast. "Right away, sir," said Graham.

Loosening his tie a quarter inch, Lenox went and sat down at the round table by the window. He noticed from this higher vantage that the skies toward the east had darkened a little. It might well rain before long.

There were two neat stacks of paper at his chair. At the top of one was the telegram from home, with that morning's clippings beneath it, and at bottom the *Times*; then, next door, the thick stack of irregularly shaped April clippings pulled from the filing cabinet, dating from the window of time when this perfect criminal claimed to have committed his perfect murder.

The first thing Lenox did was open the wire. Letters from Sussex took only around thirty-six hours to arrive, so a telegram was relatively rare.

This one brought welcome news rather than bad, thankfully.

Bound for London tomorrow STOP *Wallace* STOP *Savoy as quick visit* STOP *arriving by 2:22* STOP *dinner Edmund's* STOP *will be by yours before to pick you up if you cannot come to me sooner* STOP *all love* STOP *Mother* STOP *oh and happy birthday my dear dear dear* STOP *Mother*

This telegram would have been impenetrable to most, but it was clear as a June sky to Lenox. What it indicated was that his mother was coming here to see the family's solicitor, Wallace; the family's town house, which they kept open from September to April, wasn't worth reopening for just a night or two, so she had taken a room at the Savoy; she would like to see Charles straight away, but understood that he might be occupied; the latest she would see him was in the hour before their family dinner at his brother's house, but perhaps he would come to the Savoy earlier if it was convenient.

He was pleased at the news. He had plans to visit Lenox House in a few weeks, for the first weekend of summer, but he and his mother were, as both his brother and father had observed, like a pair of old shoes. He composed a quick reply saying that he would meet her at

Charing Cross. Then he tore the wire in two and dropped it into the wastepaper basket.

That done, he turned his attention to the articles he and Graham had clipped from the morning's papers.

Nine of their ten selections had overlapped, a high number. Graham had noticed something he hadn't, however—a small article, four paragraphs, about a sailor who had failed to report for duty in Plymouth, a notable occurrence only because he was a generally very reliable hand, a bo'sun with nine years aboard the *Culloway* who had never before failed to report.

Lenox wondered why he had missed it, then realized, looking at Graham's careful notation, that it was because it had been on a page with a larger story, about a crime in the West End. He twisted his lip in disappointment at himself.

On the other hand, it meant that he had spotted one article that Graham hadn't.

He looked to see which—ah, the dog thefts in Parkham Court. No, Graham wouldn't have considered that notable (dog theft was very common), but Lenox liked anything strange, anything aslant of common experience. In this case, slight differences: These dogs were all domestic, some of them quite doted upon. *That* was rather out of the ordinary run of things. The clipping would go in today's file, and he would remember it as he tried to weave, in his mind, thread by slender thread, a tapestry that contained a full picture of this great city's crime. Each article they cut out was another thread, its own unique shade. The names of streets as they recurred, which neighborhoods saw which types of crimes, the first and second and third most common ways thieves were caught.

He wanted to know all of it; he was young and ambitious, and very certainly determined to know all of it.

Graham returned with a cup of coffee on a silver tray. Lenox thanked him and, taking a sip, leaned back in his chair. The rain had just started, light and steady. He gazed through the window for a moment.

Then he looked up. "Well, Graham," he said, "what about this perfect crime? The letter from the *Challenger*?"

"I was not able to make a connection based upon the articles from April, sir. Perhaps you will perceive something that I have not, however." Graham reached down and arranged the array of clippings that was on the table from one month previous, seventeen in all. "The single prominent murder was the Singley one, sir."

"That," Lenox said distractedly.

The Singley case had been solved immediately; half a dozen witnesses who had seen a baker in Bromley beat his next-door neighbor on the street over a matter of honor. The neighbor had lingered thirty hours on this side of the veil before succumbing (the papers never used any other word) to his injuries.

Lenox skimmed the remaining clippings. None of them recorded anything close to as memorable as an unsolved murder.

"Very little in that period, sir, as you can see," said Graham.

Lenox leaned back, thinking. "Hm."

"Perhaps it really was a perfect murder, sir. Entirely unremarked, thought to be a natural death even."

"Interesting." Lenox sighed. "Or else of course it's the editor of this reckless newspaper stirring the pot, hoping to give everyone a fright."

"A likelier possibility, no doubt, sir."

Lenox was unsure. There had been something just authentic about the letter, something sinister. On the other hand, he might have been willing that into existence, since he was desperate for work to do. "Ah well."

Then he remembered something, though.

What was it? He narrowed his eyes, thinking.

It was the Singley manslaughter that had called it to mind. There had been something else around that time, something—

He jumped out of his chair, pushing it back. "Graham!"

"Sir?" said Graham.

But Lenox, wasting no time on a reply, hurried across the room to the filing cabinet. "The letter was printed today, May second," he said, riffling through papers quickly. "But that doesn't mean it was sent yesterday. We have no idea when it was sent. There was no date on it."

"Sir?"

"We may have pulled the articles from the wrong time, since we assumed it was *sent* yesterday, sheerly because it was printed today. Yes, look."

Graham leaned over Lenox's shoulder. "What is it, sir?"

Lenox held up a clipping, waving it in his gripped hand. "March the twenty-ninth. Here it is. We both clipped it. Of course, given the circumstances. Walnut Island."

Graham's eyebrows rose. "Walnut Island."

Lenox nodded grimly. "If the letter is referring to this, it means we are already three days past the date the letter was sent, perhaps longer."

The meaning of this dawned on Graham. "Oh no."

"Yes. If any of this is real, a second murder may be committed at any moment. Come, get your jacket, Graham, and I'll pull all the files on Walnut Island. We must fly."

CHAPTER FOUR

The offices of the rag known as the *Challenger* lay toward the cheap end of Fleet Street. Every English newspaper was quartered along this avenue, high and low; this was low. The better class of newspaper inhabited the other end of the Fleet, which was so ancient that it had been a principal route through Roman London.

Graham and Lenox alighted from a hansom cab at Ludgate Circus at a little after three o'clock. The *Challenger* was housed in a two-story building that tilted slightly left and no doubt gave a tremendous amount of business to the adjacent Ludgate Arms, a pub with a low, skulking, treacherous look to it. Despite stiff competition, journalism was probably the best-lubricated profession in the city.

NEW-MADE PIES, the pub advertised in its window.

"Interesting choice a half block from the home of Sweeney Todd," Lenox said, pointing toward the words.

This character, the villain of a penny dreadful called *The String of Pearls*, was most vivid in Londoners' minds at the moment, despite being fictional. More than three-quarters of people in a recent newspaper poll had believed him to be real.

"Intentional, perhaps," said Graham quietly in reply.

"Good point."

Lenox knocked at the door, Graham a step behind and a step to the side of him.

A porter answered. "Yes?"

Lenox held out a half-shilling. "Here to see the editor."

The coin vanished so quickly that it might have been a street trick. The door opened a tick wider. "Up, right, up, left."

They followed these directions, and were soon entering a large room filled with a surprisingly healthy glow of sunlight. The *Challenger* was a paper for the masses, but evidently the pennies of the masses added up; the building wasn't much to look at, but here inside all the desks were handsome, and the men seated at them wore natty suits as they churned out their copy, shouting to each other across the room, paper littered everywhere.

"Is the editor here?" Lenox asked of a random fellow with greasy dark hair tucked behind his ears.

He pointed at a door. "But you won't sell him anything, guv. He's bought it all and sold it for twice what he paid already."

"Thanks. I'm buying, not selling," said Lenox.

"Watch your pockets then."

The door of this lone private office was ajar. Outside sat a woman. Lenox smiled at her and handed over his card. It said CHARLES LENOX on one line, then an address on the next. (He hadn't been able to bring himself to add the words PRIVATE INVESTIGATOR between the two.) It was very plainly an expensive object, the address equally plainly an expensive one, and she sat up straighter.

"I would very much value three or four minutes of Mr. Kennington's time," Lenox said.

"Mr.—are you an acquaintance of Mr. Kennington?"

Lenox, his eyes always moving, had noticed the name on the masthead of an open copy of the *Challenger* they had passed. "He'll want to see us."

She hesitated, but a Briton could nearly always be counted upon to pay obeisance to class, and she said, rising, "Follow me."

A bulldog-looking person behind an absolutely enormous desk, a desk the size of many maids' bedrooms in London, glanced up as they entered. "Who's this?"

"This is Mr. Charles Lenox," the woman said. "And—sir?"

"Oh, only his valet, madam," Graham said, with a hard *t*.

"Valet," repeated Kennington. He accepted the card from his secretary. Between the valet and the card, he was as impressed as the secretary, ready to give them a moment. "I see. What is it that brings you across town, Mr. Lenox?"

From more salubrious precincts—was implied.

Lenox handed over the clipping of the letter about the perfect crime. "We're here about this letter."

Kennington looked at it briefly and handed it back. "Well?"

"Is it real?"

Kennington got a cautious look on his face. "It is, as it happens."

"Might we ask how it came into your possession?"

He glanced at his pocket watch. "Miss Adams, fetch the cart of incoming letters."

The secretary left. "Does that mean you still have it?" Lenox asked.

"Should do."

There was a silence. "It's a handsome office," said Lenox.

"What's your concern with the letter?"

"Ah." He had been ready for that question. "There is a family whose son has disappeared. No doubt gambling in Monaco, but we have promised to follow every lead."

Kennington frowned. The valet and that explanation didn't add up. "You're doing this for money?"

Lenox shook his head. "No, not at all. Just curiosity. I've always been interested in crime. Take them as they come. I assisted late last year on the Marbury case."

This was a curious matter of some six months before, tangentially involving a friend, which Lenox had helped solve by slipping information anonymously to the Yard. (Now he wished he had done it in person.) It was the case he thought of as his "first," even though he hadn't been the primary detective. It was after Marbury that he had decided once and for all to follow his instinct and pursue this line of work; after Marbury that he and Graham had begun clipping the newspapers.

The editor's curiosity was evidently satisfied by this explanation. "I was in gutta-percha for a while, myself, then rubber. Bought this thing last year. Circulation has doubled. We'll be moving up the street in the next year or so."

Lenox raised his eyebrows. "Congratulations."

"Bloody stories and tearjerkers—that's what people want, you know."

"I don't think there's any question about that."

"Easier than gutta-percha. Ships sink." He paused. "You're very young."

"I thank you."

Kennington laughed and pointed at Graham, though he had barely appeared to notice him. "Anyhow, you'd have to walk awhile to find the man who's going to fool this valet of yours. I'll just tell you that for free, since you aristocrats never know anything yourselves. But I've looked into a few faces in my day."

Just then Miss Adams came into the room, pushing a file box on wheels. It appeared that the *Challenger* kept thorough records. It wasn't what Lenox would have expected.

Thorough, and thoroughly organized, too. Within just a moment, Kennington had found the letter.

He held it out and then, as Lenox reached to take it, pulled it back. "A trade."

"A trade?"

"One story. A crime story. Put me onto it sometime. In the next month or two, say."

Lenox thought, and then nodded. "I accept your terms."

"Word as a gentleman?"

Graham no doubt noticed the way that Lenox's posture stiffened slightly—the anger he felt at the question even being posed—but Kennington and Miss Adams would have missed it. Lenox nodded once more. "Yes, you have my word as a gentleman."

Kennington nodded in turn at the deal he'd struck, then passed the letter to Lenox. "It arrived four days ago, I believe."

Four days!

That was a piece of absolutely crucial information. Also a frightening one.

Lenox did some quick calculations. He had reckoned that the one-month "anniversary" referred to in the letter would be four or five days off, at the earliest, May 7 perhaps—today being the second.

But it might be much, much sooner. It might be this very day.

The idea chilled his blood. "You waited to publish it?" Lenox asked.

"Figured the fellow for a crank. Still do, but we had a few spare column inches to fill, and it's excited a fair bit of reader interest. We'll probably run a follow-up head on it in the next day or two."

"How did the letter arrive?"

"Miss Adams?" Kennington said.

Evidently the secretary was responsible for such matters. "Unstamped, under our door, sir, in the middle of the night. Must have been very late, as we don't generally print until three. Between four and six, nobody is in the building."

Lenox nodded. "Thank you."

"Not at all, sir."

"Is there a spare desk where we could look the letter over?"

Kennington said there was. "Miss Adams will show you. Don't forget my crime story, Mr. Lenox. Goodbye, valet."

A moment later, Lenox and Graham were at an empty table in the newspaper's main room, both standing, leaning over to stare at the thrice-folded letter and the small blue envelope it had arrived in. Miss Adams had left them to their own devices.

The text was identical to that which the *Challenger* had printed. "Cheap paper," Lenox noted.

"Perhaps for anonymity," Graham suggested.

Lenox shook his head. "No. Because it's a cheap pen, too."

"Can you tell, sir?" Graham asked.

Lenox pointed. "Look how often he has had to go back to his inkwell. The splotches come every other word, almost. One of those metal nibs that are a dozen-a-penny. The ink's no good either."

"I see."

Lenox frowned. "Admirable penmanship, however."

"Yes, indeed, sir."

"And you see the other clue that goes along with admirable penmanship, of course."

"Sir?" said Graham.

Lenox, all of his twenty-three, was not free of arrogance, the undergraduate vice. "Come, you can see here, Graham, where he has erased his pencil lines. Faint but distinct. Beneath each line of the letter."

Now Graham frowned. "I cannot see the significance of that, sir."

"Oh. Oh." In what he hoped was a delicate way, Lenox said, "We never had lines beneath our—we were smacked on the hand if we wrote crookedly, at Harrow, with the chalk. In its chalk-holder, a great long wooden rod. I can still feel it."

"Sir?"

Lenox elaborated. "Well, it's only at the free schools that one is taught to write line upon line."

"Is it, sir?"

"I think because it is considered useful if your field is clerking." Lenox thought back to his lessons. "A gentleman's writing mustn't be too—too perfect, you see."

"Ah. Yes, sir," said Graham. "I see."

His face remained impassive. He was a fellow, Lenox's valet—or butler, perhaps, if you wished to use the slightly grander word—who learned from every direction, indiscriminately, his mind as sharp as the head of a newly fledged arrow. He would absorb this piece of information as he had every other one (that asparagus was eaten with the fingers, for instance, that one said "sofa," not "settee") and store it away forever.

Lenox felt a twinge of guilt. He smoothed the paper under his hand. "I think we have a picture of our man, at least," he said.

"Sir?" said Graham.

"Come, we'll discuss it in the hansom. We must go to Scotland Yard as quickly as possible. If the writer of the letter keeps his promise, they'll have only a day to prevent a murder. Not five or six, as I'd thought. It may even be a matter of hours."

"Yes, sir."

Lenox shook his head grimly. "It's bad, very bad, that we are the first to follow up. If the Yard cannot solve the matter, we may only hope that the next murder is not so brutal or random as the one at Walnut Island."

CHAPTER FIVE

Walnut Island—that was the case described in the clippings that Lenox had pulled from their oak filing cabinet in St. James's Square before they left for the *Challenger*.

The six articles were spread from across three days: three on the first, April 5; two on the second; and one on the third, only the *Telegraph* pursuing the story into the morning hours of April 7.

It had perhaps passed through the newspapers so quickly because, despite having several sensational elements, it had produced no clues, no leads, no identifications: nothing to add to the splashy first accounts.

Did that make it a perfect crime?

The most reliable of the three newspapers that had reported on the matter was the *Times*. Their piece had appeared on the first page of the densely typeset newspaper, datelined to London.

Thames Mystery

———

Inspectors Sinex and Exeter charged with investigation

———

Identification considered difficult; public assistance sought

———

The body of a woman was found early Thursday morning by Jacob A. Schoemaker, charman of Randall House, a residence situated upon the small islet near Twickenham known locally as Walnut Island. Schoemaker reported to police that he had discovered a sailor's trunk among the rushes near the island's east end, heavily sodden, apparently fetched there by the tide.

The trunk was clasped but not locked. Inside was the body of a woman, estimated in age as being between 20 and 40. The trunk had no identifying marks and the body was unclothed. The cause of death was strangulation. The deceased had long black hair, a prominent brow, and well-kept teeth, according to Inspector Sinex of Scotland Yard.

These and other details match no known missing person for whom the London police are actively searching, Sinex confirmed to the Times.

He added that the Yard is pursuing several promising leads. Inspectors Sinex and Exeter will jointly handle the matter going forward.

Descriptions matching those of the deceased may be forwarded either to the Times or to Scotland Yard. No statement was released by Sir Winston Kellogg, owner of Randall House, previously home to the Randall family. Sir Winston and his family are presently in Scotland.

No reward has thus far been offered.

"'Several promising leads,'" Lenox quoted angrily as he and Graham read over the article together again, heads huddled, on the way to the Yard.

It was a fairly common kind of article. London had birthed babies and buried bodies beyond counting since its foundation. Once every two or three days, it produced an unidentified corpse. Some of these corpses caught the public imagination, but few of those that involved foul play were ever solved.

On the other hand, this was the body of a young, or relatively young, woman, which was the sort the press liked to dramatize. The mention of her teeth was also a subtle indication that perhaps the police believed her to be wellborn—not a prostitute, that is, the most usual victim of violent crimes, alas.

There was also something macabre in her discovery on Walnut Island that might easily have stimulated the public imagination. It hadn't caught, however—it just hadn't. So it went.

The other five articles offered variants of the same information, none so thorough as the *Times*. The final one, in the *Telegraph,* volunteered only that Inspectors Sinex and Exeter had fielded several public visits.

Before their visit to Mr. Kennington at the *Challenger,* Lenox and Graham had combed carefully through their files from the week preceding and following March 2. There were numerous crimes contained across these 150-odd articles, including a dozen murders, but most of them had been solved, and only one other, an odd stabbing in Romford, presented features of unusual interest.

In their hansom cab on the way to the Yard, Lenox said, thoughtfully, "April fifth. A sailor's trunk is buoyant. So we may assume that it was floated down the Thames—in other words, would not need to have been dropped anywhere near the island. In fact, could have floated for days before it arrived at Walnut Island."

"Indeed, sir."

"On the other hand, such a trunk floating downriver wouldn't be likely to survive the small fry for longer than a quarter of an hour."

There were hundreds of skiffs and other flat-bottomed boats, perhaps thousands, that floated daily upon the Thames, serving every purpose imaginable. Some ferried sailors between the huge corvettes and brigs anchored near the docks. Some sold meat pies, rum, blue pictures, newspapers, anything of imaginable interest to these same sailors. Some were after river fish.

Some were merely pickers—trawling the great waterway, scavenging what they could sell, down to paper at a halfpenny per ten pounds.

"Perhaps that indicates that it was placed in the river the night before, sir. Darkness would have given the murderer cover, and the trunk a better chance of remaining undiscovered."

Lenox nodded. "My thought too."

"After midnight best of all, sir."

"Our fellow is a nocturnal soul. Slipping letters under doors at four in the morning, dropping trunks in the river after dark. Very well, then. It is dawn of April fifth that Mr. Schoemaker discovers the body."

They looked at each other, both knowing what this meant. Lenox felt sick.

"Yes, sir."

"Today is the second of May. Which means that the anniversary of the murder itself could well be tomorrow."

"At the latest, the next day, sir."

A second victim might already be dead, Lenox thought. "Yes."

"Optimistically, we could hope that it was the early morning of April fifth, sir," Graham said. "The trunk might have floated only a very short while."

Lenox nodded soberly. "Yes."

But in his heart he knew there was every chance they were already too far behind. He had never worked on a murder, and the stakes felt too high, too high.

Their hansom stalled, and Graham peered out through the window. "Two carriages stuck, passing too close, sir," he said.

Lenox pulled his notepad from his breast pocket, forcing himself to slow down and think. "Who is the murderer, Graham?" he said. "Let us assume that the letter is real—let us assume that the Walnut Island trunk is his perfect crime—who is he?"

Graham, who had been looking at the mix-up in traffic, turned his attention back to Lenox. "Why, it could be anyone in the world, sir," he said.

Lenox, brow dark, shook his head. "No, that's quite incorrect."

"Well, in London, I mean to say, sir, anyone in—"

"No," said Lenox again, forcefully. "We know a great deal." He looked through the window, and then said, under his breath, "Move, damn it all, move."

Their only hope was getting to the Yard as quickly as possible and forcing someone there to listen to them.

He tried not to think at all the jollity they had had at his expense in the last seven months—a relationship he had hoped at first might be collegial, then at least neutral, but which had proved more comic, to the inspectors there, than anything else.

Partly his own fault. If he wanted to be one of them badly enough, he would have applied for a job there. But his family could never, ever have countenanced that—and nor could he have, in fact. That was the shameful truth, that his pride came before his desire to work. So that he had become a running joke among the inspectors of the Yard, even the constables, all of whom could no doubt intuit his condescension; the gentleman detective who hung around the building, hoping to catch word of some crime he could poke his unwelcome nose into.

They would have to listen to him now. That was all there was.

"What more is it that we know about this criminal that I have missed, sir?" Graham asked curiously.

Lenox inhaled deeply. "Well. We have two sets of facts from which we may draw conclusions. The contents of the letter, and the physical object itself, which Mr. Kennington was kind enough to show us. If only he had run it earlier, a great—but anyhow."

"Sir," said Graham.

Suddenly the hansom lurched forward. They both looked through the window—the traffic had cleared. Fifteen minutes to the Yard, twelve with a rub of luck.

Lenox went on. "The question becomes where the two things line up, the letter and the letter. Leave the trunk to the side for a moment. Every letter sent in the history of the world could be traced to a single author, of course, were we only brilliant enough to untangle its minutely telling signatures. Each of us leaves a dozen on any random note of thanks, I've no doubt.

"As it is, we can do a rough job." He took that morning's clipping from the *Challenger* out of his breast pocket. "Examine the language: I would characterize it in the main as—what is the exact word? Pretentious, I suppose. And more dangerously, in my experience, grandiose as well. Take this line, about how murder is treated in England. 'Too seriously, if we are honest with ourselves about the numerousness and average intellectual capacity of our population.' Then there is the false modesty of 'my own small effort.'

"Look at the pride in that line, too. 'The generally sluggish energies of England's press and police.' In the signature, further false modesty—'A correspondent.'"

"The picture seems clear enough to me."

"A pretentious person, sir, then," said Graham.

"Even more than that. The author of this letter thinks himself far, far above the average run of man. That is confirmed, of course, by the letter's leading piece of superciliousness—this claim about a perfect crime, that he has committed a perfect crime, and will commit another.

"But lay that against the letter *itself*. Cheap paper. Cheap ink. Pencil lines erased underneath his lettering. That peculiarly admirable penmanship—I would reckon there was a prize for that at some moment in this fellow's past, perhaps second prize for penmanship in his free school, a Latin primer the prize, handed to him by someone he disdained—a minor cleric at prize-giving day, you know the kind of thing."

Lenox was gaining steam. "Because he has had hatred in his heart for a long time, our murderer. That is who we are looking for: a man of very high intelligence, very low station, and very, very great anger, Graham." Lenox shook his head, and speaking almost to himself, added, "It is a dangerous, murderously dangerous combination, that."

Graham tapped the window. "We're here, sir."

CHAPTER SIX

From the year 843 (and imagine such a year existing, sounding as modern to the ears of its chronological inhabitants as 1850 did to the chronological inhabitants of this time!) to the year of 1707, Scotland was a kingdom unto itself.

Its interests were of course entwined with England's; its fate in war often allied; its sovereignty in regard to its more powerful cousin intermittently stronger and weaker. Nevertheless, for the entirety of that period, it was the Kingdom of Scotland.

Whenever that kingdom had sent emissaries to London, whether for black-eyed negotiation or for amicable meeting, those Scotsmen had by immemorial custom stayed in a small street just behind Whitehall. Over time it had become known, first casually, then more formally, as Scotland Street; then Great Scotland Street; then, through some final invisible passage of linguistic habit by its neighbors, Scotland Yard.

A house here, backing onto 4 Whitehall Place, was the home of London's police.

It was a large private house, though in truth not larger than many fine townhouses in Mayfair. It looked in no wise like a government building—no imposing stone, nor black wrought iron. It might have been the domicile of a prosperous banker. Candles flickered in its windows.

It could remain so relatively small because the Metropolitan Police, while a large force taken all in all—many hundreds of constables were scattered around the city—had only a few members who worked from headquarters. The beats of the rest ranged across London's vastness; when they took prisoners, they usually transported them directly to the jails.

Therefore Scotland Yard (as it had come to be called as shorthand, for whatever mysterious reason, rather than Whitehall Place) could continue to reside in this small, quiet, official building with the presence of a quiet unofficial one.

A fat gooseberry-cheeked porter was seated just outside in a small booth as Lenox and Graham's cab pulled up.

Lenox sighed. "Sherman."

The porter let a laugh out from his gut as Lenox stepped down from the carriage. "Why, it's our young Lord Inspector!"

Lenox remained stone-faced. He nodded. "Mr. Sherman." The mockery of the building's inspectors—those who deployed the constables, and looked into more serious crimes—had given license for the very lowest fellow to mock him. So be it. He had business today. "Please be good enough to pass my card to Sir Richard."

The smile fell from Sherman's face. "Sir Richard."

Lenox was holding the card in an extended hand; Graham, behind him, was paying the taxi. "Yes."

"Why?"

Lenox declined even to answer this question from a bullying, gloating specimen like Sherman. He merely held the card out. At last Sherman took it, hefted his great bulk up from his stool, and went inside.

A peculiarity of Lenox's position was that he could not command even a moment of the time of Inspector Field, for instance, the most famous of the detectives who worked here, but that he could quite easily demand to see Sir Richard Mayne. This was the aristocratic head of Scotland Yard, by full title Commissioner of Police of the Metropolis.

Mayne had been born in the previous century but was modern, forward-thinking, and bright. Lenox would have liked to pick his brain at length, but had quite intentionally refused to use his name (his father's name, in truth) to meet with Mayne more than a single initial time.

This was because of his father's attitude toward Lenox's choice; one of the most unpleasant conversations of his life (he still thought of it every day, without fail) had been not long after he went down from Oxford.

"What do you mean to do?" his father had asked.

Lenox had explained that there were two things that most truly interested him, crime and travel. His father—not a voluble man—had merely looked at him for several moments. "And you mean to pursue one of these as a *career*?" he had asked finally.

"Yes," Charles had replied.

His father had been silent for a moment, and then, turning away, had said, in a voice of awful quietness, "How very unexpected."

They hadn't spoken of it again.

Lenox understood, in a way. His family had since time immemorial served England—either in the army or in Parliament—and it had been the iron lesson of their youth that in some fashion he and Edmund would do the same. Still the words had stung him. He had gone to his mother, who had smoothed Edward Lenox's censure to her son, partly persuaded him that it was only the reaction of a moment.

She had also told him to go and see Mayne. His father would never deny the introduction, whatever his disappointment in Charles's choices, she said. She had proved correct.

In the meeting that resulted, Mayne had been gracious, respectful, and essentially discouraging, believing, in all likelihood, that

Lenox was only a dilettante. Well; it was the sensible reaction, no doubt. There was as yet no proof that he wasn't. Lenox had left the meeting determined to offer that proof in the fullness of time.

After a moment, a sharp-dressed young clerk emerged with Sherman, nodded civilly to Lenox, and asked him inside. Sherman followed Lenox and Graham's entrance with an evil eye.

Mayne had a spacious office on the highest floor of the building. The clerk, who had introduced himself as Wilkinson, ushered Lenox inside; Graham waited without. No need here for a valet with a hard *t* to make an impression.

Mayne, who despite his modern ways wore long dark hair in the fashion of around 1822 and breeches rather than trousers, rose, and with a civility equal to his clerk's said, "How do you do, Mr. Lenox?"

"You are very kind to grant me a moment, Sir Richard."

Mayne gestured to a chair. "Please, sit." There was a pair of service pistols in a green velvet-lined case on his desk, decorative, as well as a silver inkstand and a desk calendar. On the wall there was an oil of their young Queen and a portrait of Sir Robert Peel, who had founded the very first police force in the city not twenty-five years earlier. "How may I help you?"

"In truth, Sir Richard, I think this a matter more suited to one of your inspectors than to yourself—knowing that your time is occupied with matters of serious administration and politics—and yet I feared I might not be able to gain their attention quickly enough for so urgent a matter."

Mayne's face remained impassive, but Lenox felt—rightly or wrongly—that the commissioner knew his inspectors made sport of the young interloper. He reddened. "Please go on," Mayne said.

Lenox passed across two clippings. One was the letter from the *Challenger*, the other the description of the Walnut Island murder taken from the *Times*. "As a means of educating myself, I am developing an archive of articles from daily papers relating to London crime." Mayne looked up, his lower lip protruding just fractionally in acknowledgment of this commitment. "I fear these two may be related."

Mayne read them slowly and deliberately. At last he held one up. "This is from the *Challenger*."

Lenox was impressed that he recognized the typeset. "Yes, sir, which might justifiably arouse your skepticism. But I took the liberty of visiting their offices. I was able to see the original letter there. It wasn't written by an editor. It may be a hoax, but in conjunction with the—"

Mayne shook his head. "No, we have been vexed by the Walnut Island matter. I have, personally." He touched a bell underneath his desk, and within what seemed a vanishing second, his clerk, Wilkinson, appeared. "Fetch the inspector on duty downstairs," Mayne said.

"Directly, sir," said Wilkinson, and withdrew.

"Thank you very much for bringing this to my attention," said Mayne to Lenox.

"Of course, Sir Richard." He paused. "I had hopes that I might pursue—having put these pieces together—that I might—"

"Do you have any additional information?"

He nearly answered that he did not, but then, decided not to waste his moment. "The letter itself presented some interesting features."

"Did it?"

Lenox explained, laying out his conjecture about the character of the man who had written it.

Just as he was finishing, the door opened again. Lenox—sitting slightly at an angle to his interlocutor—saw that it was Wilkinson, trailed by a tall, beefy, bristle-mustached young man with a hard brow and distrustful eyes.

Lenox's heart sank—it was Exeter.

He followed the work of the Yard closely, and of all the inspectors there, it was Exeter he held in the lowest regard, or perhaps just above a certain Inspector Columbus, an outright dipsomaniac. The best you could say of Exeter was that he was fairly often sober.

"Mr. Lenox, if you will be so good as to tell Inspector Exeter what you have told me, I would be exceedingly obliged. He will take you downstairs." Mayne rose, and shook hands with Lenox. "You have our sincere thanks. Please don't hesitate to call upon me again should anything similar arise—a very sharp eye, to connect the two."

"You noted the date, of course, Sir Richard," Lenox said, hating the rather high desperation in his own voice. "How close the next crime might be."

Mayne nodded. "Yes, I did. Wilkinson, find out where Sinex is working today. Exeter—take Lenox to the tearoom and make good use of his time. Consult with Sinex when he has been tracked down."

Lenox recalled that it was Exeter and Sinex who were jointly responsible for Walnut Island. "Very good, sir."

Wilkinson left. Mayne, having remained standing, left Lenox no choice but to bow slightly and say goodbye, adding his thanks again.

When they were outside the office, Graham, seated in a leather chair and reading from a thrice-folded journal that instantaneously disappeared into his inner breast pocket, rose.

Exeter sighed heavily. "Follow me."

They went to the tearoom—as ordered to—and there poured themselves cups of tea out of a great silver urn, each taking a thick white porcelain cup from the stacks of them. When they were seated at a small table, Lenox and Graham told Exeter the tale of their day, while the latter took notes, making a thorough job of it, which meant his very obvious skepticism was evidently not enough to surmount his awe of Sir Richard Mayne.

The tea was good. Resentment suffused every moment of the audience he was granting them, however.

"All but one time in a hundred, a letter like this is a hoax," he said when they were finished, setting down his pen, his tone bored in the extreme. "We get them all the time."

Lenox was tempted to say that there probably hadn't been a hundred letters "like this" in the papers in either of their lifetimes. It had some uncanny ring of truth—the erased pencil lines, the superciliousness.

Perhaps it was this that convinced Lenox that he was right—the superciliousness. There was a certain kind of criminal whose madness took in part the form of an injured sense of unrecognized brilliance.

"May we look at the trunk from Walnut Island?" Lenox asked, a throw of the dice.

"Out of the question." Exeter closed his notebook with a smack and stood up. "I'll pass this information on to Inspector Sinex. In the meanwhile, please feel free to finish your tea at your leisure. Have another cup if you like."

Exeter left the room. At the very least, Lenox thought, it would be clear to two of the Yard's two-dozen-odd inspectors that Lenox had the ear of Sir Richard Mayne.

Graham looked at him expectantly.

"Right," said Lenox, swallowing the last of his tea and standing up. "There's not much we can do, it appears, but we can try."

"Very good, sir," said Graham, standing too.

Lenox took heart from his steadfastness. "We'll have to split up."

This they did. First they walked down Whitehall, making their plans, and then they went off separately, prepared to attack the case.

They were both active late into the night, checking in periodically at prearranged times at Hungerford Bridge to exchange information.

Graham spent his time interviewing—he had a real gift for this type of work, his accent blending into whatever conversation he was having, his face somehow eliciting trust automatically, a marvel in that respect—the pilots of the small craft around this area. Lenox, meanwhile, went to the island itself, where he interviewed the man who had found the trunk.

There were few useful details here, though, and at their last meeting at Hungerford Bridge, it was difficult not to let his despair show to Graham.

It was eleven o'clock. Many hours had passed with nothing to show. The city was dark, murky, the streets unsavory. Both were exhausted. They stopped at a window and Lenox—famished—ordered them a pair of roast beef sandwiches and a jug of claret.

They ate these standing. Lenox felt slightly better when this was done. Graham had spoken to dozens of people, and come up empty. The best he could say was that there was a certain dock—Woodbridge Dock—that extended rather farther into the depths of the river than most, and which was also emptier than most, and which lay within about a mile of Walnut Island. This lay within the rough stretch of the Thames where a trunk might have been dropped to wind up in the rushes of Walnut Island, after drifting eastward for an hour or two.

"Several people mentioned it independently as the likeliest place where something might be dropped into the river and float for a while, sir, without hitting the shore," Graham said.

"Wouldn't that require quite intimate knowledge of the river, though?" Lenox said. "There must be a thousand docks within London's own limits."

Graham nodded. "It's a slight chance."

Lenox looked thoughtful. "Still, we might go out there. Better a long shot than no shot."

"By all means, sir."

They took a cab. The dock was lonely, dark, empty, windswept. Lenox saw the point the pilots had been making: Woodbridge put them a good forty yards clear of the others into the river.

They waited there, shivering and nervous, trading sips from a flask, until five in the morning, when at last Lenox said that they should go home and sleep. Even if the murderer was sincere, they probably had a day more until this dark "anniversary" he planned to celebrate, and should preserve some of their energies to spend it searching for him.

In the meanwhile, perhaps Exeter and Sinex would have found something, and a death could be avoided.

This was the fatigued but hopeful state of mind in which they went home and to their beds—one to be dashed shortly after the sun had risen the next day.

CHAPTER SEVEN

Lenox knew something was wrong in the very early light of the new day. He would have known it from the look on Graham's face as he entered the room, but even in the beat before then he had known it, and it took him a moment to realize why: Graham hadn't knocked.

Lenox rose to his elbows. "What is it?"

"Another murder, sir. Very like the first."

Graham was holding out a copy of the *Telegraph*, and Lenox took it.

Like most papers, it published a second edition after six o'clock in the morning, which was updated to include any news that had emerged since the first edition at three o'clock. As a policy Lenox subscribed to second editions, though it was usually the first edition that made its way onto London's breakfast tables.

It paid off now: 6:50, and he had most of the story.

Fifteen frantic minutes later, Graham and Lenox were rumbling through the streets of London toward the river in a cab, Lenox urging the driver on from the vehicle's interior with angry thumps of the roof. He had promised the sleepy-eyed fellow half a crown if they made it to Bankside in less than twenty minutes.

He was filled with rage, his own tiredness gone. (He had always been able to survive on very little sleep, Graham the same.)

"We had a very short window of time, sir," Graham ventured at one point.

"Mm," said Lenox in a noncommittal tone, his eyes remaining on the streets.

He didn't trust himself to say more. Instead he simmered in his emotions, angry as only the young can be, who still suspect the world to be partially within their control; as only the purehearted can be, to whom evil is a new surprise each time; angry with himself; angry with the indifferent cloudy morning sky; angry with the indifferent passersby, involved so earnestly in their meaningless daily movements.

GRUESOME AND SENSATIONAL MURDER ON RIVER THAMES

That had been the headline Graham showed him. It was from the *Telegraph*, the only paper that had carried the story in its second edition. It was a serious scoop, upon the strength of which its newsboys would sell throughout the morning, and which might even force other papers to go to a third edition, expense be cursed. Nothing else could conceivably lead the evening papers.

Nevertheless the headline had managed an error in its scant seven words. *On* the River Thames—doubtful, Lenox thought, that anyone had been murdered *on* the River Thames.

The cab crossed Southwark Bridge.

"Close," said Graham two-thirds of the way across it, breaking the silence.

This bridge was toward the eastern part of London; the affluent West End was where Lenox lived, but they had not yet made it all the way east, toward poverty, the infamous rookeries around Tottenham Court Road where men and women lived as close as moles in a burrow, in conditions scarcely less dominated by dirt, the tenements where cholera had wiped away so many thousands of souls the year before, '49.

No, solid burgher stock lived in these precincts around South-wark Bridge. St. Paul's loomed above everything. As they crossed the bridge, Lenox saw the thin townhouse facing the river where Christopher Wren had lived as St. Paul's was being built, so that he could see it from a distance each morning and evening, step back from it after a day spent amidst the dust and mortar. Not dissimilar to a detective's work.

As they neared the south bank, Lenox saw the official bustle of a police investigation. There was a swarm of ten or fifteen uniformed men keeping order, and perhaps ten times as many bystanders who had stopped to gawk. They were almost exactly where Shakespeare's Globe Theatre had been, though that was of course many centuries gone.

"This is one for Tussauds," said Graham.

Lenox nodded. No question about it. The anonymity of the Wal-nut Island murder had met its exact opposite; the murderer would have his notoriety. Nothing could be more certain. There were al-ready a few enterprising men among the crowds, one selling oysters, another copies of the *Telegraph*, no doubt at a markup. Three people were reenacting the infamous murder of Joseph O'Connor (even at a few hundred yards, Lenox could spot the top hat that always marked O'Connor as a rich man in these impromptu productions) for a small but enthusiastic group they had siphoned off—the kind of street theater that was immensely popular in London, a long and lurid per-formance that would culminate in enormous lengths of red hand-kerchief streaming from one member's collar as he convulsed upon the ground, O'Connor dying for the ten thousandth time, victim of a dashing, young, poor couple named the Mannings, who had set him for their mark.

Stand up, bow, circulate the hat for pennies, perform it again.

The Mannings were in Tussauds.

"The letter writer will find the fame he sought, sir," Graham said, echoing Lenox's own thought.

Lenox nodded. "As he counted upon."

The article had been short (little information, and a brief time in which to get it to press—the presses held for it, in all likelihood). Its subheadline had virtually summarized what the *Telegraph* actually knew, adding a nickname.

Thames Ophelia; strangled own hair; bedecked and set adrift

Then the article, whose tone was just a step down from the *Times* in ways that were subtle but obvious to the avid consumer of newsprint:

> *The body of an unknown woman was recovered just off Bankside this morning at a little after five o'clock, in remarkable circumstances. It was discovered by a clerk from the Customs House nearby, on his way to work, who immediately alerted P. C. Wright, Number 144 of K Division.*
>
> *The unfortunate woman was of dark complexion, with ringlets of dark hair upon her brow. The cause of death appeared to be strangulation of the most brutal variety. Most astonishingly, surrounding and surmounting her body were long and numerous garlands of flowers.*
>
> *She had been floated down the river on a loose board.*
>
> *Nothing else is known about the victim's identity. Members of the Metropolitan Police are present, among them Inspector Field. Sir Richard Mayne is expected to attend the scene himself shortly.*
>
> *Evening edition for further details.*

Next to this was a long history—all filler—about unsolved London murders. Nothing about Walnut Island.

As they drew closer to the site, Lenox could indeed see Inspector Charles Field, the two most respected of the plainclothes detectives of the Metropolitan Police, one of the eight original detectives of 1842. Mayne was already there as well.

Heavens, that made four: Mayne, the commissioner; Field, the preeminent detective, famous across England; and Sinex and Exeter, who had drawn the Walnut Island case.

It was hard for Lenox to imagine where he fit into this battalion of people. But he was doggedly committed that it would be somewhere.

Around Mayne and Field were a variety of police officers, some in blue, others in suit and tie. A number of constables held the crowd at bay, but the crowd saw plenty anyway. Lenox himself could perceive that all attention was centered on a small area of the river's bank, though he was angled too low to see what was there.

"I'll attempt to get through to the body," Lenox said as they came onto Bankside, the hansom attracting a few glances. "You take a scan of the crowd—the civilians, that is. Jot notes on the faces you see, clothes, telling scars, markings, but be quick about it, since there's so much to do."

Graham nodded. "Yes, sir."

It was an article of faith among the few criminal manuals available that murderers enjoyed watching the commotion they had instigated. Lenox wasn't sure if it was true, but it couldn't hurt to be safe.

He rapped the cab to stop, and steeled himself: mayhem, death, blood. Yet he knew somewhere deep in his mind, from the same mysterious depth that had noticed Graham's failure to knock on his door half an hour before, that opportunity lay within the chaos.

He wondered how quickly this would be connected to the previous morning's letter to the *Challenger*. The *Telegraph* hadn't done it. The *Challenger* would do it by the time it published its evening edition, of course. Still, for a few hours, at least, he and Graham would be among just a dozen or so men in England who suspected that two murders, a month apart, were connected.

One of those dozen or so being the murderer; and contemplating this person, Lenox felt, surfacing to his skin, a profound unease that had been lingering somewhere hidden within him for the past half hour. It had to do with: Who *was* this fellow? What kind of murderer was he?

For that matter, what was a murder?

Usually he thought he knew. It was a question that seemed to have a single simple answer. And yet in cases like this, its illimitable secondary ones occupied a great deal of his time and thought.

He had been discussing just this with Elizabeth a few weeks before, over tea in her pretty yellow drawing room—not a subject at all appropriate for either teatime or for discussion with a gentlewoman, or for a pretty yellow drawing room. But they were close enough that they could discuss all subjects with equal freedom.

"Do you know how many murders there were in Britain in 1810?" he had asked her, smiling, after she had mentioned one of his cases.

"You know that I don't. A thousand? Three thousand?"

"Nine."

"Nine thousand!"

"No, no. Nine. As in, one, two, three, four, five, six, seven, eight, nine."

Her eyes had widened. "You're making sport of me."

"Never in life. Nine convictions of murder by a magistrate, out of ten million Britons."

But of course, as he explained, that was 1810, just before the slow, significant rise in the idea of a professional police force. Nine hundred was a more likely number for how many actual murders there had been that year than nine.

All it meant was that in many ways theirs was the century in which murder had become a real notion. And the idea of *solving* a murder, of trailing a killer, was even newer. Ten years old? Twelve? Eight, if you reckoned the city's own way: Field and his seven comrades in 1842 being the first men specifically tasked with solving the identity of murderers.

Lenox was a student of past crimes in addition to the daily crime of London, and within his knowledge there were very, very few instances like this—the mix of anger, arrogance, and performance. The wantonness of it—the flowers, *Thames Ophelia*—the two strangulations—the idea of a "perfect crime." None of this was usual. It felt different, unmotivated by money (as the Mannings had been) or drunkenness or marital dispute. It simply felt different, disquietingly different.

What was a murder? Anyhow they were about to see for themselves.

CHAPTER EIGHT

They made their way into the scrum.

"Lenox," said Mayne, spotting him after a double take. "I wondered whether you might come. It would appear that your anxieties were prescient, regrettably."

"The same killer?"

"I would wager so."

Lenox nodded gravely, though doing it without any authority or experience, twenty-three, he felt an impostor—felt twenty-three going on sixteen. "I got into a cab as soon as I saw the newspaper this morning."

Mayne hesitated. "You had better come through. You know Field?"

The question was a perfunctory one. Yes, he knew Field; everyone in England knew Field. Down to his face: When a sensational case appeared in the press, there were inevitably line drawings in every paper, above the fold of the first page, portraits of the victim, the suspects, the inspector, and the witnesses, on either side of a large square picture of the scene. (Only the *Times* still refused to stoop to such illustrations.) Tomorrow Lenox would be able to see twelve different portraits of Field in twelve different papers.

The city loved him, and the counties loved him more. Criminals grinned and touched their hats when they passed him. He was a close personal friend of Charles Dickens, who rumor said was basing a character in his next novel on the inspector.

So Lenox knew Field—but didn't know him. "Charles Lenox," he said, extending a hand.

"Field. Pleased to meet you."

It was a good face, the one that would appear in the papers tomorrow. You saw why it was trusted: round, stolid, intelligent without being nervously intellectual, proper King George side-whiskers, a shirt that covered his whole neck so that he looked a high-buttoned and tightly contained bulk of human.

"The pleasure is mine," said Lenox.

Field chucked his chin toward Graham. "Who is this?"

"My valet." There was a subtle change in Field's face, and Lenox blushed. Hell and brimstone. The very first crime scene he had ever visited, and within twenty seconds he had made an utter fool of himself.

"I see."

Field turned away slightly, and Lenox wondered if he was now suddenly recollecting Lenox's name, a joke among the other inspectors, the amateur who bothered them with his occasional presence around Great Scotland Yard.

Mayne, too, looked at him oddly. "Your valet."

Lenox thought as rapidly as he could. "And assistant," he said in what sounded to his own ear like an unnaturally loud voice. "I'm a private detective, Inspector Field. I brought Mr. Graham because I was wondering, Sir Richard, if he might have permission to go to the *Challenger* and see whether another letter had arrived. They sat on the last one long enough. And the first was just braggadocios, enough that I wondered if its author might have written a sequel, out of pride."

Field turned back to him, and Lenox saw that this had been the right stroke. Among other things because it reminded everyone that

Lenox had connected the letter of the day before to Walnut Island. It also explained and disposed of Graham.

Mayne nodded. Field assessed Lenox, then said to Graham, "If you go, take Constable Bryant, over there, with the gold tooth, badge ninety-nine. They'll listen to him at the *Challenger* if they won't listen to you."

Graham had previous orders—to survey the crowd—but he was very far from simple, and nodded. "I shall return here directly afterward," he said to Lenox, wisely dropping the word "sir," and walked away.

This goodbye, too, had been clever—it gave Lenox a reason to remain indefinitely, since he had a later reunion planned here—and the young detective silently blessed his friend, who was already walking toward Constable Bryant, badge ninety-nine, of the gold tooth, for being smarter than himself.

Field had turned away again. His hands were clasped behind his back, and Lenox watched as he returned to the water. Wavelets, cresting in small dirty-white foam from the swollen deep blue of the river's center, rushed one over the other at the bank. Five or so feet beyond the reach of the water there was a lumped figure under a sheet; and in sacral hush around it, several constables with nothing to do except look solemn.

Among them was Inspector Exeter. So, he was here, too.

Lenox glanced behind him and saw that Sinex was among the crowds. More information there, probably.

"I hope I can be of assistance," Lenox said to Mayne.

"It is Field's matter entirely now."

"Not Sinex and Exeter's?"

Mayne shook his head. "They will assist Field." He paused, and some complicated arithmetic passed through his mind. "But I can let you have a look at the body."

"I'd be glad of the chance."

"I wouldn't offer too much in the way of opinion to Field, unless you see something glaring."

Lenox nodded. He had already been counting on silence as his best ally.

There had been something in Mayne's words, though. Lenox wondered, as he followed the commissioner, if perhaps Mayne and Field were at odds. One was the direct superior, but the other more famous and influential. Perhaps that had led them into conflict?

Lenox's path into the case became clear to him in that moment: he could be Mayne's own eyes.

Mayne nodded as they came up to the sheet. "I've only just arrived myself. We'll see her for the first time together." He made a sour face. "Bloody foul thing to happen," he muttered.

The crowds, sensing a convergence upon the body, pushed forward.

One of the constables, apparently first among equals, greeted Sir Richard with a grave nod, and, at the commissioner's tilted chin, stooped down to lift the sheet. A phalanx of bodies stood behind it to conceal it from the crowd.

The Thames did that job on the other side.

Lenox had a strong stomach. One or two men stepped back—perhaps because it was a woman, for most if not all of them would have seen men's bodies slumped outside of gin mills, thief-takers'—but Lenox leaned forward.

The woman was of early middle age, perhaps thirty, if he had to guess at a glance. Field, staring down at her intently, said, "You see that she is in an—unusual condition."

The woman had on a thick white dress, almost a bridal gown in the style of Queen Victoria, in fact—who had first popularized that color for wedding dresses. It was muddied and soaked through. Very long plaits of hair were extended down her body.

More remarkably, though, there were garlands of flowers up and down the body, ribboned together by their stems, piled in a crisscrossing mesh far higher than her body, thick across her chest, her midsection, her legs.

Here was the source of the headline: Thames Ophelia.

She was laid out upon a large pine bier that gave her about a foot on every side, though she was quite tall, perhaps five feet eight inches, Lenox would have guessed. This bier seemed to be unmarked, at least at first glance. In fact, the edges looked cut cleanly enough that it might at one stage have been a large door or the side of a shipping crate.

There was thick white makeup on her face, in the style of a high lady of 1790 or so. It was obscene; and her eyes were raccoonlike, black kohl smeared around them more heavily than it was on the Egpytian mummies one saw in the museums.

The whole effect was uncanny—hard to look at.

"Grim," said Mayne, more succinctly.

"Fancies himself quite a poet, this fellow," Field said. He shook his head in disgust. He gestured to the abrasions around her neck. "Strangulation again."

There was a moment of quiet. One constable very suddenly removed his tall police officer's hat, and one by one all of his fellows followed suit.

"I suppose we can cover her again," Mayne said.

But Lenox was too busy for ceremony. Instinctively, he stooped down next to Field. "What's in her hand?"

Her thin-fingered hands were just protruding from the masses of flowers. There were numerous rings on them, two or three on some of the fingers. The left hand was open but the right was tightly closed.

Field carefully pried it open, though it was clenched in rigor mortis. Indeed, her pallid body, an unnatural purplish white, all seemed clenched around that hand. Field opened it and took something out.

He held it up. "A shilling."

Field covered the body. Then he asked two constables to come forward and lift the board. They did this with ease—not too heavy.

"The body was discovered here, washed ashore?" Mayne asked.

Lenox was grateful someone else had posed the question, having committed to silence as a strategy.

One of the constables stepped forward and nodded. "A clerk from the Customs House found her, sir. Nathaniel Butler. He is accustomed to walking along the strand toward his office each morning after crossing Southwark Bridge." They all glanced up at the immense Customs House, a few hundred paces off. "He called for help. I wasn't far."

This must be P. C. Wright, of *Telegraph* fame, then. "Well done," said Mayne. "Was anyone else in the area?"

"The usual foot traffic. Light. Nobody who aroused immediate suspicion, sir. We have detained Mr. Butler as well as a seaman who was upon the shore nearby. He is still drunk, sir. Asleep in the police wagon. He may have seen something, however."

Mayne sighed. "The body may be taken in for examination, then. Field?"

Field nodded. "Yes," he said. "Though it is straightforward enough. Strangulation."

A coroner examined all victims of murder, though the bodies could pile up (quite literally) for weeks on end, due to the shortage of qualified medical examiners, a problem Lenox knew Mayne had addressed to Parliament.

Two constables covered the unfortunate woman in her makeshift shroud again, and the two who were holding the long board upon which she lay began the slow and unsteady process of taking it to the same wagon where evidently this drunken seaman was sleeping in the front seat.

Lenox's mind was full: the river; the Customs House; the shilling; the flowers; the hair; the board; the trunk; Walnut Island.

He glanced back at the crowd, which had filled in even more. There was a woman with a yoke around her neck, selling thick paper cones of piping hot porridge from the small copper buckets on either side of the yoke for a penny.

He turned away and looked across the great river. The high dome of St. Paul's stood there far, far above the low-slung buildings around it. A smokeless day, clouds chased away by the sun, the sky a pretty blue—too pure for this to have happened. A very small flock of white birds rose out of a rooftop.

There was some sense of purpose in his spirit at the moment: this was the moment that he had known would come. It struck him that it was the dome that was false to him here. The woman who had died was real. This woman had lived; she had breathed as they all breathed here upon Bankside now; now she was gone. That must count for something.

He wondered if he was as unflappable as he supposed, because his heart was also beating hard.

The cortege headed slowly toward the police wagon, and Lenox, lagging them a bit, saw something glinting in the sand and stone of the beach. It broke his reverie.

The long board on which the body had lain had left a rectangular imprint upon the sand, flattening it. He knelt down and stared closely at the area. It was empty, except for the object that had caught his eye. He used his handkerchief to lift it carefully from the sand that had threatened to bury it, like a half-buried toy forgotten at the shore by a careless child. It was a pair of silver-rimmed spectacles, the glass in them newly shattered.

CHAPTER NINE

When Lenox crossed his threshold again three hours later, he felt alive to the end of every nerve.

In an hour or two, there'd be the first newspapers of the evening. (Apparently the evening started at progressively earlier hours as the newspaper wars grew in intensity—inevitably one day soon, luncheon would mark the commencement of evening.) But for now, just now, the case was still his.

He was also—he sighed inwardly—officially on the payroll of Scotland Yard now.

Half a pound a week! He would have given ten pounds a week not to have that half a pound. His parents must never discover the fact.

Anyhow, that was all background noise. What really mattered was the sense of urgency he felt on behalf of the dead woman.

This made it slightly dispiriting when he saw the figure of Mrs. Huggins awaiting him in the entrance hall upon his return: an inevitable delay.

She was a superlative housekeeper, Mrs. Huggins. It had bloomed into a bright day, but even under the hardhearted glare of the sunlight, the rooms were dustless, impeccable, the sun exposing nothing except the virtue of the housekeeper's abilities. The very fireplaces were clean. She was a cynosure.

"Hello, Mrs. Huggins."

"Good day, Mr. Lenox," she said.

There had been a certain school-holiday giddiness in the first days he and Graham spent in this flat above St. James's Square—a maid, a cook, and a bootboy lurking in the back quarters but otherwise very little interference, two fellows in their early twenties, not much furniture, resident in London for the first time.

Then Huggins.

"I'm afraid of her," Lenox had finally whispered on the fifth day after her arrival.

It had been a stormy November morning. Graham, who had never skulked in his life, hesitated, then replied, "I am, too, sir."

She was a fine-boned, blue-eyed woman of fifty or thereabouts. Her husband had died twenty years before, leaving her the proceeds of the sale of a small but prosperous coaching inn that he had owned in Kent. She had immediately put this into 4-percent annuities and—Lenox had all this information from his mother—taken herself to London to find employment, vowing to let the money she had inherited grow behind her back, invisible, compounding itself at whatever rate it would.

Being a person of discretion and elegance, from a background of highborn servants, she had found work as the head of a large, aristocratic household, and lived thereafter upon her wages.

Lenox was her retirement. These twenty years on from her husband's death, she still wore black, but the money she'd inherited had moved more cheerfully on from its previous owner's passage out of the muck of the living world, and she was now a well-to-do woman. This, too, Lenox knew from his mother. With one eye toward retirement upon the south coast, she had decided to look for lighter work, after nearly a decade of managing the household of a certain Lady Hamilton, who had four children, nine grandchildren, twenty-seven rooms, and the most unrepentantly unfaithful husband in Parliament (not a contest with light competition).

It was clear that Mrs. Huggins didn't miss what seemed to have been, from her descriptions, like the almost inhuman labor involved in that work—by her account, she had never risen later than five, nor retired earlier than midnight—but that she did miss being a force of power and authority in the very center of London society. Lady Hamilton had breakfasted with cabinet ministers and earls. Lenox breakfasted with Graham.

Her favorite phrase was "In Lady Hamilton's household," which she could apply with a poet's ingenuity to nearly any situation; if they had been in a lifeboat upon the Pacific Ocean, subsisting on fish and rainwater, she would have managed it.

"In Lady Hamilton's household, they took only the *Times* and the *Mail*," she had said severely on her very first morning there, seeing Lenox and Graham nearly buried in newsprint over breakfast.

"Is that right?" Lenox had replied sunnily. "How dull!"

"Lord Hamilton did not find it so, I believe, sir," she had said, and brushed away—never with anything less than the utmost grace in her motions—a few of the crumbs that had fallen to the table.

The litany had gone on over the months. In Lady Hamilton's household, the pots were scoured with lye each Sunday; in Lady Hamilton's household, the houseplants were trimmed to certain dimensions (Lenox had been only very vaguely aware that there were houseplants in his possession, was still not certain from whence they had come, and could not have come within a foot of telling you their dimensions, responsibility for which he had immediately deposed in Mrs. Huggins); in Lady Hamilton's household, the charwoman never expected Sunday afternoon to herself; in Lady Hamilton's household—

Well, there alone, Lenox concluded at last, Eve had never plucked the apple from the tree and doomed mankind to its present state of fallenness.

Mrs. Huggins had at first been appalled by Graham, presumably because of his familiarity with Lenox and their idiosyncratic relationship. But Graham's discretion, the seriousness with which he took her complaints, and his obvious, unstinting dedication both to the excitements and the drudgeries of his position had won her over.

And in a queer way, she loved Lenox. His mother had been a frequent guest at Lady Hamilton's—that connection was how Mrs. Huggins had arrived in her present position—and the housekeeper had from the first extended him a long line of mental credit for that fact, and now sometimes even seemed angrily fond of him.

Not this early afternoon, however.

"Mr. Lenox, sir—"

"I am sorry to say that I am exceedingly busy today, Mrs. Huggins," Lenox said as he strode past her, tossing his light coat casually onto the console table by the door. The spectacles were carefully preserved in the pocket of his jacket, which he kept on.

"Sir—"

"I am also next door to starvation. Could you please bring me a pot of tea and a sandwich with Stilton and cranberry? I saw someone eating a sandwich of that exact description and I crave it."

She hesitated. "Yes, sir."

"The tea hotter than the devil and twice as strong, if you please."

"As you wish, sir," she said.

He went into his library.

The reprieve would be momentary. He walked to the table by the windows where he took breakfast and for a moment allowed himself to gaze at the London day.

His anger at the men and women passing each other on the streets had dissipated, the men and women hanging from the omnibuses, reclining in the new grass of the park. In its place was a feeling of tenderness. He wished they might remain innocent of such violence as he had seen this morning.

It had wounded him beyond his expectations to see that woman's body; for all that he had read about bodies like it, for all that he had been galvanized by the desire to discover the secrets of its demise.

Lenox removed a handkerchief from an inner pocket—one of the blemishless, brilliant-white handkerchiefs that Mrs. Huggins somehow produced, soft as snow.

He unfolded it and laid it upon the bare table, then took the crushed spectacles from his pocket and placed them on the handkerchief.

He sat and examined them for three or four ruminative minutes. Finally he picked up a pen and made a few notes. Their owner was a male; shortsighted; accustomed to working in low light; not rich, but not quite destitute; and it was highly possible he was not originally from London.

These conclusions matched his image of the author of the letter. Was that a coincidence of his mind's own creation? He must guard against fulfilling his wishes—stick to the object itself.

As he was finishing his transcription of his observations, Mrs. Huggins came into the room with a silver tray.

If Huggins had a redeeming virtue in Lenox's eyes—he could have lived with handkerchiefs not quite so luxuriously ivoried and softened, though it was true that Elizabeth had commented favorably on one he had lent her—it was trays like this one. Mrs. Huggins was at once a weedy woman and a natural feeder. There was some wellspring of generosity in her that never came through in her words or features, but did appear on the trays.

This one had a pot of tea, cream and sugar, several sandwiches, a plate of biscuits, and some seed-crackers heaped with a chunky orange-colored chutney, somewhere between marmalade and vinegared cabbage, which she made herself and which was of a magical deliciousness. The severest he had ever seen her was when he praised this chutney; a sure sign of her pride in it. She was a very Christian woman.

Before she had set the tray down, and before he could preempt her, she said, "In Lady Hamilton's household, Mr. Lenox, the month of May invariably meant a thorough cleaning of the rugs."

"That's fine, then. Please take a free hand with the rugs."

"And in Lady Hamilton's household, May was also the month we washed the windows from outside. It means hiring a gentleman, sir."

"Consider yourself to have a free hand with regard to the windows, too."

"Also in Lady Hamilton's household, sir—"

But here Lenox cut her off. He had already eaten a gingerbread biscuit whole, but now he looked up as sternly as it was possible to look with a youthful face and mouthful of gingerbread biscuit, emboldened, perhaps, by the morning's events.

"I am not Lady Hamilton, Mrs. Huggins," he said through the biscuit, in a choked but severe tone.

"Sir, Lady—"

He swallowed painfully quickly, just so that he could interrupt her. "I do not live in Eaton Square."

"No, sir. But Lady Hamilton, sir—"

"I do not serve on the board of the Ladies' Floral Society."

"Sir, Lady Hamilton's household—"

"The duties of that position would defeat me completely."

"Sir—"

"I do not have a dressmaker in Paris."

"If I could, sir—"

"In short, as I am attempting to convey, I am not Lady Hamilton, Mrs. Huggins."

"Sir, I—"

"If I *were* Lady Hamilton, the shock to Lord Hamilton would be profound, I imagine."

"Sir—"

"Life-altering, one might even say."

"Sir—"

He held up a hand, and for the first time saw Mrs. Huggins take

in the pair of crushed spectacles on the table alongside her beautifully overloaded tray.

She stared hard for a moment, then looked at him. The admis-
sion of defeat in her face was temporary. "I can return, sir."

"Thank you, Mrs. Huggins. Thank you."

And as she retreated, perhaps because his mind had briefly been
otherwise occupied, it suddenly came to him what had bothered him
about the area under the plank that had borne the anonymous body
of the woman, garlanded in flowers, who had presumably floated down
the Thames just as the trunk had floated to Walnut Island.

It hadn't been wet.

And neither had the plank. Each, five feet from the lapping water,
dry as a bone. He stared at the spectacles, stunned, for this fact
changed so much.

CHAPTER TEN

Graham returned at ten past two that afternoon. He looked exhausted. He didn't waste time on either an explanation or an apology for his long absence. "There's been another letter to the *Challenger,* sir," he said.

He set a folded piece of paper down in front of Lenox, who had been lingering over the remains of his lunch, thinking. He picked up the letter. "This is a copy?"

"Yes, sir. Transcribed from memory immediately after I left rather than from the letter itself, unfortunately. I had to look over the constable's shoulder."

"Why's that?"

"The editor at the *Challenger* was reluctant even to let him see it, sir. Much less myself."

"Well done then."

"I cannot promise its exactness, sir."

Lenox was reading. "I'm sure it's close enough," he said distractedly.

"We shall have the true wording when the *Challenger* publishes it, I would imagine, sir." Graham glanced over at the silent grandfather clock in the corner of the room. "They plan to run it at six this evening."

Lenox followed his valet's eyes to the clock, then settled back in his chair to read the letter carefully.

Sirs,

Did Cain wait a month? Patience likely suited Abel better—he had all of eternity before him, after all. Cain must have wished to return to violence as soon as possible. It is addictive, gentlemen— murder, I mean. Murder is addictive. I would be surprised if Cain's first was his last.

Yet I find no difficulty in imagining a wait of one month more. I have committed a second perfect crime. I observe already a livelier reaction to this one than to the first. I am gratified. The month will give me the pleasure of watching further, unwatched myself, and laying my marvelous plans.

The magical number of every civilization on earth, from the Angles to the Saxons to the Zulus, is three. Why? Impossible to say. Nevertheless, after a third perfect crime, I shall slip beneath London city's surface again. Rather like a body slipping into the water! In a century perhaps the world will know my name— Cain's name. Until then, as Abel did, I will wait.

In faith,
Your ponderous correspondent

Lenox read the letter through twice.

Then he leaned back. "Any thoughts?" he said to Graham.

"He seems madder this time."

"Yes. It was written closer to the commission of the crime. His blood was stirred up." Lenox tapped the letter against the table. "No less pretentious."

"Indeed not, sir."

"A great deal of biblical fervor."

"Arrogance, too, sir."

"I wonder why he calls himself ponderous."

"Perhaps it may be a joke, sir?"

The detective sat back in his chair thinking. "Perhaps. He does not strike me as a joking sort." Remembering himself, he gestured for Graham to sit. He rang the bell, which produced the housemaid, Clara, whom he asked to bring more tea. "It was awfully clever of you to get this, Graham."

"Thank you, sir."

"I should double your pay."

"I agree, sir."

"Well, I'm not going to, that would be absurd."

Graham smiled his inscrutable, very occasional smile. This was his favorite part of his job—there was no question about that—and though Lenox's remarks would have seemed rudely commercial in the circumstances to an outsider, to the two of them it was quite obviously a placeholder as they thought about the letter; a form of mutual reassurance, the banter.

Neither had experienced anything like that day yet. They were groping their way through it together.

"What's next, sir?"

"I'm told that in Lady Hamilton's household, May is the month they clean the rugs."

"Indeed, sir?"

"I have only secondhand information. It's hard to be sure whether Mrs. Huggins is acquainted with Lady Hamilton herself. But do not be surprised if you are moving about the rooms and there are rugs missing."

There was a pause as Graham tilted his head, acknowledging Lenox's humorous tone. "Just so, sir."

"Mm. I suppose."

"May I inquire about your morning, sir? Have the police come to any firm conclusions?"

"Ah. Yes. They did, didn't they."

They had. Two men had been placed under arrest that morning

as Lenox lurked behind the proper police force assembled at Bankside: one, the clerk from the Customs House, Nathaniel Butler, who had stumbled upon the body; and two, the half-drunk seaman who had been slumbering on the shingle nearby and then been slumbering in the police wagon.

Inspector Exeter, blundering fool that he was, had made both arrests.

Before he entered into a description of his morning, though, Lenox said, "Tell me, Graham, what do you make of these spectacles?"

They were still lying on Mrs. Huggins's unblemished handkerchief. "They're broken, sir."

Lenox laughed. "Remind me to cut your pay in half."

Graham gestured toward them. "May I?"

"By all means."

The valet picked them up and studied them in the clear daylight. At length, he murmured, "Shortsighted, male."

Lenox nodded. "My first two conclusions as well." The width of the bridge of the nose and the width of the frame were both strongly indicative that the crushed spectacles had been a man's. "What else?"

"They've been repaired, I believe, sir."

"Twice, you'll observe."

Graham frowned; then recognition appeared in his eyes as he saw what Lenox meant. One hasp was of a slightly different color both from the other and from the original silver color of the frame. There was also a small solder at the bridge. "Glasses more worth replacing than repairing if one could afford it, sir."

Lenox nodded again. It was this that had led him to conclude that the owner was neither affluent nor destitute. "Anything else?"

Graham and Lenox occasionally played this sort of schoolboy game, and Graham studied the spectacles at length in the silence of the room. (There had been a popular cheap magazine called *The Confounder* when Lenox was an undergraduate, which offered a new set of deductive games each month. They had competed over that, too.) "Not that I can see, sir."

"What do you think of the maker's mark?"

"A fairly standard one, sir."

"Not stamped with any excise number."

All goods made in London shops had to be. Graham looked again. "Ah. Not a Londoner."

"Perhaps not originally. And the name of the maker is Lancashire."

"From the north perhaps, then, sir."

"I wondered. A name can travel."

Graham put the spectacles down. "Where are they from, sir?"

Lenox frowned, before realizing that Graham was asking about where he had found the spectacles, not their origins.

He described discovering them underneath the plank that had borne the second victim's body. Then he added how struck he had been that all of it was dry—the board, the glasses, even the sand underneath the board.

"I looked up the tides."

"And?"

"I don't think the body could have been brought there by the water. It didn't rise that high onto the shore. Whereas the trunk at Walnut Island was 'heavily sodden,' if you'll recall. It had been in the water for some time."

"Interesting, sir."

"Yes, I thought so."

"It must have been easier to place the body there, sir, than to leave it to the chance of floating, being scavenged or overturned."

Lenox shook his head. "Perhaps. But what keeps returning to me, perhaps only because of that silly headline, is the myth of Ophelia, floating in the water. And then, more importantly, much more importantly, that her *clothing* was wet. Why would her *clothing* alone have been wet, Graham?"

The valet's eyes widened as he took in the significance of this observation. "Curious, sir."

Lenox laid a gentle finger on the edge of the spectacles. He was unbecomingly proud of himself. Nobody else had noticed these details—though perhaps Field had noticed, arrested the fellow, and was sitting down to luncheon.

Somehow Lenox doubted it.

To Graham, he said, "Has it occurred to you how exactly these spectacles match the description we came up with from the first letter to the *Challenger*? The clerk, underpaid, overeducated, resentful?"

"It did occur to me, sir, yes."

"But then how did they come to be *under* the plank? They have this chain to prevent them from falling. Something, incidentally, that made me wonder if their owner worked in low light, always bent over his work. A common accessory in that profession."

Graham nodded. "Yes."

"You can tell from the glass that they were broken only in the last day or two. Dirty, but not grimy. The edges of the glass still gleaming. Of course, it could be pure chance."

"But if not, how does it add up, sir—dry board, wet clothes, broken spectacles?"

Lenox paused, sighed, and then said, truthfully, "I don't know."

CHAPTER ELEVEN

After Graham had left Bankside that morning to go to the offices of the *Challenger,* and Lenox had been invited by Sir Richard Mayne to join the small band of professionals examining the body, several things happened in quick succession.

The first was the arrests. After the body had been placed in the wagon and Lenox had found the spectacles, Exeter had marched over with a man at his side. The fellow looked about forty-five or fifty to Lenox, bleary eyed, with a thick navy-issued peacoat and a white beard of four days' growth.

"I think this is our man, sir," Exeter had said, hauling him forward by the arm.

"How's that?" Mayne had asked sharply.

Exeter, young, beefy, and earnest, yanked the man's hand out of his pockets. "Near the scene of the crime—a first indication—and," he went on triumphantly, "blood fresh-caked underneath his fingernails, sir."

There was a silence, and then Field had said, "Take him to the station, then."

Mayne had nodded grudgingly. "Good work, Exeter."

The younger fellow practically clicked his heels—might have, were they standing on any surface other than sand. "Thank you, sir."

Lenox was twenty-three (and had been that age for only thirty-six hours or so), and his inclination was to be quiet; then again, his other inclination was to be brilliant.

"What is the man's name?" he asked, just as Exeter was turning away.

Field gave Lenox a sidelong glance, and Exeter turned back, said angrily, "That's none of your bother."

Mayne interjected. "Lenox has some standing here, Exeter. Lenox, this is Mr. Johanssen, an able seaman of the *Matilda*. No very coherent account of his last twenty-four hours, and he was found slumbering in a stupor nearby. According to a constable whose beat is the docks, he has been arrested in the past."

"He has blood on his hands," Exeter added angrily.

Johanssen. Many of these chaps hanging around the London dock-yards were of Swedish origin—because it was a seafaring nation, Lenox supposed. As mildly as he could, he said, "There is no blood visible on the body, so I do not see the relevance of that particular fact. May I see your hands, Johanssen?"

The white-blond sailor, whose face stood somewhere between drunk, bewildered, and belligerent, held out his hands slowly. There were abrasions on the knuckles. His thin nose had an ugly scrape on it, and his cheeks were smudged with dirt.

Field and Mayne, meanwhile, had looked back to the body upon hearing Lenox's words, as if to verify to their own satisfaction that he was right, that there was no blood on the body.

As quickly as he could, Lenox got out his notepad. He wrote four words on a sheet and tore it away.

"Could you read that?" he asked the sailor.

Johanssen looked at him suspiciously, then at the paper. "Some-thing about blood," he muttered. He had a slight Nordic accent. Then he burst out. "I've already told them I can't remember a bloody thing.

I left from the Jolly Boatman here and fell asleep. Not against any law I know about."

Lenox turned the page to Mayne and Field. It said *Johanssen's shipmates bugger him.* Not a pleasant phrase, but the one that Lenox had calculated would be quickest to send the average sailor into a rage.

"Not our letter writer, anyway," he said quietly to the two superior officers. "And the hands look to me to be from a fight, which I do not think this woman has been in. Drunkenness and fighting—fairly typical of a seaman on shore leave." He paused, then pulled out his final card. "We might also find out where the *Matilda* was a month ago. Likely not London."

This final point was the conclusive one. They all realized it at once.

A moment of deadlock passed. Field stared at Lenox. It was hard to assess his look, especially without staring him directly in the eye.

Mayne was far easier to read. "Exeter, you fool," he said. "Take the man's statement again, tell him to leave an address where he can be found, if it's not the ship, and turn him loose."

At that moment, Lenox caught Exeter's malevolent gaze.

He knew then, immediately, that he would not easily be forgiven. So be it.

The look of relief on Johanssen's face was perceptible—all he wanted was somewhere to crawl away and sleep for twelve more hours, possibly after a pork chop and a pint of ale—and Exeter, muttering something, turned away with the sailor's arm still in his grip, handling him roughly.

The crowds behind them had continued to grow. There was the shout of an oyster seller, a chaunter singing the ballad of the Melbury Murders, a man waving broadsheets for purchase.

Mayne and Lenox happened to be just off to the side, while Field was walking to the police wagon. "Listen, Lenox," Mayne had said quietly, "you happened to be right in that instance, but if you have any other observations, save them for me, would you? Hang back. There's a lad."

"Of course, sir," said Lenox just as quietly. "Thank you."

He therefore watched in silence as Field and Mayne analyzed the body at the open-doored rear of the wagon, naming the flowers (at least one of them incorrectly) and speculating about the cause of death.

There were ligature marks around the neck. Another clear case of strangulation, they agreed.

Lenox stood as close as he dared, listening intently and looking at the body himself.

Something about the ugly, rather mannish (or at least practical) brown shoes upon the corpse's feet bothered him. What was it? Graham would know what seemed off, if it didn't come to him— whatever the strange thing was.

"Teeth in good condition," Field said in a low voice at one point. "Another highborn lady."

That puzzled Lenox particularly. Two highborn women, though by that phrase Field meant only "respectable," of course, of such a class that each woman would have owned more than a single dress, never sold her body, perhaps even had had a maid. Not highborn by the standards of Lenox's sphere, that was—he clarified this in his mind for its usefulness as a fact, not out of snobbishness—but certainly by the standards of the newspapers and the Yard.

The crucial question was this: Wouldn't such women have been missed by their families and neighbors? Their absence remarked upon?

The second arrest, Field himself had made along with Exeter. It was of the clerk who had discovered the body.

His name was Nathaniel Butler, and he was terribly distraught, poor fellow. He kept protesting that he would lose his position, and that he would never, in a thousand years, murder a woman—he had merely had the misfortune to work a few hundred yards away, and live in a place that made the walk along the river the fastest way to his office.

This seemed plausible to Lenox. Field was no fool, however; in a case of high profile, such as this one, it was better not to take the one-in-a-hundred chance of letting a murderer go. Butler would have three hot meals served to him at Newgate each day, and if he was innocent, he would be free again before long.

The journalists had descended by this time. Dozens and dozens of them arrived at Bankside, shouting questions, plumbing the crowd for quotations, above all desperate for a look at the body.

Mayne wanted a word with Lenox. "What are your thoughts?" Sir Richard had asked in a low voice. "The same murderer, no doubt?"

This was before Graham's delivery of the letter, but Lenox had nodded. "The coincidence would seem to be too great for it to be otherwise."

"Yes, I agree. As does Field. He will take the case." Mayne turned a troubled look into the middle distance. "He will not take kindly to your presence beyond this morning, however. Thank you for your help."

Mayne extended his hand, and Lenox shook it. "I understand," he said. "But before you go—she was not strangled to death."

Mayne turned back. "Not strangled? Nothing could have been plainer. Indeed it was the only clear thing about the body that I saw. Floated down the Thames as brazenly as you like."

Lenox shook his head. "No."

His certainty was not a matter of overconfidence. He had had only two cases these seven months of his residency in London, each of which had taken approximately eight hours of labor, it was true. But the remaining five thousand hours—though a third of them had been spent in sleep, granted—more, on nights after he had been to his club—had not been passed idly, and his morning clippings with Graham were only one minor element of his approach to his new job.

Mostly this had been reading. He read ravenously, the sensational and stupid, the dry and didactic, consuming Scottish police statistics with the same enthusiasm as penny bloods about the Stirling-shire Decapitator.

He had taken more practical measures, too. "I have made a study of morbid anatomy recently," Lenox said, as shortly as he could, since Mayne's eyes had turned toward the departing row of police carriages. "She was not strangled."

"What makes you so sure?"

Lenox had a friend of a friend at St. Bart's, studying to be a physician there. They'd had drinks, and in exchange for a succession of subsequent rounds at his club, the fellow, Courtenay, had given Lenox a few relevant medical textbooks, with the important pages flagged, and good-humoredly answered all of Lenox's numerous questions about the variously murdered, hanged, beaten, and anonymous bodies that a medical student encountered in his studies.

"There is no bruising around the neck," Lenox said. "There are only abrasions to the skin."

"So?"

"It means her blood was no longer circulating when they were made. She was dead. Nor were there petechiae, for that matter."

Sir Richard looked halfway between angry and curious to hear a word he didn't know. "What?"

"Pinprick-sized dots of red on the skin and in the eyes. They are present as an absolute rule of strangulation."

"What killed her, then?"

"That I don't know. Poison perhaps." Mayne had looked at him indecisively for a moment. Lenox, sensing an opportunity, said, "The first murder will solve as easily as the second. Give me Walnut Island."

Mayne had paused, then nodded. "This case gives me an ill feeling. I'll put you on as a consultant at half a pound a week. I'll send Wilkinson around with a temporary badge. You report exclusively to me. Avoid Exeter. Avoid Sinex. Avoid Field in particular."

"Half a pound a week?"

"Yes."

Lenox's entire self revolted at this idea: being paid to do police work. He would often wonder, in subsequent years, what career he might have taken had he answered with the first words that came to his lips.

But this was also proof of Sir Richard's faith, and proof, in its way, that Lenox had belonged at the scene of the crime that morning, as surely as Sir Richard or Inspector Field.

So he had gulped and nodded. "Thank you."

Walnut Island was his.

CHAPTER TWELVE

N ow, just past three on the afternoon of that busy day, he and
Graham sat at the table with the broken spectacles, discussing
their potential courses of action.

"Do you think we really have a month, then, sir?" Graham asked
Lenox ruminatively.

"I rather do. He has been fairly loyal to his word thus far." Lenox
tilted his head, thinking. "He seems to be of a precise set of mind, in
the way that madmen occasionally are."

"Fanatical."

"Yes."

Lenox stood up from the breakfast table and stretched, a little tired,
then wandered toward the other end of the room, where the fireplace,
bookshelves either side of it, was burning low. He poked at it; the
great pastime of anyone who has ever wished to be lost in thought.

He was often alone in this room. The liquor stand was nearby.
Loose correspondence, too little organized, but which he had ordered
the servants not to touch, sat upon a coffee table. Above the mantel
there was a cup he had won many distant years before in school—third
place in his form's boxing contest—along with a rough-woven bag
of shag tobacco, a book turned facedown, and a small oil of Lenox

House. It was by a Frenchman. Two figures walked along the far end of the old home's pond, Lenox's grandfather and his grandfather's brother, inseparable young companions sixty years before when it was painted. Both very old men now.

There were a pair of very comfortable red armchairs in front of the fireplace; he sank down into one of them.

A month was a dangerous amount of time.

"I say," Lenox observed suddenly, "the rug is gone. The rug in front of the hearth."

Graham, who every fifteen days or so let slip a small joke at his employer's expense, said, "I hope you are not overtaxing your powers of detection at just the moment you may need them most, sir."

"Mrs. Huggins," Lenox muttered bitterly. He liked the rug. When you pushed your feet through it, the bristles stayed up stiff and lighter colored, until you smoothed them back down into their natural state of dark blue. It helped a chap cogitate. "The perfect crime, though, Graham. Think on that one."

"Sir?"

"The crime—as an end in itself. With no motive but itself. With no reason for existing but itself, the pleasure of its own symmetry and design. There's an evil thing. Murder for money or love or power is also evil, of course, but murder for itself belongs to some different class of person. I don't like it."

Graham, who had risen and was leaning, though somehow his leaning conveyed respectfulness, perhaps in the way his hands were clasped behind his back, or in the attentive tilt of his head, against the wall, absorbed this reflection. "No, sir."

The idea of the perfect crime was familiar to anyone who, like Lenox, was a student of sensational fiction. It had been especially popular in the rags this last decade, Lenox had noted; he wondered whether their murderer was a reader of the penny bloods, which gave you eight pages a week for a penny, an ongoing story contained in their sheets. (The more modern term, slowly coming into use, was "penny dreadful," but to Lenox, who had started reading them at the age of twelve, they would always be the bloods.) Even sober, middle-class novels had begun to engage with the idea of murder. Dickens himself was at work on a mystery, people murmured.

Lenox's brother had said something about this very subject a few weeks before. "They don't hang in public anymore."

"So?"

Edmund had shrugged. They'd been in the dining room at Parliament, where his brother was a backbencher, and content to remain such all his life, looking in on the occasional vote when he was really needed. (He had already avowed to anyone who listened that he would never hold office in the cabinet. On the other hand, he knew a great deal about the husbandry of pigs. He took his role as heir seriously—or perhaps it came to him naturally, the way the city felt more and more as though it was coming to Charles naturally.)

"It's different than it was thirty years ago," Edmund had said, running a fork through his boiled cabbage, the terraces by the river crowded with other MPs. "Men walking home across Hyde Park from the countinghouse, tipping their hats to each other, don't want to see a gallows being dismantled."

"No more Rotten Row."

"Right. England's bloody days are past. She's an empire now, to be managed."

Lenox let that pass, though he knew, always a better student than his brother, that empires could be bloody enough. He smiled. "So then, murder moves into the drawing room."

Edmund laughed. "Yes. It's a capital way to fall asleep, a murder mystery. I like Bulwer-Lytton myself. Decent tales, those."

"Decent murder tales," Lenox grumbled.

In the stories that circulated through Britain about the so-called perfect crime, the criminal was nearly always from the Continent—an evil, mustache-twirling aristocrat, a Bluebeard.

Not a clerk, not that he remembered.

Lenox and Graham talked through the specifics of the case for some time—the shilling in the woman's hand, the flowers, the obscuring, almost mocking thickness of the white makeup upon her face, the spectacles, the dryness of the plank upon which she was laid, the trunk on Walnut Island, and of course the letters, which now numbered two. They read these over again carefully, studying them for details.

"How will you proceed, sir?" Graham asked at last.

"Walnut Island. There's a warehouse in Ealing where the evidence of unsolved crimes is kept. Tomorrow morning I intend to go there. You'll come?"

"Only too happy, sir, if I'm not required here."

Lenox waved a dismissive hand. "I would like to go back to Bankside, too."

"I thought it was the first murder you were fixed upon solving, sir," said Graham.

"It is. But they cannot stop me from thinking about the second one. Or walking a public part of the riverside. Everyone in London will be doing the same when the papers come out."

"True, sir."

"Why the *Challenger*?" Lenox asked in a voice soft enough that it was clear he was talking three-quarters to himself. "And these two women: Where in London do you come across two wellborn women to murder, who will not be missed?"

For Mayne had been very clear: every report of a woman's disappearance in this city since the start of the year had been tracked down and resolved, for better or worse.

Graham, silent, shook his head. The air was cool; below them, in the park, the little flowers of spring moved imperceptibly in the afternoon breeze. There were clouds passing across the heavens. The authority and high-spiritedness of the noonday sun was dissipating; a moment to feel things, to ask of oneself what it all meant, the white loveliness of the sky an answer and an evasion at once, sufficient, never enough.

It was at this sort of time that Lenox's thoughts always turned to Elizabeth.

"I've kept you from your duties," Lenox said at last, after they had both stayed in silent reflection for some time. "And you no doubt need some time after your day—exhausting, I know, I know. Apologies."

"Not at all, sir."

"Could you ask Clara or Mrs. Huggins to ship in some more tea for me, before you retire? I want to sit here and gather my thoughts before I dine out."

"Of course, sir."

When he was alone, Lenox made a few fruitless lists, tore them up, scattered their remains in the fire. He leaned back and traced his fingertips along the spine of a random book on the side table next to his chair. The material was cloth, and it felt like trying to run his hand over the case: the very slight changes in texture, the very slight rises and dips, barely perceptible. Murder was a dramatic, violent act; the chase after the murderer was a matter of nuance and feel.

With that thought in mind, he took the paper notebook back up and started to write random words, connecting them with lines.

The shilling. The spectacles. Walnut Island. The Thames. Field. Mayne. Bankside. The tide. Nathaniel Butler. Death. Women. Brown hair. Strangulation.

Mrs. Huggins appeared with one of her trays.

"Ah, Mrs. Huggins," he said, "thank you."

"By all means, Mr. Lenox."

"Do you know when I can expect my rug back?"

"By tomorrow."

"Will it still bristle up in that pleasing way, or will it be softer?"

"Sir?"

He smiled. "Never mind. Thank you, Mrs. Huggins." (In a moment of levity early in their relationship, he had once called her "Madame de La Huggins," and her responding frown, though unaccompanied by reproach, had been so deep that it threatened to permanently contort her face.) "What is Graham doing?"

"Polishing silver, sir."

Lenox winced. "Do tell him to take a break, would you?"

"If you wish, sir."

"Thank you."

"Of course, sir," she said, and withdrew.

Lenox liked his tea smoky, and he took a deep draft, feeling it warm his chest. He ate quickly and happily.

His eyes began to feel lazy and soft; the fire flickered; and before long, with a mostly empty teacup cradled in two hands in his lap, he had nodded off to sleep.

He was woken by a bell. In the quick lurch from sleep, he felt momentarily confused, glanced down at his list, imagined that it was Mayne—didn't know what to think—but then remembered that of course it must be his mother, and stood up, happy at the prospect of her arrival.

CHAPTER THIRTEEN

In the house where Lenox had grown up, there was a full-length portrait of his mother. Its painter, Thomas Lawrence, had been old and grand—near the end of his life—and she had been very young. He had captured that youth, her pale face flushed with excitement, full of the future, lips parted in a slight smile. She was standing in the private study of a country house, a clean-hedged landscape visible through a window behind her, one hand resting lightly on a desk, the other holding the place in a small book, her figure slender in a brilliant lapis lazuli–colored dress.

She came into Lenox's rooms now, nearly thirty years later, and her face was aged, but in its expression identical: tender, lively, curious, warm, haughty, loving. Still always full of the future.

"There you are, Mother, hullo."

She kissed him and held his face between her hands. "You've been asleep, haven't you?"

"No!" he said indignantly.

"I must be losing my touch then." She kissed him one more time. "Is any of that tea left? I'm chilled to the bone."

"Have you been to the Savoy?"

"No, I came straight here and sent my bags there. The train was late."

Lenox glanced up at the clock—past five. "That's a nuisance."

"It always is."

"You haven't seen Wallace?"

"Wallace? Oh! No, not yet." She had poured herself the tea, deemed it (Lenox could read her gestures as well as his own mind) too cold, and had now turned her hand to tidying the tray so that it could be taken away—returned with hot water, hopefully. "Tomorrow, I suppose. You'll give me a ride to Edmund's? If so, we have an hour or so to ourselves."

"Of course."

She looked at him with a mother's eyes, and he felt her engulfing love with an unexpected sensation of gratitude. "How lovely it is to see you, Charles."

"You as well."

"Go on, then," she said, leaning forward. "I can see you have news. What is it?"

He laughed. She had always been slightly uncanny. "I do have a case."

He spun his tale. She was one of those people who bored easily, and whom you therefore wanted to entertain—even Lenox felt that, though he knew he couldn't bore her. Of all the women she met in society, she was easily the best read and usually the smartest, but she had rejected any specific channel of energy, and there was a sense of idleness in her, idleness alongside brilliance. Perhaps it was that she was one of those people who are poetic without the forced-flower unhappiness that makes for a poet—she loved nature, she felt deeply, but she never seemed to expect anything in return from that love or those feelings, as a writer would. She took violently against people; grew sick of places very quickly; treated her husband high-handedly. Virtually everyone with whom she was acquainted was in a state of continual exasperation with her, and also loved her very much.

Universally, in Lenox's experience, they wished to know what she thought of them.

For Lenox's part—his father was a figure he revered, and upon whose opinion he counted. But his mother was his best friend upon the earth.

It was rather the reverse in Edmund's case. Interesting how such things fell out.

They spent thirty minutes in intense conversation about Lenox's morning by the riverbank. It was interrupted only when the housekeeper came to take away the tea. Apparently Lenox's mother had let herself in (she had a key), because Mrs. Huggins startled at the sight of her and curtsied low.

"How are you, Mrs. Huggins?" said Lady Emma, smiling.

"Very well, ma'am, I am pleased to say."

"Would it be a terrible bother to ask for hot water?"

"I can prepare a new pot of tea instantly, of course, ma'am—if that will do, Mr. Lenox?" she said abruptly, remembering that he was in fact her employer.

"I think we can stretch to a new pot for my mother, Mrs. Huggins."

"Straightaway, sir," the housekeeper said, betraying none of the longing that no doubt lingered in her bosom to ask for news of Lady Hamilton as she left the room.

"Make sure it's the cheap stuff!" Lenox called after her.

She pretended not to hear. "Charles," said his mother chidingly. "How has she been, anyhow?"

"She is the scourge of my existence."

His mother smiled once more. "Good. A young man of your age and means in this city needs his existence scourged once an hour. You're not gambling, are you?"

He gave her a very severe and skeptical glance. This was her greatest fear, and one of the few points on which she was truly naïve. Perhaps that was because it was the great theme of so many cheap novels, an art form to which she was susceptible: vast fortunes gambled away in a single night, the red-rimmed eyes of a tragic young fellow stumbling out of a club at dawn worth nothing more than the expensive clothes on his back.

For some reason, she never suspected it of Edmund for a minute, though he was the one who in fact did enjoy a hand of whist at his club now and again. But then, Edmund had money that would never be his, in that peculiar paradoxical British first-son way—that is, he would inherit the baronetcy and Lenox House with the entrusted funds those meant. Whereas Charles, though it was less, had his own money outright, his to lose on the fall of a pair of dice if he wished.

"Still no gambling," he said. "I'm too busy with opium."

"Charles."

"And duels, of course. I may take it up at any moment, though. Your vigilance is wise."

"Charles."

"Truly I don't gamble, Mother."

"Well—mind you don't start."

"I'll wager you five pounds this minute that I haven't started by Michaelmas."

"Very droll," she said. "How is Jane?"

"She's well, I think."

"Is that all you know? You must stick together up here, you children who move to London from the country."

"It's not as if we're in the South China Sea. She has her own friends."

She smiled at him fondly. "To me you're still each about nine years old."

Impulsively, he said, "What do you think 'wondrous affable' means? Not what it *means*, the words, but what—it's a strange thing to call someone, isn't it?"

"Not someone valiant as a lion."

He frowned. "Say that again?"

"It's from Shakespeare, my dear."

"Oh."

"Nearly everything is."

He waved a glum hand. "I know it, I know it. That or the Bible or Bunyan."

"You should have paid attention in school." She stood, saying, quite directly, "I'm going to snoop until the tea comes."

They went on discussing the two women who had died upon—or beside—the Thames. For her part, Lady Emma couldn't have cared less that Lenox had elected to become a detective, and anyone who *had* cared, in her presence, would have met a lion, wondrous unaffable.

She studied the map of Russia that he had open on a card table, asking what certain ink lines on it meant, put a gloved finger to the sill of the window and came away without any dust for her effort—spied, in short, as good as her word.

The two of them had always been like this. During the two-year window after Edmund had gone to Harrow but before Lenox had, they had been closest friends; she had learned the texts and the maths his tutor set him, they had taken long walks around the grounds as his father worked on important Parliamentary matters, often dining alone together afterwards. That was unusual; but she was unusual. They often read together—Charles, adventure stories still at the time, his mother, most often, Jane Austen.

Sometimes they would talk incessantly, sometimes not at all. It didn't signify either way.

"Do you really mean to travel, Charles?" she asked. "Russia?"

"Not anytime in the next forty minutes."

"I'm being quite serious," she said, and her face was serious. "Those were the two things you said when you came down from Balliol—that you meant to travel, and you meant to be a detective. You have become a detective."

"Well, yes," he said guardedly. "I do mean to travel. Why?"

"When?"

"I don't know to any great certainty. At the moment, I really am caught up in my work, you know."

"I do know, my dear, I do know." She came and touched his cheek again. "Good Lord, how young you are."

She had always had an uncommon physical intimacy with her sons—in an age of decorum, she ruffled their hair, drew them into hugs well past their boyhood, rested a head on their shoulders: her sons. Once it had embarrassed Charles a little (there was a horrifying memory of a kiss on the cheek at Harrow in front of dozens of boys from his house, which could still make him blush), but he valued it, too, her touch.

"Twenty-three now."

"I'm so awfully proud of you."

"Are you? I haven't done anything."

"I'm proud of the man you've become, I suppose I mean."

In the far distances of his mind, a single alarm bell pealed. "Is something wrong?"

She smiled slightly and enigmatically, perhaps at his intuition, inherited from her, and sat. "You know, you're stronger than Edmund, Charles."

"Me? I am?"

"Yes."

And suddenly in that moment he realized that he *did* know this to be true, though he hadn't known he knew it. His brother was an innocent, in many ways. He belonged to the country, as their father did; Charles belonged to the city, as their mother did. His brother was larger, but Charles, slender, could bend like a reed without breaking.

"Why do you say so?"

"I worry it will hurt him terribly—it will hurt you both terribly—but—ah, well, Charles, your father. He's ill."

"Ill?"

"There is a growth in his chest."

"His chest," Lenox said dumbly.

She nodded, her face grave and sorrowful. "Dr. Rivers has given him six months to live."

"So you don't have a meeting with Wallace at all," he said, still not quite thinking logically.

"No."

He hesitated. "This can't be."

He knew perfectly well that it could, but—it couldn't. She let a moment pass, then said, "It may be less. Either way, Dr. Rivers says he'll be gone before the year is out, I fear, Charles. My poor boy." She reached for his hands and clasped them in hers. Though her voice remained steady, there were tears spilling from her eyes. "I'm so sorry to have to tell you."

CHAPTER FOURTEEN

Eleven hours later, Lenox was, as one old Irish friend from school would have called it, heavy drunk.

He had one hand on the wall of an alley. He was somewhere in West London; he knew that much. The culprit was wine, which in his heart of hearts he had never actually believed could get him properly drunk, only tipsy. As it happened, he had disproved that hypothesis this evening. He was barely upright, and only a small animal part of him was still conscious, willing the other nine-tenths of his carcass to carry on.

"Oy! Guv! Ride home!"

At the end of the alley, there was a hansom cab. It must have been just out of the stable for the morning—its horse's coat was glossy, and Lenox, had he been slightly more alert, would have noticed that its driver's jacket was brushed, too.

With almost indescribable gratitude, he nodded, lurched toward the cab, and heaved himself inside, mumbling his address.

Fifteen minutes later, he woke up with a jolt outside his own familiar home. Thank goodness for that. The driver could have made for the ends of the earth, and Lenox wouldn't have woken up to stop him. He somehow managed to pay, stumbled out, and went upstairs.

He fell asleep on the chaise in his room.

At ten the next morning he was washed, shaved, and sitting with the papers.

"Oh hell," he said to no one in particular—Graham had gone to the kitchen—when he picked up the sixth newspaper of the stack he was examining.

"Sir?"

Lenox glanced up and reddened. It was Mrs. Huggins, carrying a coffeepot. He hadn't heard her enter and wouldn't have sworn in front of her (shouldn't have sworn at all, really). "Oh, nothing, Mrs. Huggins. Apologies."

"Can I bring you anything else, sir?"

"Oh no, not as long as Graham will be by before too long."

"Only a moment, sir, I believe."

"Thank you, Mrs. Huggins," Lenox said humbly.

In fact, he didn't feel all that awful—only wretched, wretched down to the bottom of his soul. Physically he would survive: he was young, and he had slept for a little more than five hours, besides which he vaguely remembered that before he had collapsed onto the divan in his room, Graham had been coaxing him into drinking water, brick that he was.

Now, having had coffee and toast, he felt nearly human, and at that moment Graham came—as tidily dressed as ever—with a plate of bacon and eggs. Lenox had been truly drunk just four or five times in his life, and knew from those experiences that he would benefit from eating as much as possible the next morning. In the years to come, of course, he would look back with a sense of tragic hilarity at the youth who had believed these were the elements of a full recovery from a drunken night—but for now, while he was twenty-three, they were.

"Thanks very much," he said to Graham. He held the newspaper out. "Did you see this?"

He did feel fearfully low in his emotions. He had been too drunk; now this newspaper; and above all, like the thrumming of a heartbeat in his ears, the fact of his father's illness, news that right now, in a sitting room a few streets over, his mother would be gently relaying to Edmund.

Graham took the paper. "Ah. Yes, sir, I did."

The paper was the *Daily Star*. "Why on earth have they included an illustration of me? No other paper has even mentioned me! And it's—"

Lenox came up short. He had seen the answer to his own question before he was finished asking it. "Sir?" Graham said quizzically.

"It's the favorite of the police. That's what I was going to say."

Graham raised his eyebrows. "Ah."

"Exeter's revenge, I hazard. He knows my position in society will be—well, who cares. Compromised. But who cares?" Lenox shoveled a forkful of scrambled eggs into his mouth. "None of that matters. Listen here, are you ready for a trip to Ealing?"

"Yes, sir. Are you, sir?"

"Yes, I am," said Lenox indignantly. He wasn't, still foggy, still tired, but that was his own fault, and he wouldn't take it out on the victim of Walnut Island. "Get my suit ready, if you would."

"It's on the back of your door, sir."

It was a long ride to Ealing. Plenty of time to lament every bump in the road, as it jolted his tender head, and plenty of time to think.

Lenox believed himself to be a very honest person; and yet he supposed that he must not be. Because he knew that there were some men and women who couldn't have lived with themselves, keeping the news about their father a secret from Edmund.

Edmund himself, in fact, was this sort of person. So was their father. It would never have occurred to either of them—and in some self-punishing part of his soul, still full of anger at itself for his wasted night and sickly morning, Lenox realized this made them better than he was—to hesitate for a moment. They would have come to him without waiting.

Lenox and his mother were different, however. Not dishonest; "practical" would have been the generous word, "slippery" the ungenerous one. "Deceitful" the cruel one. But the deceit had been practiced from love.

After they discussed his father's condition, the night before, his mother had sighed. "The question before me now," she had said, "is how I am to tell Edmund."

"Just as you told me," Lenox had replied.

She had sighed, then smiled wanly. "He is receiving different news than you are, Charles," she said. "He is also receiving news about himself."

Lenox had felt just an instant of irritation. When you were the younger brother, you were always the younger brother; whether you minded or not; on days you forgot and days you remembered; always.

At moments of late-night introspection, he wondered if it was what had driven him into his current profession.

"Yes," he'd said.

His mother had exhaled, steadying herself. "A wife takes a vow to obey, you know. That seemed immensely serious to me when your father and I married. It does still."

"But?"

"But he would never have told you. There's no vow for a mother, either. And maybe that's because there's no—there are no words, Charles, to express the promise a mother makes to herself and her children when they are born. You can just about make up a contract between a man and woman, just. But a mother and a child—"

As she pulled up short here, deep in thought, her fingers on her chin, her eyes on the floor. She was going to have to tell Edmund, her firstborn, that he was going to assume his title, his responsibilities, his land, all far, far sooner than he had expected, too soon.

"Perhaps you should leave it until the morning," Lenox had said.

She looked up at him. "I had thought of it."

Lenox nodded. "You and he and Molly."

"He would want you there."

"I'm sure, but it's better the three of you."

"Could you manage dinner, though?"

He had managed dinner. The one thing that public school indisputably taught you was how to put a brave and cheerful face on things. (No doubt this was useful in battle.) As soon as he could do so without being noticeable, however, Lenox had made his excuses and gone off to a party with his friend Hugh, who was pleasant company on occasions like this because he was always so forlornly in love—it was a French princess at the moment—that one never felt very scrutinized.

There Lenox had gotten so roaring drunk (on wine!) and he could recall, in the cab to Ealing, that he had made a fool of himself. He had remained in close conversation in a way he never would have dreamed to do sober with Cynthia Stark, whose husband was infamously indifferent to her behavior—being, it was said, in love with his groomsman, which left Cynthia at ends too loose for her own good, her own reputation.

Wincing, he realized that he might even have discussed Elizabeth with her.

Worse still, at the next party Hugh had taken him to, near Jermyn Street, Lenox had been absolutely cut by Lord Markham, who would one day be the Duke of Rotherham, though at Harrow Lenox wouldn't have deigned to let Markham carry his cricket bat.

It might have been this slight that triggered his final plunge into drink.

"Did you see that?" he had asked Hugh indignantly.

Markham had very politely said hello to Hugh. "That's a bad family," Lenox's friend had said. "He's going to have to marry an American. The father is a gambler and the mother is addicted to laudanum, takes it in strength enough to kill horses, they say. They cut down all the timber on the property. He only wants someone to feel superior to, that's all."

"Glad I was here, then," Lenox had replied bitterly, and then—another point of shame—throwing off his friend's attempt at comfort, he had joined a party of the drunkest people, who were leading a weaving charge toward some twopenny wine bar where it was as likely as not one of them would get his throat cut.

Now, in the new day, the carriage toward Ealing rattled on, and more and more of the night came back to Lenox. He felt sickened by himself; and he pictured, somewhere behind them a few miles, Edmund suffering the news that Charles had known for a full night, standing up, and insisting that they must go see Charles immediately. *Let me do it*, his mother would say—slippery, like her younger son. Soon enough, they would all know. And it would change nothing at all. His father—his father, his only father!—would still have just six months left to live.

CHAPTER FIFTEEN

Ealing was far into outer London. As the city thinned, they passed freestanding homes with chickens running in their front yards; small groves of trees; empty fields; churches that needed their stones repaired. There were Irish flags here and there, too—by reputation, every Irishman who moved to England ended up in Ealing, and it was said that there were more than a few pubs it was wise not to enter if you spoke with an accent that originated east of the Isle of Man.

The police warehouse was a large brick building. With the help of Mayne's seal, and a little explanation, Lenox and Graham were soon enough in a private room, with all the physical evidence of the Walnut Island case laid out on a table in front of them.

"Bleak," Lenox said.

His hands were stuffed in his jacket pockets, and he felt queasy. He sat down in one of the small wooden chairs around the large central table. Light came into the room from yellowing windows, but it still felt stifling.

"Bleak," Graham agreed.

"We had better start with the trunk, I suppose."

"Very good, sir."

There were six pieces of itemized evidence here on the table, tagged with a case number (#454) and beneath it in a very fine cursive hand the words *Walnut Island* and *Unsolved*. There was also a receipt describing them. Credit to Mayne, who had organized the acquisition of this warehouse for the Met the year before and instituted a new recordkeeping system.

Three of the items were probably useless. Then again, credit to Mayne once more, for organizing a police department that retained useless evidence—which was, if Lenox's reading was an accurate indication, occasionally very useful. These were, first, a scrap of fishing net that had no doubt gotten bound up on the outside of the trunk on its journey down the Thames; second, an old ale bottle that had been among the rushes of the island as well, not far off from the trunk; and third, a chunk of driftwood that had been inside the trunk.

The other three were interesting.

The first was a tortoiseshell clasp. *Found in victim's hair,* the evidence list had recorded, and Lenox, rising from his chair, went over and touched it gently, this last personal ornament of a human being's life. She had been "unclothed," as the papers said. But this remnant of her taste, her selfhood, had slipped through that immeasurably unfair stripping-away.

The second was a woman's ring. This had been found loose in the trunk. It was not likely to have come from the victim's hand—she had swollen—and it was inscribed with a name, LIZZIE. It was made of tin silver. Cheap, though of course not free. Like the spectacles.

And then the trunk. That was third. Two knickknacks and this hulking object, a true seaman's trunk—five feet across, four feet wide, four feet deep—enough space to last a fellow with multiple uniforms and presumably the odd personal item for a voyage of two or three years. It had a rounded top. A woman curled on her side could have fit into it easily, especially a smaller one.

"What does it say about the trunk?" Lenox asked Graham, brushing his fingers over it.

Graham looked down at the inventory. "Dimensions first, sir. Then it says, *Victim found lying unclothed on left side within; cause of death strangulation. Two boards loose. Found unlocked; hasp broken. Stamped HMS Gallant (out of service thirty years; consistent with age of trunk). Water damage on all sides new.*"

"Yes, it's quite warped out of shape." Lenox could also see where it said HMS GALLANT in faded-but-still-tidy stenciled black, at the very center of its domed lid. "Anything else?"

"*Careful examination reveals no name inscribed within or without. Cleaned of corporeal fluids and remitted to locker at Ealing.* Then a date and a signature, sir."

For some time, Lenox studied the trunk's exterior. Then he opened it and looked inside with equally careful attention. Nothing here. "I wonder that it didn't open, considering that it was unlocked," he said.

"The lid looks to fit fairly firmly, sir."

Lenox nodded. "Yes, it does." He returned to the chair, his head a bit sore still. "The *Gallant* was in some of the famous battles of the Napoleonic Wars," he said.

"Was it?"

"Yes. Massive ship. Must have been thousands of these trunks issued out of it."

"Interesting, sir."

"A decent anonymous vessel for a body, in other words. Does it point the finger at someone . . . well, he would have to be over forty, wouldn't he, to have served on the ship?"

"It seems more likely to have been circulating. Peddlers use these naval trunks, sir, I have sometimes noticed."

Lenox nodded. "True. And the dockyards use them for storage on land."

"Indeed, sir."

Lenox frowned. "On the other hand, it is very rare to see one entirely unmarked, in my experience. You generally find the owner has scratched something on the underside of the lid, or—" He stood up again and one last time opened the trunk, wishing a sign would appear.

"Issued late, perhaps, sir," said Graham. "Or to someone orderly in his habits."

"Help me flip it over, would you, Graham?"

It was heavy, but they managed to move it first onto its side, then upside down. The constable outside the door peeked inside but said nothing at the noise.

Nothing personal here, either. There was a serial number printed on the bottom, G957, but that was all. "The nine hundred fifty-seventh trunk issued to an able seaman aboard the G-for—*Gallant*, I suppose, sir," Graham said.

"No doubt."

Lenox drifted away from the trunk and spent some time studying the ring and the tortoiseshell clasp; and from a sense of diligence the netting, the driftwood, and the discarded ale bottle as well.

They were back on their way to London before lunch. It was reassuring to return to the busy streets of the city's center, after the unearthly quiet of that room and its objects.

Lenox asked Graham to drop him at Edmund's house, and added that he would dine out at his club; the servants could have the afternoon off if they liked.

"That goes for you, too."

"Is there anything I can do to assist you with my free time, sir?"

Lenox paused. "Do you really want to?"

Graham looked at him gravely. "I am very invested in the solution to the case, sir."

Lenox glanced through the window, thinking. "You could clear Nathaniel Butler. I've no doubt it was the sheerest bad luck that landed him in prison, but he does match our idea—my idea, I won't ascribe it to you—of the murderer."

Graham nodded. "Very good, sir."

"Thank you, Graham. Here's my stop. I'll see you later this evening."

Edmund and Molly's house in the city was a medium-sized and unassuming place, made of that pink Georgian brick you saw too rarely nowadays. The railings were of black wrought iron, and gleamed so brightly that one might almost have been hesitant to touch them, thinking they were new painted.

Lenox, who knew better, used one to haul his sluggish body up the steps.

When he had reached the very top, though, just as he was lifting his hand to knock on the door, he held back. He hesitated, then retreated down the steps.

He walked three streets over and two streets up. The cane he sometimes carried (most often at night—she was a city where a potential weapon could come in handy with sad frequency) tapped against the pavement as he went.

He came to a little lane and turned up it, then stopped at a house, a bit larger than Edmund and Molly's.

Here he *did* knock on the door. A redoubtable housekeeper answered. "Is Lady Elizabeth in?" he asked. "I know it's out of hours, but you may tell her it is Charles Lenox, if she is not receiving."

Elizabeth was dining alone. There was a book in front of her place setting. She stood and smiled when Lenox came in, giving him her hands and her cheek. "This is a lovely surprise." She glanced down at her lunch. "It's only soup and bread and butter. Will you take some?"

"Happily, if it's no inconvenience."

"None at all."

She gestured toward a maid, who withdrew. "What are you reading?" Lenox asked.

"Only a novel."

"A good one?"

"A brilliant one. It's by a fellow named Currer Bell—and yet I have never read a man who could understand women quite so well."

"What's it called?"

"*Jane Eyre*. Have you heard of it?"

"No."

"Read it before you get married." She smiled at him once more. "You look rotten, you know."

"I feel rottener."

She gave him a concerned glance, then returned her eyes to her soup, too wellborn either to stare at him or to eat. It was a conundrum, and he laughed. "What?" she said.

"There are times one wishes one were married," he said. He smiled this time, to undercut the sadness of the words.

"There are times one wishes one weren't, or so I'm told," she replied. "Anyhow, you're twenty-three. A man shouldn't marry till he's twenty-five. So my father has always said."

He knew Elizabeth's father, who was indeed happily married. "That gives me two years. Whom shall I marry?"

She leaned back and let her eyes go up to the ceiling, thinking. His soup arrived, and there was a very orderly commotion as his place was laid, his bread cut and buttered, a glass of lemonade set next to it, the flowers in the middle of the table shifted.

When the servants were gone, she said, "Not Jane Eyre. What about Eliza Blaine?"

"She's very pretty, and sweet."

"Not smart enough, you mean. What about Eleanor?"

"We're too close."

Elizabeth thought further, and Lenox began to eat. He felt slightly better as the food went down—a hearty country soup, with carrots, potatoes, hot and salty. His friend, his dear friend, offered another name, another. She wouldn't ask him why he felt rotten until he was willing to say himself.

"That half-French girl is charming," she said. "What of her? She's rejected George Wilkes, too, so she has taste. Marie West?"

"Hm, a possibility."

She frowned. "Before I move in the autumn, I shall make it my business to find you someone to love."

There was someone he loved: her, her, her. And she was taken. He put his spoon down, and said, in a measured tone, one that tried for lightness anyhow, "I came by for a cowardly reason, I'm afraid. I couldn't face my brother."

"No?"

"No." And he observed that his voice, ridiculously, was hoarse. "Nor my mother, for that matter. Somehow my feet brought me here."

"Oh, Charles," she said, leaning forward. "I'm glad they did. What's wrong?"

CHAPTER SIXTEEN

That evening, Lenox dined at the Oxford and Cambridge Club. He had invited his friend Courtenay, the one who had provided him with medical expertise on criminal matters and pointed out the textbooks that would offer more.

"I'm pleased we're going to dine together," said Lenox right at the outset, "but I must offer warning that I had a mercenary reason to ask you."

"Did you? How mercenary?"

Lenox laughed. He liked the young, forthright, hardworking physician. His father was a clergyman in the Cotswolds. He was disappointed that his eldest son hadn't followed him into the profession, but Courtenay was a scientist to his marrow, a positivist, a scion of the Enlightenment. The second half of the century would bring miracles, he'd told Lenox once, and he hoped to be in the first row for them.

"Not very. It's about surgeons. I would like to know who the best are—the very best, regardless of whether they're here or in . . . in Burma."

"They're not in Burma." They were in the wide, red-carpeted entry hall of the private club, and started the climb up the steps to the dining room. Courtenay had been at Magdalene College, Cambridge, before moving to St. Bart's. "But it depends what you mean by a surgeon."

"Does it?"

As they sat down, Courtenay began to explain. "There are a great number of white-haired consulting surgeons whose opinion I would value very highly."

"Such as?"

Courtenay named half a dozen. "I see. And what is the other kind of surgeon?"

Just then a waiter came with a mirror-topped trolley of decanters, offering drinks. Courtenay asked for a brandy and soda, and Lenox, though he had felt strongly that very morning that the best course would probably be to join one of those Christian societies you saw in Hyde Park crusading against the evils of alcohol, found it didn't sound all that bad now that ten hours had passed, and asked for the same.

He also took a water with lemon, however. His friend Almondsley-West swore by the true cross that this was a panacea.

Courtenay took a draft of his drink once it had been poured, then put it down, pulling his cheeks back in a satisfied grimace, and said, "The other side of the coin is the actual surgery. For cutting—for sheer cutting—there are many excellent men, but only two at the very pinnacle."

"Sheer cutting," Lenox repeated.

"Yes, it's different. You need someone about twenty-nine or thirty-three, in that range, to begin with. Not past forty-five or so certainly."

"Why?"

Courtenay thought. "Hm. Well, at that age a chap has plenty of experience. But he's still young enough to have his hands. Surgeons are like sportsmen, you see. They're as good in their ways as the cricketers. When you watch them, their hands are half a step ahead of anyone else's. It saves lives. I've seen it myself, or I would think it nonsense. And even beyond that, there are always a few whose hands are—it's otherworldly, in a way—their hands are so good you can't quite believe it."

"Interesting. And do you have it?"

Courtenay shook his head ruefully. "About average, I'm afraid. Useful enough for ninety-eight of a hundred procedures, but—well, take one of these two fellows I mentioned, Anthony Callahan. Interesting tale, Callahan's. He never even intended to be a physician. He was going to be a veterinarian."

"A vet!"

"Yes. Comes from somewhere in the North. Great ruddy large fellow, solid working class. Had prepared himself quite happily to spend his life as a vet, administering to cows and horses."

"What happened?"

"Ah, so. Vets are usually apprenticed. But Callahan, being fairly bright, came down to a two-year school in London for specialization. Sort of place that produces vets for Goodwood, you know—the best. If the Queen's dog is ill, that kind of thing."

"All right."

"Well, on the first day of class, everyone received a frog to dissect. The professor was a medical surgeon. He stood there at the head of the gallery for the fifty minutes, instructing these thirty young men how to cut the frog.

"He taught the class quite normally. The instant the class was over, however, he pulled Callahan into a cab without saying anything, drove across the town, and walked them both into the office of the Dean of the Royal College of Surgeons. As Callahan tells the story, he thought he was in trouble. But it was quite the opposite. 'The best two hands I've ever seen,' the professor said. That was all. 'The best two hands I've seen in my entire life.'"

Lenox whistled low. "My."

"The rest is history. Now Callahan's charging thirty pounds for an afternoon's work. Still a lovely fellow, mind you. No airs to him."

"You said there were two. Who's the other?"

"A Scot named Thomas McConnell. Equally gifted, I think."

"Interesting."

"Yes, people scrum to watch them."

The menu lay forgotten in Lenox's hands. "What do you mean?"

"There are seats in the theater. Generally not hard to come by. But for Callahan and McConnell, students line up an hour or two beforehand. I've done it myself. Even then it can be hit-or-miss. I saw Callahan do the prettiest excision of a diseased liver about a month ago, though, you wouldn't have believed it."

"I wouldn't have had any idea what I was looking at."

Courtenay grinned. "No, true."

They ordered, and the conversation moved on to other matters. Courtenay was very good company, the second brandy and soda far silkier than the first. After they ate dessert, Lenox asked about petechiae and poisoning, the ghost of a self-doubt in his mind, but his friend confirmed his suspicions entirely, and then they spent a great deal of time talking in confidence about the case.

"Get me the coroner's report on the first body if you like," Courtenay said.

"I doubt it will even be ready. The backlog is disgraceful—eight weeks more often than not. But could there be anything to learn?"

"Oh, certainly, always."

"I will try, then," said Lenox. "I say, thank you."

"Not at all."

They lingered with cigars after supper, drinking port in the billiards room and watching as two older men cleansed the table of its red and white balls over and over, their expertise unerring. At last Courtenay and Lenox took a free table and tried their own impression of the feat; unconvincing. Not bad fun, though.

The next morning, very early, Lenox went to Harley Street, the slender thoroughfare where every doctor in England of consequence had an office, armed with a list of addresses. Like a broom salesman, he went door to door making his inquiries; by nine o'clock, he had booked two people to travel to Lenox House that week to see his father, on successive days.

One was named Sir Riley Callum; he had white hair, and fell into Courtenay's category of consultants. The other was Thomas McConnell. (Callahan, fine anatomizer of frogs, was vacationing in Somerset for two weeks.) The idea was that if Callum advised cutting, McConnell would be there the next day to do it. Lenox saw neither of them—they each had secretaries. He met their outrageous prices for traveling so far and losing a day's work without demur or negotiation.

He felt better when that had been done.

He thought back to seeing his brother the afternoon before. Their mother had already boarded the train home. They were in Edmund's front room, which was strewn with souvenirs of the country—a horsehair chair, portraits of dogs they had known, walking sticks suitable for a heath but not a cobblestone street—all across it.

They knew the same information now, though they had received it in a sequence to which only Charles and his mother were privy.

Edmund had poured his brother a glass of ginger ale (at this point, a few hours before his dinner with Courtenay, Charles was still at the tail end of his previous night's regrets) and come over to sit down, his face full of sadness and strength.

"What a dreadful hand to have been dealt," he said. "For father, I mean."

"Mother, too." Lenox looked at his elder brother. "And you, you shall have to be the baronet."

"That doesn't mean anything." Now it was Edmund's turn to pause. "I wonder how he'll take it."

"Very calmly," said Lenox without any doubt.

Edmund nodded. "Yes, he will, won't he."

Their father was a trim, crisp sort of person, with a clipped gray mustache and short hair, his wife balancing his occasional tautness with her sense of humor and creativity; they were a match.

The quality Lenox thought of as belonging to him more than any other was that he was true blue, down to his fibers. He was only ever himself. He would sooner have put his head beneath a guillotine than told a lie, or cheated a man. He was known across Sussex for his generosity—just as an example, he leased his lands for five lifetimes, generally, rather than three, and his tenants thus had a sense of continuity like few anywhere else—but it was also known that he would come down very, very hard on anyone who stepped out of line. He would evict a man in a day if the fellow didn't live up to his standards—a thief, for instance, or anyone violent.

He had declined to come to London to get a second opinion on his condition, according to their mother. Charles had decided (and told his brother, over the ginger ale) that London would have to visit the country. He himself planned to go down to Lenox House that week, as soon as he had seen to one or two things about the case.

CHAPTER SEVENTEEN

The case: a month was a dangerous amount of time, as he tried to remind himself every hour. Just long enough to let it slip through one's fingers.

After he had visited the offices of Sir Riley Callum and Thomas McConnell, he returned home. The papers, which he had taken with him and read along the way back, were full of nothing but the Thames Ophelia, as she was now universally known. His own name did not come up again, blessedly. He had taken scissors in the small leather valise he carried, and even as the carriage rattled, he carefully sliced the stories he wanted to preserve for his archive. It reassured him not to miss a day of the practice.

When he returned home, he found that Graham's own newspapers had been dissected and sorted, too.

"How do you do, sir," Graham said, greeting him near the breakfast table, where he had been.

"The rug is back."

"Yes, sir," said Graham.

It did look cleaner. "Mrs. Huggins!" shouted Lenox.

The housekeeper appeared after a moment. "Sir?"

Lenox glanced at the clock. It was only ten, but he was starving.

"Could you please ask them to make me a sandwich with cold chicken and some of that chutney you made, if we still have any. And a pot of tea. And see if we have any shortbread biscuits, those square ones, and if we don't, please fire the cook. Then go get some yourself, because I want those, too."

"I'll—I'll bring the food, sir," said the housekeeper, who perhaps hadn't foreseen her employer's having accomplished enough business of an unpleasant nature in the morning that he would be in quite such a cavalierly commanding frame of mind. "Just a few moments, if you please."

"Thank you, Mrs. Huggins. The rug looks marvelous, incidentally."

"Oh, I'm pleased you think so, sir!" she said, and looked positively happy for the first time in a long while.

Lenox felt guilty. "Well, not at all, not at all. And don't really fire the cook."

"We have shortbread, sir."

This was the first thing that might have passed as a joke in the long tripartite acquaintance of Lenox, Graham, and Mrs. Huggins, and as she withdrew, the detective and the valet exchanged a look of raised eyebrows.

"Well," said Lenox, sighing. "Walnut Island."

"Yes, sir."

"I'm going to the dockyards after I eat. You read the papers this morning, from the look of it?"

"Yes, sir."

"They've not gotten far."

"That was my conclusion, too, sir."

Lenox threw himself down into a chair. "It may in fact be possible that we are the ones who can do it, you know," he said.

"I hope we may help, sir."

Reading between the lines—for of course outwardly, the press's opinion being of paramount importance, everything was presented in terms of the rapidest progress, Field was "intensely focused on a handful of suspects," Mayne was "confident an arrest would be made within the week"—the police themselves had made no advancement whatsoever.

That was to say, there was no name to attach to either woman; nobody had come forward to claim the body, or had recognized the sketch of her face distributed by police; the papers reported no new witnesses.

Fleet Street would soon grow restless. Innumerable articles, all with nothing to say.

Except that of the *Challenger*, of course. It published the two letters the murderer had written under a banner headline so large and provocative that Lenox had spotted it thirty times that morning already.

"You looked into Nathaniel Butler?" Lenox asked, shuffling through the clippings he had pulled out of his carrying case. He pointed to Graham's usual chair. "Please, sit."

"I did, sir," said Graham.

"And?"

"I believe he is innocent, sir." He pushed across a piece of paper. "To begin with, he was away from London for three days on either side of the first murder."

"That would be a perfect crime," Lenox pointed out.

"Very true, sir, and yet it would be hard to imagine a less perfect crime than the second. He reported it to the police himself. That seems very stupid."

"Or the act of an obsessive."

"Perhaps. But a third obsession, sir, in addition to the letter writing and the—" Graham's imperturbable face looked briefly perplexed, and then he alit on the word. "The symbolism, sir? Furthermore, I met Mr. Butler in prison."

"How did he strike you?"

"He is utterly bewildered and afraid, sir. I wouldn't credit him with the intelligence to plan a luncheon."

"Hm."

"He was wearing glasses with a chain on them, I feel bound to report as well."

Lenox considered this, tapping the table with a finger. Then he picked up the dossier Graham had prepared and began to read it.

All the relevant details of Butler's life (date of birth, current address, employer, salary) were here. He was married and had two children. He was relatively prosperous by a clerk's standards—his wife had brought two adjacent townhouses into the marriage—which was another strike against Lenox's portrait of the killer. Though it was important, he thought, not to let that become binding in his thoughts.

"It would be just like Field to arrest this poor clerk and prove right," he said. "Where was Butler during the week he was away from London?"

"Visiting his mother in Birmingham, sir. She is ailing, and he was owed vacation. His family was with him."

"You have confirmed this?"

Graham nodded, and Lenox trusted the nod implicitly. "Still, he might have returned in the night to do it. Not all that far, Birmingham."

"Anything is possible, sir."

"Alas."

Lenox's early lunch arrived, and he fell upon it like a horde of Visigoths sacking a city. It was gone before long. He swirled the last of his tea, drank it off, and then, picking up his newspapers so that he might finish clipping them along the way, left to go to the dockyards.

He arrived at the navy's own shipping yard half an hour later. This was an enormous and busy building just along the river, with a heavy smell of fish and old seagoing equipment.

He knew that a friend of a friend, or really a friend-of-several-friends, a fellow he'd met once or twice, was in charge here, Captain William Ampleforth. He sent his card upstairs and was beckoned up not much later. He was here to cross his t's and dot his i's, as his most odious schoolmaster had exhorted them every day to do with completely unthinking repetitiveness. ("Boys, you'll conquer the world if you'll only . . . ," and so forth. Thus far none of them had conquered the world that Lenox could see, his old schoolmates. For the most part, they seemed to be drinking in various London clubs and bars.)

Ampleforth was a genial and generous soul, red cheeked, that particular kind of round-faced naval homebody who feels best at home in an officers' mess. He immediately offered Lenox a tot of rum, and they drank together. Then they discussed the murders, which were all anyone was talking about along the river, according to the captain.

Lenox explained that he was looking into them.

"Bloody mess," Ampleforth said. "This clerk they've arrested is the man, I suppose?"

"He may be."

"There's plenty of violence for an Englishman to do at sea," Ampleforth said, shaking his head. "This chap needs Bedlam."

"He'll get it," Lenox replied.

"Anyhow, what was it you wanted from me?"

"Ah yes. It's about a seaman's trunk. Have you ever seen one that belonged to the *Gallant*?"

"I imagine so. Why?"

Lenox explained about Walnut Island. It was news to Ampleforth—evidently, to his credit, not a regular reader of the *Challenger*. (The other papers would get the murderer's letters into the evening editions.) "It had 'HMS *Gallant*' stenciled on its lid," Lenox said, "and on the bottom was printed 'G957,' which I assume is because it was issued by the ship. No other markings."

Ampleforth frowned. "G957?" he said.

"Yes. Why, does that seem unusual?"

"Not unusual so much as not usual, if you see what I mean. We're not too precious about our lockers in the navy, so long as they match the dimensions. Most sailors are on a dozen different ships before they're nineteen."

Lenox was puzzled. "Hm. I see. So that marking—"

"It wouldn't have come from the *Gallant*, anyhow. Just the manufacturer's mark, I suppose."

"And what about the stencil on the lid?"

"Well, that would be quite normal—except I would have expected it to be scratched in with a knife." Ampleforth thought of something. "Look here, draw me a picture of this trunk, would you?"

Lenox did so as quickly and well as he could, its brass handles, its rounded top. Ampleforth took it and immediately shook his head. "No, no, no," he said.

"What is it?"

Ampleforth turned the sheet around. "If there is one thing we value aboard a ship, it is space. Well—water, but after water, space." He started to sketch himself. "Look. A seaman's trunk is always flat, like this, so it can be stacked. Always."

Lenox felt a buzz of excitement, as yet still mysterious. "I see."

"What's more, I've never seen a trunk yet with just two markings on it."

"Perhaps it could have come from a private ship, not a naval ship?"

"They have the same exact customs, when it comes to that kind of thing, a thousand times in a thousand. All their men are retired from our service. And anyhow, it says the *Gallant*'s name on it."

Lenox sat back. He was deeply uneasy. It was like the board from the second murder not being wet; he had made the mistake of believing what he had been manipulated to believe, that it was a seaman's locker he had been dealing with, first because the articles they had clipped said so, second because of the words HMS GALLANT on its lid.

"Then what kind of locker is it?" Lenox asked.

"I've no idea at all. I'll tell you what, ring for my clerk. Let's ask him."

Ampleforth hit a bell. Meanwhile, for the first time, Lenox had the feeling of his mind meeting the murderer's own—the planning it had taken to stencil HMS GALLANT on the box, the careful misdirection, the hideousness of the two women's deaths, the dry board but the wet clothing—and he felt a chill of fear somewhere deep inside.

CHAPTER EIGHTEEN

Lenox, Ampleforth, and Ampleforth's clerk spent some time discussing the trunk. Lenox asked them repeatedly if perhaps some privileged traveler aboard the HMS *Gallant*—a paying passenger—might have brought this trunk. But no, Ampleforth insisted, the navy was highly regulatory of onboard baggage, and had been twice as strict when the *Gallant* was still seaworthy thirty years prior.

But what was the purpose of the concealment?

G957, he had in his mind; the ruse of the *Gallant* must be designed to cover, somehow, for that G, explain it away.

He thanked Ampleforth, owed him dinner he said, then took a carriage home in a thoughtful mood. It was just past one o'clock. In his rooms there was a raft of morning mail—a note from Elizabeth asking if he was going to Lady Ledderer's that evening, a bill from the bookstore, a close friend from Oxford who was in Ceylon and sent very funny intermittent updates about his life there. A telegram from his mother, too.

Thinking of you STOP *send word if there is aught I can do* STOP

That "aught" came from the previous century, and so, Lenox thought with a pang, did his parents. And while he might, they would not see the next.

As he was contemplating this, tapping the folded telegram against the table, Mrs. Huggins came in. Apparently she had been encouraged by Lenox's praise of her work on the rugs, unfortunately. She now presented him with a long list—it ran to a second page!—of things she thought should be done around the house because it was spring.

There was nothing Lenox wanted less in the world than to have a long conference with his housekeeper assessing the "state of curtains (2nd bedroom)."

He looked at the list with at least a simulation of thoughtfulness.

"Why don't you go ahead with the first four, and then we'll revisit the rest with Graham," he said after a moment.

She looked on the verge of mentioning that in Lady Hamilton's household, orders five through nineteen would have been executed as a matter of course. But, perhaps sensing that she had already pressed her luck, she acceded and withdrew.

Lenox composed a telegram to his mother.

Huggins will be death of me STOP *otherwise holding steady* STOP *looking forward Lenox House two days time* STOP *bringing doctors* STOP *they will not stop overnight* STOP *prepare Father* STOP *Charles*

He thought that he ought to go see his brother. But there was so much to do; and in the end, he decided that he would visit Sir Richard Mayne instead.

Mayne received him curtly, but this attitude seemed to be more global in nature than in any way specific to Lenox.

"Well?" he said.

"A few things," Lenox replied in a tone of corresponding briskness.

He felt his youth. Presumably when he was older, he wouldn't be so terrified in situations like this one. The happy anticipation of that future was of no comfort to him now, though. "The first is Nathaniel Butler."

"Yes? What about him?"

"Multiple people have confirmed that he was in Birmingham for several days on either side of the first murder."

Mayne frowned. "Hm. Field won't like letting him go."

"That's your business, of course. The next thing is the trunk."

"The trunk?"

Lenox explained, and Mayne's curiosity was piqued. He wanted to know if G957 was a useful clue. "It almost must be," he said. "At any rate, it's among our best leads so far."

"I'm attempting to solve the puzzle," said Lenox.

Mayne waved an irritable hand. "We don't talk like that here, it's not a novel," he said. "Just get at it. Do you need a man or two?"

Lenox, swallowing, said that that would be useful, certainly. "My plan was to go to a few shops that sell trunks. I could write up a list."

"Have it to me by the end of the day—keep it sharpish, mind—and I will assign you a constable."

The end of the day, sharpish. Lenox hated that half pound a week with all his heart. "Very well," he said.

Sir Richard, perhaps remembering that he was speaking with the son of a Member of Parliament and an aristocrat, shook his head. "Sorry, Lenox. Not myself. The press. Was that all?"

"No. There was one more thing, in fact."

"Eh?"

"It's about the two women."

"I should hope so."

"Specifically where they might have disappeared from. It's been bothering me."

"Go on."

"Does Inspector Field have a theory?"

"Prostitutes." Some look of irritation must have passed over Lenox's face, however briefly, because Sir Richard said, "What, you think it unlikely?"

"We know very specifically that their teeth are those of wellborn women. It was mentioned in the first article ever written about Walnut Island."

"A prostitute may have decent teeth."

"It's not common. What's more, the second body, what I saw of it—"

Here Lenox ran aground, though.

How could he explain that his instinct told him it was the body of a person who had a decent place to sleep, decent food to eat?

A tortoiseshell comb for her hair.

Mayne nodded. "No. I take your point," he said. "I am inclined to agree."

"There is an easy way to find out more. If the medical surveyor makes a venereal examination . . ."

Mayne turned—he was standing, pacing—and picked up a piece of paper. "I am pressing them like all get-out to examine the body. They are as slow as that hippopotamus."

Lenox shrugged. "In that case, I think it is our task to discover where these women might have come from. Nobody has reported them gone. Nobody has written in, I assume, saying that one or both match the description of someone missing?"

Mayne shook his head. "No. But what do you propose?"

"I think we must wire the police service in every county and ask if they are missing either one or two women."

"The replies will be a flood—every girl who eloped to Gretna Green with the local blackguard, or went bad and came to London."

"My assistant and I shall go through them, even if they are overwhelming in number," Lenox said stoutly. "And if the descriptions you provide are precise, regarding height, weight, eye color, hair color, age—the comb and the ring from Walnut Island."

Mayne hesitated, and then nodded. "Very well. It shall be done. The replies to be forwarded to you?"

"I am happy for Field to share the work, or to take it myself."

"Leave Field to Field," said Mayne. "You shall have the replies if you want them. Is that all?"

"For now."

"Good day, then," said Mayne, sitting down and looking at his papers. He glanced up at Lenox. "You're doing good work. I thank you."

The young detective—he could call himself that, he thought!—left Scotland Yard aloft on that compliment.

The last several months had been so frustrating, so endless, so full of self-doubt. There was every chance he might scrap this detective work yet, of course. Politics had always interested him, and he had the means and the inclination to travel. Either might make for a career, though the diplomatic corps seemed a hard road.

He would rather not join the army or the navy—the worst parts of school, extended over a lifetime.

But it gave him a coursing feeling in his veins to be on a scent, to be doing what he had envisioned doing. For the first time it all seemed worth it. Lord Markham be damned.

There was a wire waiting for him at home—briefly and irrationally he hoped it might be the first response from one of the remote constabularies of England, but that would take days, even longer, no doubt—and as he tore it open, he saw it was from his mother.

Recall now Huggins highly susceptible to cats STOP *Love* STOP *Mother*

Susceptible to cats! Lenox had only a moment to pause over this odd declaration before Mrs. Huggins herself entered, announcing that he had a guest, Mr. Rupert Clarkson.

CHAPTER NINETEEN

W ho on earth is Mr. Rupert Clarkson?" Lenox asked.

She did not know. "I cannot say, sir. He offers his card."

Lenox took this. "How strongly does he smell of drink?"

"Not at all, sir," said the housekeeper indignantly. "Over the years, I have—"

"Is he selling any variety of unguent or tonic out of a briefcase? Play straight with me, Mrs. Huggins."

Mrs. Huggins looked scandalized. "Indeed not, sir! He appears to be a respectable person—appears to be a—"

Lenox sighed dramatically, but the card bore out this informal assessment. It was a gentleman's card, with a gentleman's address near Oxford Street. "Ship him in, ship him in," Lenox said, interrupting. "But don't immediately start offering him roast beef sandwiches or he's liable to stay forever."

"As you please, sir."

"I'll ring if there's anything we need."

Almost all of Lenox's guests fell into one of three categories, distributed into about equal parts: Elizabeth, Edmund, or Someone Else, generally a friend or relative. Five or six times Lenox had hosted small dinner parties, usually as a prelude to some evening out—a ball, for instance (there was one this week), or a concert. Two had been arranged expressly as a favor to his friend Hugh, who, having been for a long while ardently and unrequitedly in love with their friend Eleanor, and being of a poetic bent, had made all the arrangements on those occasions himself.

At any rate, none of his visitors were like the Mr. Rupert Clarkson who entered the room now: ancient, apparently foul tempered, and present without explanation.

He was for some reason in high dudgeon. "You're Charles Lenox?" he asked with suspicion, as if someone had been passing bad checks under that name.

"I am, Mr. Clarkson," said Lenox, rising. "I don't believe we're acquainted."

Clarkson stared at him very baldly, toe to cap. "You're young."

Lenox was sorely tempted to reply *You're old*, but that would have been unkind, and he was not an unkind person, even when the situation justified it. ("That will get you shot one day," Edmund had predicted when Charles first moved to London, in their initial conversation about his decision to become a detective. "You'll be in a pub, on the verge of arresting a murderer, and he'll beg you to let him have a swift half of porter, and then while you're paying for it, he'll shoot you." "Thank you for that cheerful prognostication," Charles had said. He had added with some vehemence that he wouldn't pay for the drink; though in his heart he knew that it was true he *would* let the fellow have his drink, his brother had got him at least that right.)

Instead of replying, he merely waited for Clarkson to state his business.

After a moment or two, the old man removed his hat and sat down, making himself very free with one of Lenox's armchairs. "Please, sit," Lenox said, settling down opposite him. "Can I help you in some way, Mr. Clarkson?"

"A private detective, the papers said you were."

"Oh! The papers!"

"That's what they said. Were they wrong?"

Lenox shook his head. "No. It's true."

Lenox's mind had done a strange little flip. It was some push-me-pull-you of regret at having appeared in the paper, but tinctured with pride, and surmounted by an immediate excitement. Could this be a case, a veritable case?

"Much experience?" said Clarkson.

"A fair amount," said Lenox blithely.

"Well, you're what I need. A private detective. The police have no interest. And they shouldn't have any interest, what's more. No crime that I can discern has been committed."

Lenox was curious. "I would be happy to hear more."

"What are your fees?"

"Negotiable."

"Would a pound a day do?"

It was something Lenox hadn't even considered, especially; a privilege, he was conscious. Hugh was fearfully poor, a situation he had no expectation of changing, since his parents were also poor, unless he found his way into some viable concern.

"At the moment, Scotland Yard has retained my services. There's also the matter of expenses."

Clarkson took out a billfold. He put two ten-pound notes down on the side table. "When my credit has run out from these, you will let me know."

"I haven't accepted the case yet, Mr. Clarkson. Would you care to tell me about it?"

"Picky, are you?"

Lenox frowned. "Yes, as it happens, I am."

Clarkson shifted his chair, and seemed to really look Lenox in the eye for the first time. He had close-cropped white hair and wore round spectacles. His clothes were expensive and new. His watch chain was gold. A rich fellow.

"I need help," he said.

This piqued Lenox's sympathy. "What kind of help?"

Clarkson leaned forward in his chair with both his hands on his cane, which rested on the floor and came up to about the level of his chin. "That's more difficult to say."

"Start wherever you like."

Clarkson nodded. "Very well. A word about myself. I am an engineer, a retired engineer now. I was born in Shropshire and educated in London. I married early in life, but my wife died thirty years ago, of influenza. After that loss, my business became the primary interest of my life, and I did handsomely out of it. We're a firm that designs agricultural equipment. We possess several dozen patents. Three years ago, I retired and sold out to two young men, though I still consult with them for an annual fee."

"I see."

"I don't know any of this to be relevant, but it gives you a sense of my history."

"Did you and your wife have children?" Lenox asked.

"No," Clarkson said. "Nor did I remarry."

"And your problem?"

Now Lenox's interlocutor looked less certain of himself. "It's—well, it's this way, Mr. Lenox. I have a house in town here and another in Dulwich, where I often spend a day or two a week. It's a good practical arrangement for a gentleman at my time of life."

"I've no doubt."

"I often entertain friends at both—Dulwich if they like fishing, London if they like dining, as those are my two chief interests in retirement. Wine, especially. I have several congenial former colleagues who were erstwhile active in the city, too, and share one or the other of these two interests."

Lenox nodded. "I see."

Lenox knew Dulwich, a village north of the city, picturesque and very green, with a brook running through it. It would have taken only fifty minutes or an hour to get there, though in its rural beauty, it felt as if it were much deeper into the countryside.

"I wouldn't have said anything odd could happen to me, at my age. I'm seventy-one, I may add. My medical man pledges to me that I have the fitness of a fellow two decades younger. The fishing, I believe—and a temperate appetite."

"And what's happened?" Lenox pressed gently.

Clarkson looked discomfited. "It sounds mad, but I assure you I am in control of my faculties, Mr. Lenox."

"Nothing could be plainer."

The older man looked relieved, and it was clear that at least some of what Lenox had perceived as ill temper was nervousness. "Well, quite."

"And so?" said Lenox.

At last Clarkson came to the point. "About a month ago, I was in Dulwich for four nights. I returned home to London, and the house was as I had left it, with one small exception. There was a five-pound note in an envelope on my desk."

Lenox frowned. "That was not yours?"

"That was not mine." Clarkson looked at him sharply. "I know what you'll say—that I'm an old man, and forgot I had left it there. It's not true. For one thing, I am very careful about money. For another, it was not my envelope—did not come from my stationery drawer. And most important: I returned to Dulwich the next week, and there, on my desk, was the same exact thing. A five-pound note in an envelope."

"Was anything written on either of them?"

"No." Clarkson reached into his jacket pocket. "Nor on any of the four subsequent envelopes. Six in all."

He presented them to Lenox triumphantly. He took them. They were exactly as described: identical plain white envelopes, each with a single five-pound note in it and nothing more.

"That's queer," said Lenox. He looked up. "It's rather a lot of money."

"I know."

Thirty pounds was around the annual salary of many servants, and would have gone very far indeed outside London in particular, where a handsome house could be had for seven or eight pounds a year.

"Do you have servants?"

"Yes, but they travel with me between Dulwich and London, except for the charwoman in each place, who only comes in for the day."

"Was there any lock broken in either place? Or window? Anything missing?"

"No. I was very, very scrupulous in ascertaining to my own satisfaction that nothing was missing, no lock broken or window left open." Lenox didn't doubt that. Clarkson seemed generally scrupulous. "The last time I went to Dulwich, I left my valet behind to guard my home in London. He reported no intruder, nothing unusual. I asked him to wire me each evening with news of whether anything had appeared on my desk. Nothing had."

"And?"

"And when I returned, there it was, the fifth time."

"And this valet—"

"Ha!" said Clarkson, thumping his cane slightly. "I thought the same thing. He was the guilty party—if guilt you can call it. I therefore returned to London but left behind a young housemaid, Lily, whom I hired expressly from an agency in Dulwich for the week I would be away."

"And?"

"Her experience was identical to my valet's. The wire each evening. No intruders, no visitors. And there, when I arrived: the last envelope. This was yesterday."

"Who has keys to your residences?"

"Only my servants and I."

"I see."

"I am going mad, Mr. Lenox. I have no idea what to do. I saw your name in the paper, and here we are."

Lenox frowned. "These are deep waters, I fear, Mr. Clarkson."

"Can you help me?"

Lenox had two ideas of what might be happening. One sinister. "I believe I can, yes. You will have to be patient, however, and for that reason you may want to seek assistance elsewhere. I am due in the country for a few days this week, and I am assisting the Yard, as you know."

Clarkson looked incalculably relieved. "No, I leave it entirely in your hands. I am not someone money is winkled out of easily, but I would spend ten times what I am giving you to know what is happening, and how." He caught himself. "Not that you have license— when I say ten times—but I see that your own circumstances seem comfortable, and I know you will not swindle me."

"I am not engaged in the business primarily for financial reasons," Lenox said stiffly. He stood. "Leave the envelopes with me, and do me the favor of writing down, here, on this pad, your two addresses, the names of all your household staff, and the names of your usual round of acquaintance—the people you see most often, the shops you frequent, that sort of thing. Anything that could conceivably be germane, however remote the likelihood may seem to you. Then we shall see what we can do."

CHAPTER TWENTY

The next morning, Lenox was up at a little before six o'clock. Not much later he was standing in the chill air by the river, his arms long behind his back, stretching out the muscles in his chest and shoulders. He wore light shoes of white cotton and a dark blue tunic, left over from his Balliol days.

He took a moment to gaze around. The world was so fragile at this hour; so individual, each tree, in the early pink light, utterly itself, still unblended into the busy day. The buildings across the Thames were quiet, alone with themselves. The secretive water rose and fell, rose and fell.

With a last stretch of his arms, he stepped into the little scull that bobbed along the bankside. It dipped low to one side as he settled into his seat, then regained its equilibrium.

He had seen Graham as he left the flat by St. James's Square that morning. "There you are," he'd said. Graham was arranging the morning newspapers, which had been dropped at the door. "Good heavens. Where on earth did you get off to yesterday?"

"I apologize, sir," said Graham. "I was absent—well, accidentally, sir. It was in reference to the case. I thought you would want me to pursue it."

"Did you find anything?" Lenox asked.

"Not yet. I need just the morning, sir."

Lenox looked at him curiously. "Take the afternoon, if you need that too. I'm late, and meant to be on the two nineteen to Markethouse, but take the afternoon, obviously, take as long as you need. Consider yourself relieved of all other duties. You can come down to the country by train later than I do if need be."

"Very good, sir. I do not anticipate missing the train. But my apologies again, sir."

Lenox waved a hand. He was already walking to the door. If you were on the river too late, it became fairly impassable. "You can disappear for a year if you like," he called. "But leave a note. Back shortly."

Lenox had never been a superior rower—there were lads in the first boat at Oxford quite literally twice as fast down a river—but he had always been a happy one. It had been part of his life longer than he could remember. There was a pond at Lenox House that he and Edmund had raced across countless times in thick-planked dullard rowboats, and as a schoolboy, Lenox had once finished first in lightweight pairs. He placed upon the small medal from that day a far greater value than he did any of his academic prizes.

Now he steered this small, lissome craft out onto the Thames. It was a scull Harrow had sold off the year before to make room for newer models, and he had snapped it up when he heard the news. It suited him perfectly. He liked to go out before dawn, when he still had a chance at fairly clear racing. There was a specially fitted little mirror in the bow of the boat that enabled him to see what lay behind him, and his eyes had somehow managed the trick of looking at it continually without focusing on it, so that he could take in the scope of the sky, too, and the great ships with their crisscrossed nettings, nearly as intricate as life.

He rowed west for about twenty minutes, looped a small islet with a single hut on it, and then returned, pulling for his life.

There was something he loved in the contrast between the

immense physical effort rowing took and the noiseless glide of the scull; in the pounding of his heart and the stillness of the city. The inattention to his own thoughts—he had a very active mind—let him in on a higher, wordless form of attention, he sometimes thought.

When he had gotten back, Collins, the boathouse keeper, helped him stow the scull and its oars, then gave him two towels, one cold and wet, the other dry. He would scrub the scull down shortly. Lenox thanked him cheerfully, red faced and already feeling the increased optimism he always did after a strenuous exercise, and walked home with the second towel around his neck, occasionally scrubbing his sweat-soaked hair.

The day was just starting. His clothing attracted two looks from black-suited, black-hatted gentlemen on their way to the counting-houses. By the time he was home, it was bright, the light of the morning gone.

He felt better. Even the 2:19 train to Markethouse did not daunt him—or panic him quite so much, at least, for he still felt its full imminent weight.

He sat with the newspapers and ate a gratuitously enormous breakfast (Mrs. Huggins looked on with a conflicted mixture of admonition and pride) of eggs, kippers, bacon, toast, marmalade, tea, and suet pudding.

When it was gone to the last scraping, he lit a pipe, settled back contentedly in his chair, put his feet up, and began to examine the papers more closely.

The story of the Thames Ophelia had been rounded into smoothness by time, the aggregation of opinion and fact turning it into a tightly made snowball.

The general opinion had it that the author of the letters to the *Challenger* was a lunatic, perhaps escaped from one of the madhouses. Lenox—who did not doubt that his quarry was a lunatic, but had a very different opinion of what he would look like outwardly—read with interest various philosophical experts who ruminated on the intellect of such a soul. They seemed to agree unanimously that he would probably be homeless, likely prone to bursts of violence, dangerous at close quarters. Not Lenox's opinion, either.

Field, however, cautiously endorsed it to the *Caller*, to which he had granted his lone interview. They ran Lenox's portrait again. Its analog in real life burned red.

Walnut Island was revived and combed through. Poor Nathaniel Butler got a decent coal-raking.

The *Challenger*'s circulation had doubled, Lenox read in an editor's note from their own pages.

Not an insignificant fact, even if exaggerated; he stored it, with dozens of others, in his roving, searching, hoarding mind. It could even be a motive for murder.

When Mrs. Huggins came in to freshen his teapot, she said, "If I could have just two hours of your time this morning, Mr. Lenox, I believe we could satisfactorily resolve several outstanding issues that require our immediate attention."

"Two *hours?*" said Lenox, blanching.

"I have recommended at previous moments—it has fallen on deaf ears, I know!—that we have a meeting each morning to address the continuing maintenance of the household. In Lady Hamilton's—"

"This is a very, very busy time," Lenox said, trying desperately to head her off. It was clear she was in an undemocratic mood. "Even half an hour would be difficult to spare at the moment, Mrs. Huggins."

"At a bare minimum I must ask, if I am to continue in my role—"

"Mrs. Huggins!"

"If I am to continue in my role," she went on doggedly, "I must ask for an answer to the first nine questions on the list I presented you. Sir."

Lenox looked at the list, which he had forgotten. Since yesterday, he had been successfully able to elude her, his time consumed by the case, but he knew when he was pinned. This was the Mrs. Huggins of the previous seven months. Anyhow, no English aristocrat can defy a nursemaid for longer than a day or two. This was probably the likeliest way to beat the country in a war, in fact.

"Very well," he said. "Before lunch."

"Thank you, sir," she said.

It was in a considerably gloomier cast of mind that he returned to the papers. It did seem hard that he should pay this woman to yell at him. But he perked up when he heard the sound of the door—it was Graham, he could tell from the footfall.

The valet looked tired, though as usual, he was dressed unimpeachably, and his face was impassive. "There you are," Lenox said.

"Good morning, sir. Are you at your leisure to discuss the case now?"

"Always."

"I have not been so successful as I hoped I might be," he said, "but I have at least identified the type of trunk in which the first victim was found."

Lenox brought his feet down from the table. "But that's marvelous."

"I had hoped to track down its exact source. My hopes were high yesterday afternoon. I passed a shipping and luggage store, and stopped in. I drew a picture of the trunk, and to my surprise, they all said that though it was of a common enough sort, in those dimensions it seemed certain to them to come from a manufacturer in Manchester called Wilton's. Apparently it is most commonly sold for overland trips in England and Scotland, because it conforms to the luggage racks in the cars of nearly all British Railway transport trains."

"Good heavens, Graham, what a brilliant discovery."

"I wired Wilton's—without your permission, I am afraid, thinking the time might be—" But Lenox waved a hand, hurrying him up; the money was well spent, of course. "At any rate, they were not able to say what the mark meant. It is not theirs."

"The trunk, or the mark?"

"The mark. The trunk is most assuredly theirs."

This caused Lenox a moment of pause. At last, he said, "Are the trunks cheap or expensive?"

"Expensive, sir."

G957. "And they were sure nobody else might have made it, this trunk?"

"From my description, they seemed extremely sure it was theirs. They alone have 'F-shaped holes' in the brass around the lock—that is their signature."

"Our trunk had F-shaped holes." He could picture them. "It's conclusive."

"I note, as well, sir, that they did not commence production of the trunk until after the HMS *Gallant* was permanently retired."

Lenox's mind was racing. He had many thoughts now; many thoughts. He sprang to his feet and ran to the door. "Beautifully done, Graham. Pack my things for the country, please—if you have the energy—don't bother if you don't—I'll be back."

He was gone for two hours, which he used to see first Mayne, and subsequently Exeter and Field.

It was a productive use of his time. Finally he felt they had momentum. He returned to the flat at a sprint, hazardously close to his train's departure time.

Fortunately, Graham was waiting in the hall. "Your luggage is in a taxi downstairs, sir. I think we can still make it."

"Thank goodness," said Lenox.

Just at that moment, however, Mrs. Huggins appeared. Her face was thunder. Lenox realized, with a plunging feeling, that he had utterly forgotten his word to her.

She had realized the same. "I have been deceived, sir. I have, in my long career, endeavored to be conscientious about—"

"Mrs. Huggins—"

"My position here being what it is, I see no choice but to tender—"

"Mrs. Huggins," he interjected desperately, one eye on the ticking seconds of the carriage clock on his front hall table, "do you know cats?"

This brought her up short. "Cats, sir?"

"Cats, yes. Those animals you see with tails, and everything like that. They eat birds."

"Do I *know* any cats?" said Mrs. Huggins. "To begin with, they don't all eat birds—they are very loving—"

"Listen, I must be off, but I have been thinking, and I have realized that what this house needs is a cat. I'll be away for a few days, but can I leave the selection of the cat in your responsibility? It would mean the world to me if you could handle it."

"Oh!" She looked much changed. "I—I suppose I could."

"Thank you so much, Mrs. Huggins. I leave it entirely in your hands, about the cat. Color, and if it has—whiskers, I suppose?—do they all have whiskers?—anyway, everything—all the details—whiskers and all—"

"Very good, sir," she said solemnly, and watched without speaking as Lenox and Graham, released from her ire, took their rapid leave.

CHAPTER TWENTY-ONE

It was a long train ride south to Sussex. Everything in the countryside was the surprised fluttering green of spring. The trees, the little sprays of random pink in huge meadows, made Lenox's heart ache in a way he couldn't quite fathom, something to do with home, something to do with his father.

At Markethouse, he sent Graham ahead with his luggage on a cart. He wanted to walk to Lenox House by himself. First he passed through the small town, with its two churches, greengrocer's, village square, the public houses (one bright and jaunty, the other low and lurking, each about as reputable as the other once you got inside).

As he passed down Whitcomb Lane, someone a distance away called out "Welcome back, Master Duck!" which was a village nickname that he had been given after a cricket match when he went out for a duck (the term in cricket parlance for making zero runs), to his very great humiliation.

He rolled his eyes, touched his hat—he suspected who it was, an older opponent from that day named Arnold, a blacksmith—and thought of Elizabeth, who had honeymooned in part in Italy, telling him that their word for nickname was "injury." True more often than you'd like.

"I was out for forty the next match, and we won handily!" he shouted back.

There was a guffaw by way of reply.

By this time, he was at the edge of the town, Markethouse. It took him trekking across a half mile of rough countryside to get to the handsome black gates of Lenox House. The shadows were now long, the sunlight a heavy gold. In the gatehouse was old Carter, who had retired into this position at twenty after sustaining a bad wound in the army, and had sat here with a stone flask of hot tea and a newspaper (hopefully he changed it out occasionally) for the approximately fifty years since.

"Father nearby?" Lenox said after greeting him.

"Shooting on the small lawn, sir," Carter, wiry, sharp eyed, known as the village's best poacher, said immediately.

"Shooting, is it? Well, did my things come?"

"They did, sir, right quick."

There was a long avenue from the front gate to Lenox House itself. The dirt road was lined with symmetrical rows of lime trees, which his grandfather had planted years before. A pretty walk. He heard the crack of a gun, then twenty yards later heard it again, and smiled to himself.

The house itself was a small but picturesque one, mirrored prettily now in the pond that sat in front of it, two long wings in the shape of an L. The great lawn lay to the west side of the house, and led to the formal gardens. But it was to the small lawn, chapel side of the house, that he made his way.

"Hullo!" he yelled out well before he turned the corner, just to be safe. "Don't shoot!"

"Come round unless you're a clay pigeon!" the call came back.

He found his father sitting in a small wooden chair, with a leather seat that sank low. It looked designed to fold. He'd never seen his father shoot from a chair.

He stood up, smiling. "You've come back to Sussex, have you?" he said.

"Yes, sir," said Lenox, going forward and grasping his father's outstretched hand.

Nearby was Terrance, an old servant of around 150 years old, with heavy jowls and the gloomiest face in Christendom. He was dressed in a checkered jacket so threadbare that it looked as if it would dissolve in sunlight. Its pockets were bulging. He stood at the trap, holding a clay pigeon that he had just pulled from one of them. "Welcome back, Master Charles," he said.

"Thank you, Terrance. The air is considerably fresher here, I'll say."

"Perhaps it'll keep you out of the papers, too."

Lenox scowled at the old servant, who said pretty much what he pleased these days. His father smiled. "Your mother will be happy you've decided to visit."

"Yes, just a quick one," said Lenox, forcing a smile of his own.

"Care for a shot?"

"Eh? Oh—go on."

There was about twenty minutes of light left, and they traded rounds of shots. This was his father's best gun. On his first attempt, Lenox missed twice. ("I'll have to fetch 'em, of course," Terrance muttered in a voice he either did or did not believe to be under his breath, but which regardless could have halted traffic in the Strand.) But then he got the measure of the light and the surroundings, and fired off several good shots, culminating in a double.

"Very fine shooting," his father said, and Terrance grunted, which in his case was roughly equivalent to a notarized letter of praise from the Queen.

His father took the gun back with a "thankee"—in certain mannerisms, he was still very, very old-fashioned, plucked from 1740-odd—and sat in his chair. He split every pigeon cleanly in half, sighed with happiness after the tenth, and broke the shotgun over his arm as he stood up.

He turned to Charles. "Now, that's a lovely evening. Son back at home, clay taught its lesson, and Terrance has something to complain about because you missed those two."

Lenox's father was named Edward. He was a half inch shorter than either of his sons, and he always seemed to walk back in his shoes, as if he were assessing the world carefully. He had gray hair, a gray mustache, and very shrewd, watchful hazel eyes, which Lenox had inherited, though in other respects he more resembled his mother.

Sir Edward had spent his career in Parliament. Twice he had declined positions in the cabinet. This had always gnawed at Charles, though not at Edmund. There were eight hundred baronets in England, and five hundred peers; several hundred members of Parliament; but only twelve in a cabinet. Lenox, churlish though he knew it was, had sometimes felt among people of his class (at Harrow, especially) that he was always just shy of the mark: second son; not in the peerage, though for the most part he could not have given a fig for that, because the Lenoxes had been on their land twice as long as most of those newish Elizabethan earls; his father never prime minister or anything so exalted as that.

A disgraceful way to feel. Nevertheless, real.

Edmund, though, who had a slower metabolism and had been raised from the instant of his birth in the knowledge that he would inherit, said he thought that his father, first, always kept his primary loyalty in the countryside, not Thames-side, and second, preferred the flexibility of being in every significant meeting of his party without being bound to a single duty within it—the treasury, say, or the war department.

Lenox could understand the wisdom of this. But there were moments when he wondered if his father could have been more, done more, gone higher.

None of that was to imply that his father was in any way a diminished figure in his eyes. On the contrary, Lenox knew instinctively that his own father was more right, more substantial, more significant, than any of the dukes' sons he knew could ever say their own were. Indeed, Sir Edward was like a royal to his sons—*more* important than the Queen, in some indefinable way—and it was commonly said in town that he was the best baronet the family had produced.

He was sixty-one now. As they walked toward the house's side door, Lenox glanced surreptitiously, but could detect no real change in the older man's physical appearance.

"The newspaper, then," he said mildly as they reached the mudroom.

Charles had been dreading the revival of that question. "Yes, sir. I didn't know you took the *Daily Star* in Sussex now."

His father tilted his head. "News will always reach you if it's bad," he said. "It's the kind people are most eager to give."

They went to the large double sink and both washed their hands. "It's not all bad to be invited in to consult," Charles said.

His father looked up very quickly. "No! No, not at all. I didn't mean objectively bad news, you know. Any man can turn any piece of information to his pleasure. The devil can cite Scripture, and all that. One of the curses of each of us being a person, you know." He shook out his hands, drops flying from them in the golden light. "I'm going to change for supper. I expect your mother will want to see you, though. She'll be in her study."

Charles nodded, dried his hands, then walked through the entrance hall, up a short flight of stairs, and into the study.

His mother had a small, beautiful room on the second floor of the house, full of her personality, with a small desk whose fine intricacy had fascinated Charles endlessly when he played underneath it as a boy; the wallpaper was a pale lilac, and there was always a clean scent here that didn't exist in the rest of the house, too light to be perfume, never absent.

"You're here!" she said with an enormous smile when he knocked on the open door.

He came in and returned her embrace. "Susceptible to cats," he said.

"You got my wire!"

"I did. You might have been clearer! I wasn't sure if it was from you or if the French government had sent an encoded message to the wrong fellow."

"And yet I'll bet you four pounds she was susceptible. Wasn't she?"

He frowned. "Have you taken up gambling? I hate to see that vice in someone your age."

She hit his arm in frustration. "Was she?"

Lenox smiled and said that yes, his mother had been right, or at any rate right enough to buy him ten minutes of freedom, though the Lord alone could know what the consequences would be. Some hissing, scratching creature, no doubt. It was almost too great a cliché—a widow who liked cats.

Here his mother interjected, though, that it wasn't like that at all. According to Lady Hamilton, Mrs. Huggins had grown up solely with dogs. It was her husband who had loved cats.

That was moderately interesting, and Mrs. Huggins took them through ten minutes of conversation. His mother rang the bell and asked for a whisky and soda for her son, and a Chartreuse for herself. "The curate and his wife are coming to supper this evening, and Jane's father," she said. "Nothing very out of the ordinary. By the way, you looked lovely in the paper! They captured you beautifully, I thought. I've half a mind to write the draftsman and buy the portrait."

"When are they arriving?"

"Not for half an hour."

"Oh? Listen, then. I have two doctors coming down on Thursday and Friday."

She frowned. "Yes, you wired."

"They're the two best men in London. One a consultant, the second a surgeon. I did a great deal of looking into it."

She shook her head. "Well—may you live in interesting times, they say the Chinese tell each other. For now I shall just be happy to have you back here. I can't tell you how happy. Go get changed for dinner, you look like you came from a long day of cleaning chimneys."

CHAPTER TWENTY-TWO

Graham was in Lenox's room (when each boy turned fourteen, they had moved from the east wing of the house, where the several small rooms comprising the nursery were warrened, to the south wing, where the bedrooms befitting adults were situated) and was brushing his suit there.

"Good evening, sir," he said.

"Good evening, Graham. They were civil to you downstairs?"

"Exceedingly so, sir. Mr. Crump shared a glass of wine with me from his personal cellar."

That was the butler, a stern old fellow. "That was decent of him. I say, Graham, about that trunk."

"Yes, sir?"

Lenox was loosening his cuffs, preparing to change. There was a bowl of hot water at the mirror into which he dipped his hands and face, and he patted them dry with a towel. "You said it was sold primarily for train trips."

"Yes, sir."

Lenox shook his head in frustration. "Then I am more convinced than ever that these two women are not from London."

"Sir?"

In his meeting with Mayne that morning before departing for Lenox House, Charles had described Graham's inquiries about the Walnut Island trunk.

Mayne and Exeter, who had been present, said that Field's investigation was heavily focused on four prostitutes missing near Shoreditch. Three of them were of the precise physical description of the victims.

Nevertheless, Lenox saw two difficulties in the search, which made it exasperating that Field had expended so much time upon it. The first was that prostitutes were a fluid population—they might return home to the country, go to another part of the city, or to another city altogether, for that matter. Take up with a single suitor. Save enough to buy an apprenticeship in a dress shop. Virtually anything.

("Still, you must concede that four is a high number," Mayne had said.

"I'm not sure," Lenox had replied. Exeter had looked outraged at this impudence, but Lenox was already more confident with Mayne, if still deferential. "We don't know how many there are in general.")

The second was that they had only two victims, not four, to account for, and both had died within the few days before their discovery.

Lenox took a fresh shirt from Graham. "I think they were transported by trunk. One of them, at least. And our killer—bear in mind he believes himself to be committing the perfect crime, and is at a very minimum quite clever—stenciled the name of the HMS *Gallant* on one to make it seem local to London."

"Throw us off the scent, sir."

"Yes," said Lenox. "The question is what it means that both bodies were found on the river."

"Doesn't it imply that the man lives near the river, sir?" asked Graham.

This had been the working theory of the police, and until now the two of them had accepted it.

Lenox tilted his head, thinking. "It's possible," he said. In his room there was a small leatherbound book he had received from his aunt Martha before he left for school. It was filled with intricate maps of London. He went and got it from the shelf now. "On the other hand. Consider: He would want to spend as little time as possible in public carrying the bodies. Do you agree?"

"Of course," said Graham.

Lenox found the page he was looking for. "Let us theorize, then." He turned the book to Graham. His finger was on a spot. "Look at this spot."

"Waterloo Bridge, sir," Graham said.

Lenox nodded. "Two train stations within a stone's throw of it. Charing Cross and Waterloo. The two busiest in London, perhaps?"

"One would need to look at the numbers, sir. Victoria Station and King's Cross, among—"

Lenox waved a hand. "But—"

"Yes, sir," said Graham, making a rare interruption to concede the point. "Among the busiest, certainly."

Lenox tapped the book. "Then I think it is this. Our murderer is going to another city to commit these murders, returning by rail, and then disposing of the bodies on the river as quickly as he can. He is coming into Charing Cross or Waterloo to do it."

Graham frowned. "But why, sir, would he risk traveling across England with a corpse, and then be so immediately eager to get rid of it?"

Lenox smiled, shaking his head. "Yes, that's the question. My first instinct would be to say that he has killed two women from a population small enough that they would be noticed. But we might well have heard of that—a village missing two women, for instance."

"Most likely, sir."

"Therefore I think we must look to motive."

"Motive, sir."

"Our Walnut Island trunk—designed to deceive. Our Ophelia—

never floated upon the water, merely left upon the bank. Again, designed to deceive."

"There is method to the madness, you think, sir," said Graham. "The perfect-crime business."

Lenox had sat back upon the bed, and crossed one leg over the other. The fire at the other end of the room was low, and the evening was cold. Still, he stared at the page. "Yes, I think he knows a hawk from a handsaw," Lenox muttered.

If he wasn't purely a madman, chasing the "perfect murder," what was he, this killer?

A bell rang. Cocktail hour. That must mean someone had arrived, and Lenox registered dimly that he had heard a carriage a few minutes before, though he had assumed that it was the mail or the butcher or someone like that.

But it was no doubt Jane's father, the Earl of Houghton.

"Your tie, sir," Graham said.

He put it on Lenox as the latter stared down at the map of London. "You realize one person this implicates."

"Sir?"

"Nathaniel Butler."

Graham and Lenox's eyes met in the mirror. "A trip from Birmingham to Charing Cross, sir?"

"Yes, exactly. Two trips, in the dead of night."

Graham accepted this impassively, though Lenox, who knew him, saw that he still didn't believe Nathaniel Butler capable of the murders. "The heavier or lighter of the black jackets, sir?" he asked.

"Eh?" Lenox was distracted, still staring at the map. "Oh. The heavier, I suppose."

"It's true the wind is southerly, sir."

Lenox smiled.

Over the next days, Lenox, his father, and his mother settled into a happy pattern.

The single rule of these happy hours was apparently that nobody mention Sir Edward Lenox's health; or at least, nobody did. There had been two years when Edmund was at school and Charles wasn't, which Lenox was reminded of. (They weren't all that distant, after all.) He and his mother spent their mornings together, while his father attended to the estate; except that instead of doing his schoolwork—though he and Graham did doggedly continue to take cuttings from the newspapers—Lenox was now focused obsessively on the case, making list after list, drawing maps, immobile in thought for extended periods as he tried to circle closer to the personality of the person he was chasing.

At lunch all three of them read. It had been a shock to Charles when he learned at the age of nine or ten that there were families that didn't do this: the soup coming in (always something fresh and full of vegetables, soup being his father's favorite food, though Edmund would argue him into a powder, tirelessly, that soup couldn't be a person's favorite "food"), then a chop and some potatoes, and usually fruit from the hothouse for dessert, each of the three absorbed in some kind of reading. For his father, generally a Parliamentary report or a biography; for his mother, a novel or poetry; for Charles, though in his youth he would have been reading a tale of adventure, the reports of London newspapers.

Lenox had always considered this silent state of affairs highly companionable, though Elizabeth had once said they all ought to be institutionalized.

Then, in the afternoon of these few days, he and his father would find an hour or two to spend together. On the first they shot again, then bowled cricket to each other on the great lawn as Terrance fetched the cherry-red balls, calling fours and sixes (quite unfairly, Lenox thought) by eye. Eventually Lenox's father ran short of breath, and Charles bowled to the old servant, who would only tap the ball, but whom it was impossible to spin anything whatsoever past: a truly maddening state of affairs.

The second day, Lenox and his father went on a long ride over the whole land.

Lenox had grown up on horseback, and his father never looked more natural than atop his beloved charcoal gray gelding, Clarence, a beast of great sensitivity and almost human intelligence. His father had an extremely light seat, a formal refinement in riding that had always seemed to his son to arise from the earth itself, through the animal, and into his limbs, as though by some mysterious ancestral grace.

Lenox loved to ride with his father almost more than anything on earth. It had nearly always been Edmund (who, though he adored horses, looked like a sack of wheat tied to a saddle when he was aboard one) who took these sorts of rides with Sir Edward, however. Lenox had understood that this was part of his elder brother's birthright, and that some transmission of—what? duty, knowledge, familiarity?— took place on their outings.

But occasionally his father would invite him, and the two of them were a more natural pair, could ride far harder together; and even now Charles took a childish pleasure in that.

They rode very hard now, floating as lightly as two tufts of down across the great upslope that lay west of the house, two miles in all.

At the top, his father pulled up, breathing heavily, grinning.

"I do love a thundering good ride better than anything," he said, smacking Clarence's haunch proudly.

"Likewise," said Charles, heart pounding from the exercise.

His father stared back the long distance toward the house and the pond for a while. "Most anything," he said, clarifying.

They rode back. Soon enough it was time for supper. Three or four times a week Lenox's parents had someone or other to dine (often just a particularly close friend of his father's named Johnson, who owned a good deal of farmland) or went out themselves.

There was no reading at supper, of course. (That would have been

indisputably eccentric.) To Charles's surprise, they were both in-
ordinately curious about his life in London, his parents. They quizzed
him endlessly about his friends, about which public houses and shops
received his custom, about whether he ever saw Lady Quilt or that
young Cynthia or the Reverend Marblehead, about what hour he
rose, about Mrs. Huggins. Even about his case.

At any rate, three days passed in this contented state of affairs;
"most anything" the closest Edward Lenox came to acknowledging
his position; and then the doctors began to arrive.

CHAPTER TWENTY-THREE

As in most country houses, the dogcart at Lenox House was in perhaps eight times greater use than the carriage. But the carriage was here: now painted a glossy maroon, Lenox arms on the door, easing down slightly earthward on whichever side it was stepped into. Four black horses, groomed and beautiful, ridden out every morning by Hitchens and his stableboy two by two, were ready to pull it.

Lenox and Graham went together to pick up Sir Riley Callum, the consulting surgeon Courtenay had recommended. He stepped from the train, and Lenox's first thought was that in looks there was virtually nothing more you could have asked of him: his white-haired head might have been the model for a marble bust, and he stood marvelously erect, a man with delicate papery skin and keen gray eyes that seemed to survey and anatomize the world with bloodless precision.

They might as well have taken the dogcart for him, though. He was closeted with Lenox's father for about ninety minutes, spoke briefly with Lenox's two parents, politely but firmly declined Lenox's company on the return trip to the train station, and left.

Lenox was in the ballroom, vast and empty, sitting with his legs up in a window and staring at the clean-shorn hedges of the formal gardens, when his mother came down. "Nothing to be done, he says."

Lenox stood up. "That's all he said?"

"He concurred with the opinion of the other doctors your father has seen." She bit her lip. Her arms were crossed. "No surgical options."

"None?" said Lenox, stunned.

"He offered some palliative advice. Though your father won't stop smoking his pipe, of course."

"No," Lenox said in an indistinct voice. More plausible that the sun should stop rising in the east. He looked up at his mother. "Shall I cancel Dr. McConnell?"

"Hadn't you better? Your father will see him, but there doesn't seem much point."

He didn't, though. Something in his mother at the moment she said that—well, he had never known her bright, lively face so drained of life. He decided he would keep the appointment.

What a mystery one's parents were! Lenox would have said that his mother was by far the better equipped for this kind of loss—she was so universally beloved by her friends, so interested in life, so alive herself—and yet he saw now that in fact he had been exactly wrong. His father would have borne the loss of his mother. He would have been shattered, but he also didn't have quite so strong a sense that *his* life was important. Perhaps it came of being the steward of a title and of land. If it had been she who received this diagnosis, Sir Edward would have known that his loss was only personal and, however inwardly bereft, carried on.

But for Emma Lenox, all of life was personal. The way she teased, her easy gift for being in a room—all these warm traits would be adrift on cold waters without her husband, Lenox saw for the first time.

The next morning, Graham and Lenox sat in the carriage again. They were, as usual, discussing the crimes in London. The first thing they did was stop into the telegraph office—very new—to see if anything had arrived from Mrs. Huggins, who was under strict orders to forward anything from Scotland Yard, regardless of expense.

Nothing there, however.

As they waited on a bench near the small train station, with its pink shutters pulled back so that the newsagent and the small tea shop looked appealingly open, inviting, Lenox said, "I've been thinking about the letters."

Indeed, he had read them over and over, until he had made copies because he was afraid he would rub the newsprint too much to read.

"Have you, sir?"

"Is he really trying to commit perfect crimes, do you think?"

Lenox's valet was never one to reply before thinking, and he sat for some time, pondering the question. For his part, Lenox valued these silences, which often allowed questions he had to resonate in his own mind.

"Why do you ask, sir?" said Graham at last.

"Because!" Lenox burst out. "Think about every article you and I have clipped in the last seven months. What did they all have in common?"

"Sir?"

"None of them was a perfect crime! No—they were all driven by money or anger. Every single one."

"And yet he has written these letters, sir."

"Come at it from another angle. Why has he killed women? They are infinitely scarcer—men pass in and out of London all the time, men are passed stupefied by drink in every corner of the city. Slit a man's neck and walk away. That is the perfect crime."

"On the other hand, that very fact suggests an obsessiveness, sir. He has chosen two women of similar health and appearance."

A loose conflagration of birds burst from a tree nearby, in ragged unison. "True," said Lenox. "But what about these lurid flowers, the Thames 'Ophelia,' showy, literary, guaranteed to attract the press's attention. Sheer misdirection. He has already done it once: the HMS *Gallant*."

Graham, who looked less convinced, said, "Perhaps, sir. You think there is some base motive involved here, then, and all of this is— window dressing, sir, I suppose you would call it."

Lenox reflected on the question. "I don't know," he said at last. "What's funny is that you are right about the two women. I retain in my mind the same image of the murderer I had after the first letter.

"Perhaps both things are true—that he is the arrogant, misused person of the letters, and also that he is acting out of some other motive. Because the letters are too convincing. They are too well in character to be false, to be truly false."

Just then a whistle sounded, and around a curve of poplar trees the train appeared, chuffing black smoke. The few souls on the station's platform stepped forward, as people waiting for trains always do a moment or two early.

Lenox stood up. He had the certainty in his breast that they were getting closer and closer—from Sussex!—than the police were in London.

It was odd. Almost for the first time since Oxford, he believed that perhaps this was what he was meant to do, after all. Some combination of reasoning, psychological insight, and curiosity (some combination of qualities that he couldn't even name, strictly) made him fit for this work, and perhaps for no other.

Youth is dramatic, his mother would have replied to that. He smiled faintly to himself, though visibly enough that Graham looked at him, at a slant.

Only four people stepped off the train at Markethouse. It was clear which one of them was the doctor from London—for one thing, he stepped from the first-class carriage, while the rest bundled out of third, and for another, he wore a high white collar and a cravat and carried a leather medical bag, while the rest immediately set about offering proof to any interested party that they were in an advanced state of inebriation.

"Dr. McConnell?" said Lenox, going forward with his hand out-stretched. "Thank you for making the journey. I'm Charles Lenox."

"Delighted to meet you," said the doctor, extending his own hand and smiling. "A very pleasant journey, too, all in all."

"Here's the carriage to shoot us along. Can my valet take your bag?"

"This? No, it barely weighs a thing."

Lenox's first impression of Thomas McConnell was that he liked him enormously. It was hard not to. He was tall and extremely handsome, with strong features and hair that he wore in a fringe below his collar. His eyes sparkled with intelligence and interest, and he emanated goodwill, amiability, a readiness to be pleased. For a doctor to retain his decency seemed nearly impossible—death, paraded before you every moment, in all its dull spangled variety. Yet here was a person who had, one felt.

His accent was fairly English now, slipping home to Scotland here and there for certain words. On the way to Lenox House (Graham sat on the box with the driver, rather than inside the carriage), he listened attentively as Lenox described the little he knew of his father's case. He also accepted the report of Sir Riley Callum, which had arrived that morning by mail.

The doctor read this carefully. The trip was a short one, and they were turning past Carter at the gatehouse when McConnell closed the report. "Does your father seem to be in good spirits?" he asked, his face serious and attentive.

"I think so."

"Mm." The doctor tapped his door where his hand lay, thinking. Then he turned to Lenox. "In any case, I will spend some time with him."

"You do not think of cutting today, then," said Lenox, his heart sinking. He had hoped that McConnell would dismiss Callum's report as pessimistic.

"It is almost always impossible to say without seeing the patient," Dr. McConnell said gently.

They drew down the avenue; the clouds above were black, ominous, and as they went inside, the first drops of a heavy rain began to fall on the marble steps leading into Lenox House.

CHAPTER TWENTY-FOUR

Lenox remained in Sussex another thirty-six hours, half of that Saturday and the full of the subsequent Sunday, not leaving until the last train from Markethouse to London, the 9:39. He was hesitant to leave, but wanted to have a week in the city—Scotland Yard at work, Mayne in the offices—in order to move forward with the case.

A month was a short time; he repeated this to himself morning, noon, night. June 2.

On the second afternoon, he and his father rode out again. They rode farther than they ever had together, though not farther than Sir Edward and Edmund, who had rambled all across the county over the years.

Beneath the downs under the village of Somerton was a small creek, and after a hard hour's riding, they stopped there and let their thirsty horses drink and recover.

His father was stripped down to his shirtsleeves, and soaked his arms and neck in the stream, too. There was a contented look on his face. He dried himself with a broad piece of cloth tied to his saddlebags, then took out some figs, cheese, and bread, which he divided between them. Charles accepted the victuals gratefully, famished.

At the house his mother would be having a hearty tea, but he wouldn't have traded spots.

After they had caught their breath, Lenox's father said, quite unexpectedly, "I wonder whom you think of marrying."

"I? I don't have anyone in particular in mind, sir."

His father nodded. "You're very young. I only wondered."

"Not twenty-two anymore," Charles replied, smiling.

"No indeed."

There had been a young lady at Oxford, the daughter of a don, named Cynthia, and he wondered if this was what his father meant. He had introduced his parents to her; at one time, when he was in her father's grand bookish musty Norham Gardens house every afternoon, he had thought he would certainly marry her.

In the end, she had married rather beneath herself, to a fellow named Allerton. He was one of the handsomest chaps who had ever drawn breath—utterly decent, too, but extremely stupid. She hadn't cared; nothing could have been clearer. She treasured him. Beauty, Lenox had learned: there was a force in the world. This fellow's beauty had mattered more than Lenox's openhearted affection.

He could give himself a pang very easily thinking of Cynthia. (The wedding was only eight months in the past; the silver tea set he had given them hadn't had time to tarnish.) She was modern, with a slim, beautiful figure. But if he looked just beyond the middle distance of his emotion, to whatever far-off place he was journeying toward, he knew that it hadn't been she who got away.

Because his thoughts had turned to Cynthia, it surprised him when, a moment later, his father said, "And is Lady Elizabeth well? She likes London life?"

"She has been to see the hippopotamus."

"Half the cabinet has, too," said his father. "Appalling waste of time."

"So I told her."

There was a fractional pause, and for a passing second Lenox thought his father might mention his son's career—or his ambitions to travel, which he seemed to dislike just as strongly, another dilettante's choice.

But all he said was, "Shall we ride back?"

"If you think the horses are ready."

"Oh yes. Clarence had another few miles in him when we stopped, and he's the older of the pair."

They set off in loud, happy silence.

That question was the closest his father had come to mentioning his condition, Lenox reflected as they rode. Then there was a fence to jump and the thought was chased from his mind. He was conscious, however, to remember each of these moments; and it was a queer feeling to know that he was doing so.

McConnell had been a more delicate, interested, and thoughtful party than Sir Riley Callum, who was perhaps overburdened by his own greatness and had seemed irritated at the disadvantage in which it placed him (a knight of the realm!) that mere money had drawn him four hours across the country.

But the result was the same. A slight shake of Lenox's mother head after the two-hour visit, and he felt as if he had been leveled by a gust of wind.

Charles had returned with McConnell to the station, Graham on the box. He liked the Scot, who seemed, now, sober and respectful, but not overplaying the role. "He will have a very fair quality of life," the doctor had said.

"Right until the end?"

McConnell had pulled out a pad of paper. "I could prescribe a medicine, but look—you live in London. Have you seen Mother Bailey's Quieting Syrup?"

"Yes."

It was advertised widely—a colicky baby's best remedy. McConnell was writing the name down. "It is essentially pure poppy. There is nobody on earth whose pain it wouldn't relieve."

"Poppy."

"The most jaded denizen of the filthiest opium den would find relief from it," McConnell said lightheartedly—attempting to be lighthearted.

"Thank you," said Lenox.

"On the bottle they dose by weight. You can extrapolate."

"Amazing that this is the best modern medicine can do," Lenox said.

McConnell shook his head angrily, in a way that implied he agreed. "Yes," he said.

But Lenox had only, with this idle comment, been delaying the question he dreaded asking. "When will he need it?"

They were halfway through Markethouse, every bump in its road familiar to Charles. "In five months," said McConnell.

"And is there some other expert, some physician who perhaps could—?"

"There is not," said McConnell sympathetically but firmly. "The growth is too large, and the symptoms all indicate that the disease is present in other regions of his body."

Lenox nodded. "Very well. Thank you."

"I will be in touch every two weeks. If there is some surgical option that could provide relief at the end, I will be happy to return—more than happy. You needn't bother about the doubled fee. That's my secretary. He's on a salary, but he gets a gleam of gold in his eye."

The carriage had stopped. Lenox looked at his watch. "It is still thirty minutes until the next train. I shall wait with you."

McConnell shook his head. "Please, go back. Thirty minutes will be enough to find my way around the town. I like a small town. I grew up in one."

They shook hands and the rangy doctor strode off, bag at his side. His immense good health and handsome face seemed somehow not like a rebuke to his patients, but a form of love for them, faith in them.

Lenox watched him go down Cowman's Lane—he didn't turn back, a final gracefulness—and then tapped the door of the carriage to indicate that they could return home.

How silly it had seemed, the handsome carriage; the vanity of it; the vanity of the world. Those were his rather muddled thoughts after dropping the second doctor at the station.

He had been so sure he could fix it. Arrogance.

Still, it was good to have the following days with his parents. Edmund was arriving soon, and Lenox had been setting his mind to the next five months. He wished to be here as often as possible. After June 2, he would, one way or the other, spend most of his time at Lenox House.

After midnight on that Sunday evening—so at the outset of Monday, really—Lenox and Graham arrived at Charing Cross. It was a rainy night in London, heavy fog.

To his surprise, his brother was waiting for them there. He lifted a hand and smiled. "There you are," he said. "To the minute."

"Goodness, Edmund," said Charles. "What on earth brings you to meet us?"

"Oh?" Edmund took one of the small bags that Graham and Charles had divided between them, having declined a porter. "Just a thought that I would."

They took a cab back to Lenox's flat, which was slumbering—he had offered no advance notice of the timing of his return—and together made up a bickering fire, then settled comfortably with two drinks. Graham had retreated to the back part of the flat to unpack.

"How do they seem?" Edmund said.

Charles reflected for a moment. "Father seems himself. Mother a wreck."

"And the doctors are in agreement?"

"Yes."

"Five months."

Charles nodded. "Or six. Thereabouts."

"October," said Edmund.

The strangest look came over his face. It was one of those moments when a hundred roads forward fall away. From now on, like their father, he would be concerned with the health of trees on their land, the happiness of their tenants, the expense of fixing a wall four centuries old.

But it was also infused by a purer grief than perhaps Charles had experienced, he saw. He realized that even this week he had still been looking for his father's—approval, perhaps, or respect. For Edmund, his father was closer to an equal. He needed nothing from Sir Edward before his death; what a keen edge that added to his sorrow, and what a keener one it took away.

Charles was quiet. At last, he said, "Molly will go with you?"

"Oh? Yes, and the boy."

That was their son, James. "I say, get Molly to draw."

This was rather elliptical, but Edmund nodded straightaway. His wife—a person of the country—had rather fewer attainments, in French or pianoforte or whatever you liked, than most of the women they knew. But she had an innate gift for likeness in drawing. Her small line drawings, often made in half distraction at a party and left behind, were unerringly alive, and whenever Charles was next in whatever home they had been in, he would find that Molly's scrap of paper had been framed and placed in some honored place.

It had to do with her deep well of kindheartedness. She drew the best person everyone was, somehow, without ever flattering them in the least.

The two brothers sat and discussed the country (the cricket, the horses, the shooting, the season), and their talk gave way here and there to memory. At last, near two o'clock, Edmund stood up and said he supposed he had better go. He asked if there was anything he could do for his brother before he left town.

"You don't have any Mother Bailey's Quieting Syrup, do you? I could use some."

Edmund gave him a strange look but smiled. "You're an odd duck, Charles. Ha—look at that, Duck! My mind must have been working behind my back."

"The only way it ever does."

"Very funny." Edmund paused. "If Father—goes, as it were, Mother will remain exactly where she is. None of this dowager—well, you know."

Charles laughed. "Yes. We have talked about it a hundred times or so."

Nevertheless, he was glad to hear it once more. They shook hands, and Charles walked Edmund down to a hansom cab in the streets, which were lost in a swirling, relentless fog; he returned upstairs drained, very grateful that he had a brother.

CHAPTER TWENTY-FIVE

Lenox stood up, one hand in his jacket pocket, the other holding a cup of tea, and stared at the riot of paper on the breakfast table. "If someone wanted to be out of countenance for twelve days or so, it would be hard to think of a better prescription than this."

Graham sighed, just barely audibly. "Indeed, sir."

It was the next morning. They had been up since seven o'clock, reading the letters and wires that had come in from various parts of England, describing the women who had gone missing within the past two months.

There were thirty in all. Their collective history was a grim one. Maude Lyons of Bournemouth, whose husband was known to be a violent man, had last been seen with him near a deep and rocky local ravine, being dragged against her will by the arm; he was mum on her whereabouts. Miss Adeline Bold, fourteen, of Liverpool, ward of an uncle it emerged had been interfering with her; last seen near docks; suspected runaway. It was difficult to imagine a happy outcome for her.

And so on. There were one or two slightly lighter notes. For instance it was hard not to absolve Sara Cather of Manchester. She was "missing" in the technical sense of the word, and had been since her husband died of what looked suspiciously like strychnine poisoning. That was no good. But the last sightings of her contained reports that she had a broken arm and a battered face; her sister, in Trafford, refused the police entrance, and slammed the door in their faces with a declaration that they could "all go and [expletive] pigs" before they would see her sister.

Lenox and Graham spent some time speculating about what expletive might have been omitted here.

In the end, there were four out of the thirty women who, first, matched the rough description of both women (younger than forty, dark curls, decent teeth, fair-skinned), and second, whose disappearances were genuinely enigmatic.

They came from Glasgow, Liverpool, Leeds, and Cardiff.

"No two from a single city," Lenox said, contemplating the pile.

"No, sir."

"That would have been useful. Still, all four cities have direct trains to Waterloo or Charing Cross, if we believe that our murderer brought the bodies to London with the aim of disposing of them instantly, and therefore chose the river."

"You believe the river itself is irrelevant, then, sir?" said Graham.

Lenox shook his head and thought for a moment. "I do not know, sincerely. The HMS *Gallant* in the first murder and the bizarre affectation of the flowers, the bier in the second. Both murders seem to be centered obsessively on the Thames, the water."

"The shilling, sir."

"Yes, exactly."

This was the detail the press loved most, certain that it referred to the payment the blind boatman received for ferrying the dead across the River Styx. "But you believe these may be deceptions, sir," Graham said.

"I believe it's possible."

If they were, the London press was certainly deceived, in the shilling and in all other matters. They were in an absolute uproar of worry. There were twenty-five days until the next murder, but it might as well have been twenty-five minutes. The newspapers published hundreds of articles providing amateur analysis of the two letters the *Challenger* had received. If the first murder attracted too little notice for the murderer's attention, the second must have more than gratified his least realistic dreams of same—it was a case with just the lurid amount of detail, just the sense of menace, just the tantalizing number of clues, to capture the entire public's imagination.

Even that morning, as he walked from St. James's Park to Scotland Yard, Lenox saw evidence of the case everywhere. On a newsstand, there were penny ballads about the murders for sale, special editions of all the cheaper newspapers and magazines, even in one case threepence for a cheap mug depicting the *Thames Ophelia*.

He called on Scotland Yard at a little after nine o'clock. Mayne, Sinex, and Exeter were closeted together.

"Good morning, Lenox," Mayne said.

"Good morning, sir."

The commissioner didn't seem especially delighted to see him, but he was positively doting compared to Sinex and Exeter, in their stiff tall blue hats indoors. "Walnut Island?" Mayne said.

He had been impressed with Lenox's discovery that the trunk didn't come from the *Gallant*, and the name of the firm in Manchester that had likely made it.

He had been less interested in Lenox's speculations about the letters and his (now-consuming) interest in the spectacles and the dryness of the second victim's bier on Bankside. Perhaps because they weren't new facts.

"As you know, sir, I've sorted through the wires from the other constabularies. These four candidates seem more likely." Lenox passed across a list. "We've sent them the sketches by mail."

Mayne nodded curtly. One intelligent thing Field had done was to have quick likenesses taken of the two dead women before their bodies were transported to the morgue. "Anything else?"

"I do have a theory."

"A theory," Sinex said dryly.

This Sinex was a man of middle age, immensely strong, with the tidy square-jawed face of a particularly fearsome stepfather. Lenox knew Exeter better, but he didn't like either of them. Nor, as far as he could tell, had either of them made a single iota of progress in the case. "Indeed, Mr. Sinex," said Lenox.

"Pray tell."

Lenox had in his jacket pocket (he wished to hell and back that he had thrown the sprig of lavender Graham had placed in his buttonhole that morning in the gutter on his way in) his book of London's maps. He showed it to them now.

"We've seen London," said Exeter, younger and stupider than Sinex but probably more ill inclined to Lenox.

"You know where Waterloo and Charing Cross are, then," Lenox replied. "I believe that is how the victims came into our city. As I have said from the start, it is most likely to me that they are from elsewhere. I think the location proves it."

He explained the idea, which had seemed so persuasive to him in Sussex, in a tone that he wished were a little more commanding.

Mayne listened, to his credit, and said, "That would explain the trunk in the Walnut Island case."

"Yes, sir."

He added that he still thought Field should expand his range of victims. "Mr. Field's business is Mr. Field's business," Sinex said.

Mayne nodded, though not with the air of someone completely enamored of that fact. "He thanks you for your contribution on Walnut Island, incidentally."

Lenox flushed. "Thank you, sir."

"Let us know if you have anything else," Mayne said. "In the meanwhile, collect your pay."

Lenox's stomach fell. "Oh."

"It's downstairs. It looks odd on the board that you haven't collected it two Mondays in a row."

"I would like to look at the evidence from the second murder, if it's at the warehouse in Ealing."

"That should be fine," said Mayne.

"The door upon which she was laid, in particular," said Lenox.

To his surprise, Sinex, who was just in his peripheral vision, leaned forward in agitation. "Absolutely not."

Mayne's gaze shifted from Lenox to the senior inspector, mildly surprised. "No?"

Sinex answered. "It's Field's case—then mine—and Exeter's."

"What can another pair of eyes hurt?" said Lenox, humbly he hoped.

Sinex answered. "Every pair of eyes in London is on us already. We must keep the circle small."

"I think I can help."

Sinex, red faced, stood up. "Collect your bloody pay, and stay away from Ealing!"

Mayne gave way. "You'd better leave it, Lenox."

Lenox did not collect his pay—he would say he had forgotten—and returned home in a brown study, lost in the mazes of his own mind, tracing the footsteps he had walked over again and again on each case, the painstaking steps, but unable to add another step to either.

When he got home, he went into the breakfast room. Graham had organized all the telegraphs.

"You've sent the sketches to the four cities?" Lenox asked.

"Yes, sir. First-class."

Lenox threw himself into his chair by the window. The day was reprovingly beautiful, hot and clear. He thought of Edmund, on the train down to Markethouse with Molly and their boy right now.

What a clatter, to travel in a great retinue like that.

Imagine doing it with Elizabeth, though, his mind told him, until he pushed the thought away.

Edmund and his father would take a ride that afternoon, and he couldn't help it in himself, he felt a pang of jealousy, and wasn't quite sure of why—and he felt very old, very young, very new in London, implacably ancient too; felt all the ages of his body live inside it simultaneously just for an instant.

He must have been some time, but when he came out of his reverie he stood bolt upright. "I think I've got something, Graham."

"Sir?"

"It's the door, of course. How dim I've been."

"Sir?" said Graham again.

Another fellow might have bothered Lenox with a lot of chatter, but Graham was silent until Lenox spoke again. "Do me a favor, will you. The place that makes the trunks."

"Wilton's, sir."

"Yes, Wilton's. Wire them and ask for a list of everywhere they've sold to in London, with quantities. Paid return—however many words they need."

"Very well, sir."

"There must be trunkmakers in London," Lenox muttered.

"Sir?"

"Nothing, nothing. Just send the wire as quickly as possible. Ask for a reply before end of business."

Graham, already standing up, said, "Yes, sir."

"I'll be back before tea. I'm for Ealing."

CHAPTER TWENTY-SIX

There was a ball the next evening, a Tuesday.

Lenox arrived at five thirty, an hour and a half late, and the line of carriages up Clarges Street was impassable. He hopped down at the intersection some ways off, looking natty, he rather thought, in his black jacket and black trousers, low-heeled boots, with white gloves in one hand. It was not completely unpleasant to be in futile love. For one thing, it saved quite a lot of trouble (he had given no thought whatsoever to his dance card for the evening) and for another—well, he would see Elizabeth tonight, and because she was a married woman, it would be perfectly respectable to spend his time speaking with her.

The ball was to be given by Mrs. Huggins's own Lady Hamilton (of all people!) and had a Russian theme, to which Lenox had acceded by bringing a bag of potatoes. She greeted him at the door with a laugh at this house present and an affectionate kiss on the cheek, in a tarlatan gown, rather frowsty looking in the warm late afternoon—but she had a lemon ice to sip.

After they had chatted he walked to the back garden—the orchestra milling amongst themselves in the ballroom wouldn't begin to play for another hour—and almost immediately ran into a punch bowl the size of a small bathtub, sitting on a heavy oak table, with a single momentous piece of ice floating in it.

There were small double-handled punch cups, and Lenox accepted one from a servant. The drink was delightfully refreshing; a taste of citrus and spice on its edge, just thin enough to simulate the effect of hydration, and no doubt deadly alcoholic.

It was the kind of ball at which one had to say hello to everyone, or no one—at least, he recognized everyone. He nodded more or less at random. He stood until he had finished his drink, when he heard a voice behind him and turned.

"Mr. Lenox!"

It was Thomas McConnell, the young Scottish doctor. "How do you do?" asked Lenox, shaking his hand.

"It's like being on board an omnibus."

Lenox laughed. "Do doctors take omnibuses? All carriages, I should imagine. Or litters, borne by eunuchs."

"No, I was a very poor student once. Or rather a passable student, who was very poor."

The small garden behind the house was, indeed, as full of people as the street outside was of carriages; the harassed waiters, moving through with trays, could barely remain civil as they shoved the highest members of the aristocracy in order to pass. This was the zenith—as far as the ball went—of the slightly older crowd, the married ones, the parents and grandparents, since the dancing, it was conceded, the later part of the night, belonged to the youth.

"I realize that I don't know whether you are married or—attached," Lenox said to McConnell.

Now the doctor smiled. "Attachment is more common in the unmarried than the married, I sometimes think."

"Not always."

"Not always," McConnell replied with a graceful incline of his head. "But to answer your question—no, I am neither married nor attached. Too much at work. The Hamiltons invited me, I fear, only because they were imposed upon to do so by one or two friends."

It would have been rude to point out that five hundred people would be at the ball, all told—the driver of the omnibus himself was no doubt here—but Lenox was saved from answering when he saw a friend approaching him.

Her name was Lady Lucia Chatham. "There you are, Charles," she said. "Give me some more of that punch, wouldn't you? I've never been so bored in my life."

There were some who reckoned Lucia the most beautiful single woman in London. She was very thin, and wore a pink muslin dress of barely any contour, in the minimal style in fashion at that moment. (The enormous crinoline bustles, whose skirts would have made the party feel twice as crowded, had fallen blessedly out of favor that spring.) Her long blond hair was intricately knotted with lilies, half-falling, half-up. She was rather breathtaking—indeed, McConnell's breath looked rather taken.

"Lucia, may I introduce you to—"

"You can introduce me to Satan himself after you have refilled my glass of punch, my dear—hand it—yes. Ahh. Infinitely better."

This was the fashion, too; a certain looseness of manner, particularly among friends. She smiled winsomely at McConnell to cut her rudeness, and he, enchanted, bowed when they were at last introduced.

Lenox thought that perhaps he would let the two of them talk. He was extremely fond of Lucia, who was part of his small circle, but also found her tiring. (Her beauty would have meant more to him on an earth that didn't hold Elizabeth.) But then someone saw McConnell and grabbed him urgently, and Lenox and Lucia were left alone.

"I think I see a sort of bower there, under the elm tree, Charles," she said, threading her arm through his. "Shall we go and sit? Can't we?"

Her arm was a provocation to every Georgian grandmother in the garden, and Lenox resented being used as an accessory to her daringness. On the other hand, it wasn't completely awful to be the center of attention; and she smelled of divinity, loveliness, youth.

"We'd better refill our punch glasses before we sit."

She sighed. "I always suspected you of being a genius."

"So did I." On a small wrought iron bench together they whispered about their friends. Lucia was entertaining—truly entertaining—and Lenox let himself float on the soft puff of her wit and charm. What a lovely wife she would make for someone, someday. An eventful wife, but a lovely one. She had told him before that she could never move to the country, as Elizabeth proposed to do. Funny: neither could Lenox, yet it was Elizabeth whose spell he was under.

The shadows in the garden started to grow a little longer. They were positioned to rebuff almost everyone (including Lucia's nominal chaperone). Just when it had seemed as if it couldn't possibly get more crowded, it did.

"If there is a God, I won't have to dance with Laurence."

This was the man the city expected Lucia Chatham to marry. He had no title, but there were probably not ten richer men under thirty in Her Majesty's isles. It was said you could ride Devon on his land, one end to the other. Probably an exaggeration.

"I doubt there is a God, in that case."

She smiled at him. "You're too clever, you know that, Charles."

"Am I?"

"I want to be told that I shan't have to dance with him—that you'll dance with me instead."

"I'll dance with you instead."

"Do you mean it?" She took out her card. One of her thin wrists she laid across his knee, examining it, and he felt a shocking thrill, something very real. "My first and fifth and eighth dances are yours, if you'll take them from me."

"I?"

She looked up at him with her large eyes. "Say you will."

"I would be the luckiest man here, of course," he said.

She smiled and wrote his name down. His own card, which was blank, she took from his jacket pocket—it was peeking out—and wrote her name upon it. "There. That's settled." She leaned back, stretching her arms. "What happens if I am drunker than I expected, Charles?"

"What happens if I'm drunker than I expected?" he replied, laughing.

"Nothing will happen to either of us, is the answer." They were strangely alone in the little bower, despite the incredible din of the party, and it didn't feel wrong when she gave him a very quick kiss on the cheek. "See?"

He realized they were both probably very much drunker than they had thought.

"There you two are!"

Charles and Lucia both looked up, startled, no doubt with guilt in their faces. Elizabeth and their friend Hugh stood in front of them. Elizabeth was wearing a blue dress, light brown curls falling around her face. There was that Gioconda smile in her eyes: it was how Lenox had always pictured Jane Austen, deep brown eyes that missed nothing, took it in, saw the humor and the irony in it, and refused to pass judgment.

"Hugh is going to commit suicide. The princess isn't here."

"How are you going to do it, Hugh?" asked Lenox.

He sighed. "Probably the river."

"You can be the third victim!" said Lucia.

Elizabeth caught Lenox's eye. The princess was not a proper princess—or, she was, but a French one, and therefore a tier beneath their duchesses, because the French were backward in virtually everything. The Princesse de Parme. She was odd looking; also exceptionally alluring, somehow. She was here for the season, and Hugh had fallen hard for her, having finally given up on their friend Eleanor.

Just at that moment, the orchestra struck up inside. Lucia grabbed Charles's arm. "This is my dance, Charles! Come, let's go, let's go."

"I'm yours, my dear," said Lenox, offering his arm.

"We'll be late for the switch—the best bit—hurry, would you, hurry. Hugh, if you're dancing, come along."

"Back in a moment," Lenox said to Hugh and Elizabeth. (Elizabeth wouldn't dance at all—Hugh's card he had no doubt kept strictly clear, poetic soul that he was.) "Save a little daylight for us."

He felt Elizabeth's eyes on him as he walked half a step behind Lucia, inside to dance. He was certainly much drunker than he had thought.

CHAPTER TWENTY-SEVEN

Lenox wobbled into consciousness late the next morning, first barely aware he was there, then aware that it was unpleasant to be there, then finally awake enough to realize that he was awake. It was late. Cripes, could suns be this bright? Who allowed that? With intense irritation, he pulled a pillow over his eyes.

He had the most awful taste in his mouth. He reached blindly and realized, with gratitude, that there was a glass of cider with chips of ice in it next to his bed. Graham, bless his soul. He sipped it and then shoved the pillow on top of his face again.

He felt shame down to the bottom of his soul. Twice in two weeks, to be as hungover as a parson, when for three years at Oxford he had kept a clear head.

As he lay there, the night began to return to him in bits. Above all he remembered the gliding, carefree, dizzyingly happy feeling of dance after dance with Lucia Chatham—she had scratched Laurence off her card for the ninth dance and given it to Charles, to scandalized murmurs in the room, which had seemed quite funny to them at the time—and the equally happy sensation that Elizabeth, sitting with the other married women along the side of the grand pink and gold room, so many of them much older than she, never stopped watching them. He had a vague recollection of her face growing dark, and the wholly unbecoming gladness that it gave him to wound her. How awful a part of him. Then there had been the orchestra packing up, the final drinks, the thinning of the crowds, the grandiose plans with Hugh and Lucia and Eleanor for day trips the following afternoon. . . .

Could his father really be dying?

Deep in the night, when it had finally been time to go home, he'd realized that through the whole night this question had been passing through some deep and wintry ravine in his mind, on a journey that even he could see only from afar.

Lenox had never been a drinker, and in the cold, lonely moonlight outside his flat he had, in a moment of lucidity, wondered if this was why he had agreed with Lucia to scandalize everyone at the ball, to be the center of attention, to drink too much.

He forced himself up onto his elbows, blinking hard and angrily at the windows. Next to the glass of cider was some toast. He ate it, and when it hit his stomach, he felt immediately a little more human. ("A morning head lasts twenty minutes at your age," he remembered his mother telling him when he set out for Oxford. "Treasure that. It will all change when you're thirty. Then again when you're forty.")

He reached for a notebook next to his bed. The last page he had written in was from his trip to the police warehouse in Ealing. It was headed with that name:

EALING
Shoes ✗
Door ✓✗
Trunk ✓
Flowers ✓
Spectacles ✗
Shilling ✓✗
Strangulation ✗

Lenox studied this for some time. Where he had made a checkmark, he felt fairly confident; an *x*, still confused; both, he thought he had some idea of what was going on.

He pushed the small white button on his side table, which was wired to clang a bell in the servants' quarters. He rarely did this, since he considered it, if not rude, at least imperious. But his limbs felt as though they were full of wet sand, and he desperately wanted some more iced cider, some toast, and some very strong tea.

It was Graham who appeared. "Hello," said Lenox moodily.

"Good morning, sir."

"Ha! A wry observation. What time did I come home?"

"I did not notice the hour, sir."

"Please be so kind as to stop lying."

"Four o'clock, sir."

"Hm." Lenox rubbed his face. "What time is it now?"

"Just before eleven."

"It's not looking likely that I'll make six o'clock church service."

"No, sir."

"I suppose I'll go to hell."

"I couldn't speculate, sir."

Lenox held up his list. "I want to ask you something. But could you get me some more of that—more of both of those?" He gestured at the cider, the toast. "They are the only reason I'm speaking to you this politely."

"Not at all, sir. As for the—"

Just then a raw-cheeked young footman came in without knocking (he had been employed for under a month here, Roger was his name, a very decent fellow of around fifteen with bright orange hair) and bearing a silver tray with the things Lenox had asked for, and also tea, milk, sugar, and a plate of digestive biscuits. He put it on the small circular dining table near Lenox's bedroom window about as inelegantly as any human possibly could have done, then withdrew, tripping over the threshold on the way out.

"He's doing very well for someone who was born nine days ago," Lenox observed.

"Come now, sir," said Graham, smiling.

That chastisement was quite right. None of these people were responsible for his condition—and it was base in him to take it out on them.

He vaulted out of the bed, ignoring the screech of his nerve endings, and went to the breakfast table. "I apologize."

"Not at all, sir."

"And the papers?"

"Would you like to read them in here?" Graham asked.

"I cannot face Mrs. Huggins."

The bedroom was a place she did not breach, at least not while Lenox was present. "She has been mostly absent, sir," said Graham.

Lenox looked at his valet curiously. *Absent?*

"Yes, sir," said Graham, with an imperceptible shrug. "I have seen her—dressed to go outdoors—now and again. But she has mostly been away from the apartments, sir."

"Anyway, I don't mind eating in here. I'll take the papers if it's not too much trouble."

"By all means, sir."

Graham was at the door when Lenox had a thought. "Wait. Graham."

"Sir?"

Lenox was staring down at the list in his hand. He took a sip of tea.

"Do you remember my telling you how bothered I was by the shoes of the second victim? The Ophelia?"

"I do, sir."

Lenox studied the list in silence for another moment. "I think," said Lenox slowly. "I think I know why they bothered me."

"Why, sir?"

"They were not part of the picture."

"The picture, sir?"

"The delicate nymph, laid out upon the board. The flowers, the white dress—wet, don't forget, though the board was dry! And yet she was wearing the kind of shoes that Mrs. Huggins might."

Graham tilted his head, thinking. "The significance is not quite clear to me, sir."

"Haste," said Lenox. "Something in his plan went wrong."

"Such as, sir?"

But Lenox was in a study, staring at his piece of paper. Finally, he looked up and said, "No word back from Wilton's?"

"Not yet, sir."

"Hm. Tomorrow, perhaps." He looked at the paper and muttered, "By God, I'd like to get him."

The sun flashed across the window, and Lenox winced. He looked up. At the ball the evening before, he had met Lord Billingsley, who was the current and 17th Earl of Sedgewood. The Sedgewoods and the Lenoxes were related, though the Sedgewoods were much grander—they would have considered the Lenoxes a cadet branch of the family, while the Lenoxes, who were as prideful as the next group of men and women God had chosen to place on earth, considered themselves in key respects better than the Sedgewoods.

Nevertheless, Billingsley and Lenox's father were deep friends, with twined roots. There were few men the earl met on equal terms, but Edward Lenox was one of them.

Charles, drunk, had greeted his second cousin with affection—he had spent many weeks at Sedgewood House as a child—and was taken aback when his relative's lined old face remained stony.

He couldn't remember the exact words. That nobody else would say it, but Charles was making an embarrassment of himself as a detective; that his father deserved better; his brother; that he had better not expect to remain in society much longer if he chose to stay on this course.

No doubt the old earl, deferred to by probably tens of thousands of people in the course of his life, had expected Lenox to immediately internalize this piece of chastisement. But now, with morning come, all he could think was that he had a strong feeling about the door; he was sure he knew about the trunk; and he was quite certain that if his hunch was right, he would have his hand on the murderer's collar the next day.

Let them try and stop him then.

CHAPTER TWENTY-EIGHT

At a shade before six o'clock on Thursday morning—feeling fit as a fiddle, Lady Hamilton's ball a distant memory—Lenox stood by the river and watched its gray waters reconstitute themselves over and over, rise, fall, sweep, crest, wave, dip, splash.

It could be argued that the Thames hadn't changed in seven thousand years. Or—that it changed at every second, and in every decade, and in every century, while remaining eternally itself. The millions of boats that had passed down it, just think! Yet here it was, dark, flat, as stark as a god. They said a body a day was fished from its waters. They said every Londoner drank thirteen cups out of it one way or another between dawn and dusk, in wine, in beer, as water itself. King John had signed the Magna Carta on one of its islands. Millions of generations of fish plucked from it. A city rising, falling, rising around it. And none of it changing the river even slightly; not really.

How separate humans were from nature, thought Lenox.

He was standing on Bankside. In fact, he was at precisely the point where the second "perfect" had been discovered. (That was the awful nickname the press had settled on for the two victims, and for their murderer, simply "The London Murderer." No doubt that gratified him, its exclusivity: *The*.)

He could see four bridges. One was Westminster Bridge, which touched Parliament, and a memory came to him unbidden of his father taking him and Edmund to the House of Commons when they were, oh, perhaps five and eight.

"Do you know why the bridge is green?" he'd asked them as they pulled across it.

"Why, Papa?" Edmund had said—it was for him, this trip, though Charles had suspected of himself, even then, that he might like to go into that grand building every day and decide what the nation should think.

"It matches the color of the benches in the Commons exactly," his father had said with a soft smile. "Vanity, isn't it? But pleasant."

Now, eighteen years later, Lenox turned around, away from the river and its bridges, and examined the thin shingle behind him.

Facing the Thames here was a row of warehouses, interspersed with thinner countinghouses, almost all of them to do with the great shipping concerns around them—rather as, on the water itself, small fry lived in the wake of the whalers, outfitters, accountants, the kind.

Lenox's scull was tied onto one of the posts scattered at intervals along the river. He was red and sweating, deep in thought: the spectacles, the door. He looked down at the small pebbles mixed into the sand.

At last, he took out his notebook and scanned the buildings in front of him one by one. The address was Bankside, as simple as that—here, numbers 30 through 114, roughly.

He stared for a long, long time—perhaps twenty minutes—without anyone passing by, and finally, with a sigh and a feeling of significance, a certainty that this was the day, he got back into his scull.

The vital thing was to hear back from Wilton's, the trunkmakers, Lenox thought. The earliest they might conceivably write was nine o'clock, so naturally he started to look for their wire at around eight fifteen.

It kept on not arriving. He would have settled for a note from one of the constabularies, the identity of one of the perfects. Nor did that arrive, however.

Instead Lenox and Graham spent the morning catching up on their newspapers. (Crime went on occurring around London, which seemed rather unfair.) There was one note: Mayne reported that Sinex was irate that Lenox had gone to Ealing against direct orders, and demanding that Lenox be fired summarily.

Moreover, he had still yet to pick up his pay. He would do that in person today, Mayne said; or Mayne would follow Sinex's advice.

Lenox crumpled this message and hurled it across the room to the fireplace, though it fell just short. On the side table nearby were the two ten-pound notes of Rupert Clarkson, like a couple of shreds from the tattered flag of his dignity.

He sat in silence for a long time, then burst out at a charwoman who was passing through the front hall. "Where on *earth* is Mrs. Huggins?" he called to her.

She looked absolutely terrified, and Lenox felt instantly guilty. "I can't say, m'Lord."

Lenox was not a lord. "If you see her"—this was hardly likely, given that she was leaving—"tell her to come here immediately. Graham, do you know where she is?"

Graham first nodded in courtly fashion to the charwoman, who had been standing rooted to her spot, and now hustled away. "She was here this morning, sir."

"Was she? How splendid for her. Nevertheless, please inform her that I intend to stop her pay if she is not present during working hours."

"The house has never looked finer, sir."

Lenox looked around, and saw to his intense irritation that this was indeed true. There were beautiful vases of hydrangeas on every surface; every dustless surface. It was just like Mrs. Huggins to be most superlative in her work as she was shirking it. "It looks fine," he said shortly.

"Shall I send the wire?" Graham asked.

It was on the table, waiting—a wire to Wilton's, asking for their progress. "Not till eleven o'clock."

They waited, and at eleven on the dot, Graham went out to send it. Meanwhile Lenox went to collect his pay. His name was in bright red on a white board by the pay window, as if he'd committed some crime; the man behind the counter laughed nastily at him.

"Not many's too good for their pay," he said.

Evidently Lenox was—known, here, too. "Nor am I."

"Here you are, then."

"It comes in coins?"

"'It comes in coins,'" he replied in falsetto.

Lenox gave the coins to every beggar who asked for them along his path home, indiscriminately. Then he almost traced his step to ask for them back, because he hated the arrogance of the gesture. But of course, it was too late. Half the coins were no doubt spent already.

He wished he could cast himself back to that morning on Bankside, when it had all seemed so clear.

Wilton's had responded. Graham handed over the telegram when Lenox entered. Lenox read it. "Damn them."

"Sir?"

He passed across the wire, which read, with infuriating economy given that it was postpaid,

Assembling STOP **Regards** STOP

"No indication of when it might arrive," Lenox said.

"Would you care to tell me your theory, sir?"

"No, because I don't want to be wrong," said Lenox bluntly.

Graham nodded. "I understand, sir."

The day was saved, unexpectedly, at a little before noon. There was a ring at the door; it was Elizabeth.

At seeing her, Lenox felt, first, a sudden consciousness of shame at how he had behaved Tuesday night, though he could see no clear reason for it, and second, the release of the nervous tension in his limbs, the toll of that morning of waiting.

"Hello, Charles," she said. "I was just out calling and I thought I would make you give me lunch."

"I'm a terrible cook."

She smiled. "Come now."

As they ate their lunch, which was quite good in the end—salmon with lemon and asparagus, a baked cauliflower with cheese, a silver dish of peas with a lump of butter melting over them—the two of them discussed Lady Hamilton's, their friends, Hugh's doomed love, Lucia's likely one.

Afterwards, a cup of coffee in her hands, Elizabeth wandered the study. She stopped in front of a map of Russia. "Tell me," she said, "do you really mean to go?"

"Indeed I do, my lady."

"It snows more or less continuously, no?"

"Sometimes less, and sometimes discontinuously." He smiled. "Summer is not an English invention."

She traced her finger along a route that Lenox had drawn on the map. It took him by train from St. Petersburg to Moscow, with stops marked by small blue circles along the way. "What are these?"

"Monasteries. You can walk from one to the next."

"You shall become very spiritually enlightened one of these days."

Lenox shook his head. "May it arrive soon."

For the first time, she looked at him directly in the eye. "I owe you an apology."

"Do you? I can't imagine you do."

"I do; and you know why. I was very censorious at the ball—and your behavior was none of my business at all."

He stared back at her.

By the time he had realized that she was not merely his closest friend (her youth had been an obstruction to that realization, a fatal one), she had accepted a proposal. This was the closest either had come to speaking a word about their emotions since then.

"As my closest friend," Lenox said, "you are forgiven. In fact, you could move to a Russian monastery, and I would visit you there."

She smiled. "The country won't seem so far then."

There was a ring at the door.

Lenox's heart leapt. Graham came tearing in, if it was possible one could tear into a room in a manner befitting the gravity of a butler. "The telegram, sir."

Lenox opened it.

It was very long, a list of all sales the company had made in London within the last five years, though because Wilton's were based in Manchester, it wasn't so prohibitively long that it was impossible to scan. At the top: they had sold 1,900 trunks to a muslin importer in Lambeth; 1,750 to a dry goods company in Greenwich—the list went on, down to ten trunks entrusted to the Oxford and Cambridge Club.

For shipping food, Lenox would wager.

And then he saw it. "Here!" he cried. "Graham, order a cab. We have to go to Bankside. Elizabeth, goodbye—I'm sorry—I shall see you this evening, I hope—at Clarissa's—but I must go."

"Go, go," she said, "go."

CHAPTER TWENTY-NINE

An hour and a half later, Lenox, Graham, Sir Richard Mayne, and Inspector Exeter were in a hansom on the way from Scotland Yard to Bankside, the former two on a bench facing the latter.

Exeter looked mad as a whipped horse. He hadn't wanted to come. Mayne had overruled him, but did seem filled with skepticism now, worn down by his subordinate's ire. "Well—you had better explain," he said to Lenox.

Lenox nodded. "Of course." He coughed into the crook of his elbow, to give himself time to collect his thoughts. "Very well, first, then:

"As you know, it has bothered me for some time that the door itself upon which the second victim's body was laid was dry, dry all over—underneath, on top."

"Yes, you've mentioned it thirty times or so," said Exeter.

"Because I found it curious."

"Inspector Field did not."

"I will tell you why I think it has been bothering me.

"The board and the body together were heavy, at least some two hundred pounds. That, combined with the fact that they were dry, leads me to strongly believe that they came, crucially, from very close by, if we believe the murderer to be a single person, as I think we all do."

Lenox paused to let this sink in. Mayne merely grunted. "Hm."

It wasn't lost on any of the four of them that Lenox had given an address on Bankside to the driver. They looked at him expectantly, and he went on. "The fact that the body itself was wet was only an attempt at disguise, to make us believe that she had floated down the river, like the trunk that landed at Walnut Island—when the trunk actually *had* floated downriver. From Bankside, I would bet money."

All four men were silent, and in that instant caught someone a stone's throw down the street (they were on Whitehall) singing the ballad of the "Perfect Crimes," a two-stanza ditty composed to aid in the sale of a gaudy and mostly fabricated little pamphlet about the murders. Lenox was thoroughly sick of the melody, and Mayne, if his face was any indication—the pamphlet was not generous toward him—felt similarly.

"And where specifically are we heading now?" he asked Lenox.

They had begun to pull across the fatal river itself. Lenox, though confident in his logic, felt a bundle of nerves. More than once he had asked himself what someone his age could do—and more than once answered himself, more stoutly than he felt, that if it was within Exeter's capabilities to solve a crime, it was also within his own. At his very dullest he couldn't be duller than Exeter.

Lenox passed the telegram he had received from Wilton's over to Mayne. "That is a list of everyone in London who has made an order for Wilton's trunks—that is, the kind in which the first victim's body was discovered—in the last five years."

Mayne frowned, staring down at the long list of names. "And?"

Lenox handed over a second piece of paper. "This morning I wrote down the addresses of every building near our spot on Bankside. Then I looked up their names."

Mayne had caught on before Lenox finished speaking, and was cross-referencing the two lists, pointer finger bouncing back and forth between the two sheets.

He found it, and looked up at Lenox, suddenly no longer a skeptic. "Corcoran and Sons?" he said pressingly. "What is Corcoran and Sons?"

Lenox shook his head. "I only know that it's a business. I'm not yet sure in which line." He pointed at an enormous warehouse along Bankside, number 38. "There it is, however. I think many of our answers lie inside."

The carriage stopped. All of them stared at the huge brick building, whose anonymity seemed suddenly ominous.

Two constables traveled with Mayne at all times, and everyone inside could feel it when they jumped down from the rails outside. A moment later, the two doors opened.

The four men inside piled out. Both constables, who flanked them as they walked toward the warehouse, were short, one dark and one fair; they were called Middleton and Becker. Mayne nodded at them, and then said, "Well, Lenox, this is your show."

Lenox nodded, more optimistically than he felt. "Follow me."

After receiving the wire that early afternoon, Lenox had come to this very spot alone. It hadn't been easy to loiter; there were dozens of men about, ferrying goods to a pier nearby, counting pallets, that sort of thing.

But he had found what he wanted.

The warehouse comprised a large ground-level story with vast windows, where goods were held, and two shorter stories above it, which contained offices. Everything on the building was salt- and weather-worn, battered, rough, as indeed everything along the river was after more than a month's distance from its last painting or polishing. Salt could eat anything, of course—a brush of it from an incoming shipment, a little time, and its tale was told.

There were two dinghies upended outside the colossal main doors, and various mysterious seagoing paraphernalia, all of it tattered and smudged.

There were also seven or eight trunks lying about. They were of just exactly the type in which the Walnut Island body had been discovered.

Lenox first led them to one of these, which sat about twenty yards from the warehouse. He upended it. "Oy, what're thee!" shouted a gruff voice.

It belonged to a foreman, striding toward them. But Mayne and even Exeter were ignoring him. The constables, Middleton and Becker, convoyed in front of their boss, ready to explain.

On the underside of the trunk, it said G811.

Lenox gestured toward the others. "The others are the same," he said. "An in-house marking. Now follow me, if you will."

It was with a brisker step that Mayne obeyed this request. The G811 was monumentally significant, of course: it put a trunk from this warehouse directly on Walnut Island, the site where the first victim had been discovered. The warehouse itself was only a hundred paces from the site where the second had been.

It was beyond conceivable coincidence.

Lenox led them around the eastern corner of the building, gaining strength from that thought. There were fewer windows here, and a series of smaller doors, presumably entrances to various separate working sections of the warehouse.

There were seven of these doors in all (Lenox had counted), and all were stripped and salt-worn, like everything else here.

All the doors except one.

It was painted a fresh blue-gray color. It was quite obviously new.

"Where's the one it replaced?" Mayne asked.

"In Ealing, unless I am much mistaken."

"In Ealing."

"I went and saw the door yesterday, despite Inspector Sinex's objection. It matches the dimensions of this one to the inch, as well as the color of the others. It was substantially more worn, however. A large hole near the handle—risk of a burglary. In other words, it had reached the time when it needed to be replaced."

"So it would have been lying about," Mayne said.

Lenox nodded. "Forty yards from the river here."

"Then why the flowers? The shilling?"

Lenox shrugged. "Why the HMS *Gallant?*" He turned the handle of the new door. "I propose that we attempt to find out."

They went inside.

What greeted them in the warehouse was the sight of hundreds of Wilton's trunks, scattered about in various places. The business of Corcoran and Sons became clear quickly: they evidently took in goods from the ships on the Thames and transported them overland across the British Isles. There was no single dominant good here; being packed into various trunks, by hefty men, there were piles of muslin and fine lace, cases of liquor—luxury goods, all of them.

It was plain to see how the Walnut Island trunk could have gone missing without being missed.

An enormous fellow in shirtsleeves, with long side-whiskers and huge arms, was striding toward them. "Private premises," he said. "Who are you?"

Four police badges emerged at once—even Mayne's, which he couldn't have frequent occasion to display.

"We need to see the person in charge of this business," he said.

The man frowned. "He's away, Mr. Corcoran."

"Where?"

"Looking for his daughter."

A jolt of electricity went through Lenox's spine. "His daughter? Where has she gone?"

"She eloped to Gretna Green, the fool. Turned down ten thousand pounds a year by defying Mr. Corcoran—for love."

This last word was spoken in the most derisive tone. "Then who is in charge?" said Exeter impatiently.

The man frowned. "In charge of what? I'm King Jerry the First as far as this particular floor is concerned."

"And upstairs?" said Mayne. "Who is in charge there? We have serious questions to ask."

"About the perfect?"

Mayne looked at him. "How did you know that? What is your name?"

"I'm Blackstone. As for how—happened on our part of the river. Six of you. Doesn't take a genius." His massive shoulders rose and dipped just slightly. Obvious. "You'd better see Mr. Corcoran's senior manager, I suppose. Nobody down here knows anything. I'd've whipped it straight out of them. Two women, like that. An absolute disgrace. You should read the pamphlet they've going about that tells what happened."

CHAPTER THIRTY

The senior manager of Corcoran and Sons was a tall man who managed to stoop his way into middle height, slope-shouldered, head sunk down to his chest. He had white-blond hair shaped into two diverging and immovable planes, and a middle manager's face, with owlish spectacles and a furrow of shortsightedness in his brow.

Old, battered spectacles, Lenox noticed.

Blackstone had accompanied them up to this office, which was small but commanded a pretty view of the water. (Mr. Corcoran's own much larger office was just next door, at the corner of the building.) In the vast room outside the two private offices there sat fourteen clerks working, and Lenox had scanned their faces—all turned to see the visitors—closely, looking for signs of his man.

No new spectacles there, either; nobody he recognized, or whose face drew his notice.

"Scotland Yard, Mr. Cairn," said Blackstone.

Mr. Cairn, who was sitting, peered at them over his spectacles and sighed. "Scotland Yard?" he said. "Mr. Corcoran is away."

Lenox thought it odd that he assumed they wanted to see Corcoran. "Our business is not necessarily with Mr. Corcoran," he said.

Cairn looked slightly surprised. "I assumed it was about his daughter."

"She eloped, we understand?"

Cairn hesitated, and then said, "Thank you, Blackstone." When the foreman was gone, he said, with a pained look on his face, "Yes, Eliza Corcoran has eloped, I'm afraid. The fellow an utter bounder. Not a penny to his name, and full to the brim with lies."

"How do you know?" asked Mayne.

"Mr. Corcoran has had him investigated."

"He has been gone a month, Corcoran?"

"A month? No, two weeks. He decided at last that he had better go himself. Miss Corcoran had left a long, hysterical letter about true love and that sort of rot." Cairn shook his head. Evidently this was not a workplace filled with very great credulity about the concept of love. "Mr. Corcoran has tracked her to Glasgow. Now it is a matter of hunting them to ground, paying this fellow off, and bringing his daughter home. Mr. Corcoran and I asked Scotland Yard for help some time ago. While I have you, I should like to note that we received none."

"What is this man's name?" asked Mayne.

"Leckie. Or so he says. I told Mr. Corcoran I would bet anything he's a Spaniard. Swarthy."

"An accent?"

"No," admitted Cairn grudgingly.

"When did she elope?" asked Lenox.

"About five weeks ago."

Lenox and Graham exchanged a look. Mayne, who was no fool, saw it pass between them, and immediately cottoned on.

Exeter, who was closer to a fool, saw only that they were all looking at one another, and started to look at each of them suspiciously, as if they were keeping a secret from him.

"What does she look like, Miss Eliza Corcoran?" asked Lenox.

Cairn frowned. "She's fair, fair-haired. Rather shorter than most, and largish." His voice became confidential. "Plump, one would admit if one were pressed. Therefore, in her insecurity, vulnerable to this vile sort of predator. Leckie."

Lenox, who had been sure this young woman was the victim of Walnut Island, felt disappointed—the body in the trunk had been slender, with dark ringlets of hair—then chided himself for it. Eliza Corcoran was at least alive, whatever circumstances she had worked herself into.

"Has she been corresponding with her father since she disappeared?" he asked.

"Yes." Cairn shook his head again. "Reckless girl."

"Eliza Corcoran? I take it you knew her, then?"

"Oh, yes. I've been here for thirty years—a third again as long as she's been alive."

Lenox nodded. "And your trunks are from Wilton's?" he asked

Cairn looked at him curiously, thrown by the change of subject. "Our most recent batch. We have been looking for a cheaper supplier, actually, but there are only half a dozen who make that type in England. Why?"

"What is the marking stamped on each one?"

"They are marked with a G, for goods, which is the railway's preference, to distinguish them from personal items, and then with a number from our warehouse, which is ours. That way the trunks with which we ship liquor aren't later used to ship—well, delicate furs, for example."

"It's a luxury goods company, then," Mayne said.

"Yes. Buy overseas, sell to England." He looked at them all now, suddenly concerned. "What is this about? Our books are clean, you know. We haven't had a case of theft inside the company in three years, either. We pay too well. One stolen shipment about eighteen months ago, but our insurance covered that."

"Who is out sick today?" said Lenox.

"Out? What, sick?"

"Yes, that, or has been excused early?"

Cairn gave him a strange look. "Nobody."

"Nobody?"

"I can assure you we hire no malingerers here, sir. It's a very, very good job for a clerk. Several have been promoted to the managerial level, here or at other firms."

"There were fourteen men in the room we passed through to get to your office. There are fifteen desks."

Exeter scoffed. "An extra desk."

"It had been in use this morning, or I am much in error," Lenox said curtly.

Mayne was staring at him. "How did you count so quickly?"

Lenox hadn't counted quickly—he had just known, the way one knew the word "tangerine" at a glance without thinking about the *t* or the *a* or the *n* or the *g* or any of the rest of it. His mind worked that way. It always had.

"I thought it might be useful," he said, however, by way of reply.

Cairn frowned and stood up. "They should all be present. You are right, Inspector—"

"Lenox. Mr. Lenox."

"You are right, Inspector Lenox, in saying that we have fifteen clerks, and that all of them are present today."

Lenox felt his pulse rise. The murderer might be fleeing even now.

Cairn circled them to get to his door, which he opened, going out into the main clerks' room. He surveyed this with an expert eye. "Hm," he said to himself.

"Well?" asked Mayne.

The senior manager tapped the nearest clerk on the shoulder. "Where is Pond?" he said.

The fellow, who was young and plump, possessed of a very earnest face, looked up like a rabbit peeking from its hole in the ground at the scent of spring air, and turned his eyes toward the empty desk on the other side of the room. "The loo, sir, perhaps?" he said. "I saw him at his desk earlier."

Cairn stepped forward, as if to make an announcement. But Lenox grabbed his arm. "Perhaps we could speak in your office," he said.

The six large men pushed their way (very noticeably, and rather comically) back into the small office. Cairn took his seat, his back to the beautiful view of the river and the city. "What's this about?" he asked again.

"Can you tell us anything about Pond? What is his first name?"

"Jonathan."

"Where is he from?"

"Listen, I'll go find him right now. He's in the loo, no doubt. Though we expect a great deal of our clerks, that's one privilege we allow them in the job." Cairn had sharpened up. "Anyhow," he said, "I really must insist upon asking what this is about, if not Eliza Corcoran."

"It's about the murder that happened on Bankside," said Mayne.

Cairn looked about to reply, then paused, nonplussed. Evidently his foreman was quicker to the draw than he was. "The murder?"

"Yes."

"Did Pond see something?"

Lenox looked at his watch. Mayne wasn't taking charge of the situation quickly enough. "Go find him if you can, Mr. Cairn," he said. "Becker, Middleton, get downstairs as quickly as possible and cover the exits."

Mayne looked at him, and then, suddenly realizing what Lenox thought, nodded: Pond might already be on the run.

"Exeter," he said quickly, "you could do the same. Mr. Graham, if you were so inclined, you might also help them. Mr. Cairn, Lenox, and I will follow you. We must hope that there is a simple explanation for Mr. Pond's absence from his desk."

The four men left, Exeter leading them, and the remaining three followed, striding out of the clerks' office and then three abreast down a wide hallway.

Cairn, more serious now, didn't speak, but was half a step ahead. This was a prosperous concern, Lenox thought. Brass light fixtures, mahogany paneling, gleaming wood floors.

Cairn went into the bathroom (indoor plumbing, no less) and emerged after a moment. "Empty," he said, looking a bit more concerned now.

For his part, Lenox was utterly sure something was wrong.

The certainty derived from a single reason, which was the signature appended to the second letter the *Challenger* had received: *In faith, your ponderous correspondent.*

The fellow, feeling too clever by half, hadn't been able to resist inserting his name in the letter twice. *Pon*derous corres*pond*ent.

Cairn, with a more urgent step, said, "He may be in our records room. I feel absolutely sure that Pond is not—cannot be *involved*, if that is a serious consideration of yours, and if he had seen something, I know that unless he were under some threat, he would have, that he—"

Mayne cut off Cairn's anxious chatter. "We only wish to speak to him."

The records room was two long hallways down from the central office, in a dim and musty corner that faced South London, the part of the building without a view of the river.

At that moment, Lenox considered that if Pond wasn't here, Graham might get hurt. A wave of guilt passed through him. Middleton and Becker had whistles and training, but if Pond were very desperate—and Graham were alone, separated from the constables or Exeter—

But Pond was here, after all, he was here.

They discovered this when Cairn pushed open the door of the records room (the name embossed in gold leaf, money here, money, Lenox's mind racing to store all that he saw) and stepped inside.

There was a confused instant, Lenox and Mayne following him

inside, in which Cairn said, "Mr. Pond, there you are. The police are here and would—"

And then, a gunshot.

Lenox had shot guns his whole life, but he had never heard a sound as earsplittingly loud as this one, a gun fired in an enclosed space.

"Good God," said Mayne, and Lenox at the same moment said, "Cairn!"

But it wasn't the senior manager who had been shot. Cairn turned back to them, his face whiter than chalk, said, "But he's shot himself—he—he—"

And then fainted dead away.

CHAPTER THIRTY-ONE

Mayne stooped down to help Cairn. Lenox vaulted the manager, half-tripping over his bulk, righted himself, and then went to find Jonathan Pond.

It didn't take long. The records room was a long dusty hall, with bookcases lining either side of a central corridor. Slumped back against one of these bookcases was a young man in a clerk's standard-issue black suit and white shirt. He had a bullet hole in his temple.

He was also still alive.

Lenox, who had taken such forensic interest in violence these past seven months, read about it over and over, cataloged it, clipped it from the newspaper, pinned each variety of it entomologically in its place, felt a complete change overtake him, seeing it in person.

He stood frozen, suppressing the urge to run.

A detective. By God. What had he been thinking?

Behind him he could vaguely hear the arrival of people drawn by the noise, as well as the ministrations of Mayne.

He forced himself down to one knee. Pond's eyes were wide, terrified. He was gulping, strangled, as animal as a horse with a broken leg. He tried to speak, but either couldn't or didn't. He gave a great convulsion, and then, blood pouring from the corners of his mouth, heaved a breath.

It was his last; he was dead.

Lenox, who had seven months before spent most of his days in the golden sun of Oxford, debating whether to have another biscuit from the tray in the common room, found himself staring for the first time at a person who had been living one second, dead the next.

The moment lasted three eternities. Finally, Lenox heard Mayne behind him. Cairn, his carefully slicked hair fallen obscenely out of shape, like the day, had staggered to his feet and was following the Commissioner of the Yard.

"This was Mr. Jonathan Pond?" Mayne said.

"It—it is," said Cairn, and then, without warning, half turned and vomited into the space between two of the tall bookshelves.

"Oh hell," Mayne muttered.

Lenox stooped down lower by the body. He had already recovered his composure—a little bit of it, anyway. (Was this what his friends who were soldiers experienced? His cousin Josiah Lenox, in the Dragoons, Elizabeth's husband, a dozen Old Harrovians he knew in the Coldstreams and the Grenadiers?)

Very gently, he touched the shining spectacles that hung from a chain around Pond's motionless neck. "Brand new," he said quietly.

Mayne stooped next to him, his face red. He wasn't used to working out of the office. "Yes." He stood up. His face was grim. "Now the mystery starts, I'm afraid."

Lenox nodded, standing. He had been thinking the same thing. "The two women."

Almost immediately the press arrived, within what seemed like a shockingly short time, ten minutes perhaps. Two of them had already managed to insinuate themselves into the building by the time Mayne and Lenox had returned to the main office, leaving Pond under the guard of the constables. They'd already gotten Pond's name and begun to ask questions when Middleton appeared at Cairn's office, dragging one in each hand.

Mayne gave them a dressing-down—but of course, they already had enough to begin writing their articles, as he knew full well.

"If the headline is anything other than 'Third Murder Averted,' you'll both be in my sights," he told them angrily. "Dead in my sights, I tell you. Interfering with a police investigation, among other things. Middleton, take their names and credentials. I know this one, Capston from the *Mail*."

Graham had followed Middleton in to find Lenox. "What's the scene outside?" Lenox asked. "Have you looked?"

"Only through the windows. Bedlam, sir. Press, crowds."

"Stay close, would you. Second set of eyes and ears."

"Of course, sir."

Cairn, having been taken to the washstand to clean himself, was now back in his office. He was very obviously much shaken. Lenox left, going to Corcoran's office at the corner of the building.

Here, as he'd expected, he found a bottle of brandy on a small table beside an enormous brown chesterfield. He took three glasses and poured healthy slugs, bringing them back. Ostensibly this was an act of generosity toward Cairn, and indeed it did steady him—he slicked his hair back into its careful shape after the first swallow, a marginal return to decorum—but Lenox needed it, too.

Even Mayne looked grateful.

They took some basic information about Pond (address—a lodging house in Kensington—salary, history).

Then they began to pull the clerks in one by one. None of them had much to say against Pond; nor for him. He was a quiet little fellow, according to one, and another said that he was fairly good at his job—airs, though, uppity, rather "literary." A third clerk said that he had quite liked Pond, though the fellow drank every once in a while and when he did grew pontifical and swaggering, and also had been shirking since Corcoran took away to look for his daughter.

Lenox glanced at Cairn to see if this was a surprise, but evidently the senior manager could be no further destabilized that day—his brandy glass had been drained to the last drop, and he was gazing vacantly into space.

"What would you have said of Pond?" Lenox asked him curiously between interviews.

"Eh? Why—nothing!" said Cairn, crumpled down in his chair. "That he was a clerk at Corcoran and Sons! Not a job to throw away! And you mean to tell me that he was somehow involved in these two murders you see plastered everywhere—in the news—and the company—"

Here he trailed off. "Would you please tell us about Eliza Corcoran one more time?" Lenox asked.

Cairn walked them through the timeline again. She had eloped about five weeks earlier with this Peter Leckie character. (Gretna Green was infamously the first village across the border from England and into Scotland, which had much more tolerant laws regarding marriage.) She and her husband stood to inherit the firm *if* her father approved the match; he was the "son" of Corcoran and Sons, and, since he was a widower, Eliza was his only family. Even after her elopement, he had retained hopes that he might draw Eliza back to reason, Cairn said—that was why he had finally left the business two weeks before.

"It was a mad thing to do," Cairn said. "The firm is worth hundreds of thousands of pounds. She could have married a duke."

They resumed their interviews with the clerks. All of them agreed that it had been a strange period. Mr. Corcoran himself seemed to inspire a great deal of awe in them. He was evidently a short, thin man, but possessed of the iron will of a towering magnate, and two or three clerks mentioned how strange it had been to see him so out of countenance over his daughter.

None of them could even remember Pond mentioning the "perfects"—which seemed odd, in retrospect.

When they were finished with their interviews, Lenox, Mayne, and Graham checked in with the constables in the warehouse, who were conducting their own interviews for the sake of thoroughness, then made their way through the remarkable throng of people outside, some press, some civilian, all shouting questions at them.

"My heavens," said Mayne after he had struggled, red faced, into a police carriage.

Lenox, Exeter, and Graham just barely made it in after him. The four then went together to Pond's lodgings.

His salary had been ninety pounds a year, too little to do much beyond subsist and hope on in this great city. He was apparently a northerner—several of the clerks had commented on his Birmingham accent, "Brummie"—who had come here to seek his fortune.

The house of Mrs. Hutchinson was brick, with a small forecourt where a lone chicken made its residence. There was an advertisement for two rooms to let in the window. It would be three soon enough.

"So you had us wire all over creation when the answer was on Bankside, eh, Lenox," Exeter said as they climbed the stairs.

"At least he found the answer on Bankside," said Mayne shortly.

Mrs. Hutchinson herself, a scowling woman who could have stood on her toes without brushing a five-foot ceiling, let them in. "Good Lord, more of ye," she said.

"More of us?" said Mayne.

To their surprise, they found that Exeter's partner, Inspector Sinex, was already in the room. He nodded curtly at Mayne, ignored Exeter, and glowered at Lenox and Graham. "What are they doing here?"

There was a very tense moment and then Graham said, perfectly calmly, "What are you doing here?"

Sinex whirled on the valet. "That's none of your bloody business."

It did seem strange. He said he had gotten the address from Cairn, and, not wanting to wade into the mess from which the other four had come—the whole warehouse, the clerks' offices—he had come here to begin his part of the investigation.

He held up a thick stack of papers: the *Challenger*. "A popular paper," said Mayne, frowning.

Sinex shook his head grimly. "No. Look at the dates." All four of them leaned forward. "Ten copies each from the dates of the publication of the two letters. Trophies of his first publication."

It was growing darker now, and they called upon Mrs. Hutchinson to bring in candles. She grumbled, but Lenox handed her a few shillings, telling her to use them for her costs, and she cheered up and said she would go to the corner shop for more. Mayne added a few shillings of his own and requested a sandwich. By the time she had returned, Mrs. Hutchinson was much chattier ("I barely ever saw the boy after he moved here in May, out vast early, in vast late, these clerks, you know") and was warmly enough inclined toward them to offer them a pot of tea.

CHAPTER THIRTY-TWO

They remained for several hours, going carefully through the possessions of the dead man. By the end of half an hour, they were all more or less certain that he was their criminal, their self-described perfect criminal—though a more imperfect outcome to his endeavors could hardly be conceived.

It was a plain room, with a small bed, a teas-maid, an armoire, a desk, and a chair. There was one black suit in the closet, along with two white shirts and a rather shabby brown tweed suit next to them, perhaps his northern suit.

He had left behind nothing quite so definite as a journal. But when Lenox looked down at his list of items at the end of the evening, it seemed overwhelming proof of Pond's guilt.

The first thing they found were flowers pressed in a copy of the Bible, each of which matched one of those from the overwhelming profusion of flowers on the second body.

"Where did he get the money for those, I wonder?" Lenox asked out loud. "They must have been five pounds at least, those flowers. A week or two's wages."

"Perhaps a week's salary on flowers doesn't seem very much when you have a vision," said Graham.

Sinex was holding up a small stack of papers. "Look at this."

Lenox and Mayne came over: a series of doodles of a woman lying on her back, eyes closed, presumably dead, covered in flowers. "Well," said Lenox, sighing.

"One of the clerks mentioned that Pond was a good draftsman," Graham said.

"Yes—gifted."

Exeter looked at Lenox as if he were mad. "He was sick in the head."

"There have been gifted men who were sick in the head before, and there will be again," said Lenox, handing the drawings to Mayne. "It is one of the world's many flaws."

It was Graham who had the idea to bring out Pond's clothes to inspect them; when he pulled the brown tweed suit out, sand fell from its cuffs, and it smelled distinctly of the riverside, in a way that his black suit did not.

But the most unsettling discovery was Lenox's own: beneath the mattress, there was an envelope with two locks of dark, curly hair in it.

They were divided by sheets of paper. A third space was open.

Mayne crossed himself. "May the Lord preserve them," he said.

But who would the third woman have been? There was one tantalizing clue. On the reverse of one of the drawings was the name *Susan*, written twice.

There were other artifacts of life in the room. On the desk was a small row of books, mostly schoolboy novels. There were a few short but affectionate letters signed by Pond's mother; Lenox made a note of her address in Birmingham. There were Pond's pay stubs from Corcoran and Sons. In a small lockbox, which Sinex levered open with suspicious adroitness, were a few coins, a pound note, an old train ticket, and a small cameo portrait.

Lenox studied it in the candlelight. "Dark, curly hair," he said.

Finally, when it was too dark to see anything, Mayne sighed. "Well, we shall reconvene in the morning, gentlemen."

There was so much Lenox still wanted to know. But they had covered the room thoroughly, and the press had found its way here now.

The three men of the Yard were taking the evidence back to headquarters. "Is there any point stopping back at Bankside?" Lenox asked.

"Not that I can see. You have your badge, however—" Sinex snorted. "—so feel free to do as you please."

Mayne, Exeter, and Sinex ignored the journalists outside and pushed through. Lenox and Graham trailed them by ten feet or so, thanking Mrs. Hutchinson (who had been strongly encouraged to remain mum for her own safety, and looked properly cowed at the idea that she would be a target) and followed their example in ignoring the journalists.

Graham and Lenox escaped the press, then walked a block or two in silence. At last Lenox said, "There's no point in it, but I think I would like to go back to Bankside." An overwhelming day.

Graham nodded. "I feel similarly, sir."

They got into a hansom. Lenox spent the drive brooding, trying, trying, trying to put the pieces together, to figure out whom Jonathan Pond had killed, and why.

How could two women simply disappear?

Lenox wasn't convinced that his wires across Britain had been useless. Mightn't the bodies have come to London by train? His thoughts returned to that little cameo in the lockbox. And the name: Susan.

There was still an enormous crush of people outside Corcoran and Sons, just barely held at bay by a hastily strung rope and a row of constables. It was like a carnival. Lenox showed his identification and pushed through.

There were two clerks remaining in the large office with fifteen desks in it. Both looked up when Lenox and Graham came in.

"Still here?" Lenox said.

"The business doesn't stop for much," one of them said ruefully—Jones, Lenox remembered his name would be. "Large shipment tomorrow."

"Will it be a distraction if we look through Mr. Pond's desk?"

"Not at all, sir," said Jones. "Let us know if we can help."

"Thank you," said Lenox quietly. He felt sorry for them. They had known Pond. He stood there for a moment, hands in trousers, and at last said, "Tell me, can you believe it of him? Of Pond? That he was a murderer?"

The two clerks glanced at each other. But after a beat both nodded, reluctantly. "He wasn't a bad chap," said Jones. "Or never seemed a bad chap. But he had very grand ideas of himself. He was very down on most of us—cutting, you know. And then, I suppose the rest of us have . . . He never had a girl that he spoke of, or any interest but his literary goings-on."

"He kept to himself," added Carrington.

Lenox nodded. "Thank you."

For the first time, he began to believe that they had really caught a murderer. But he hadn't expected it to be like this! The terrible inconclusiveness of it—Pond's death—Cairn's pale face, and his thudding fall—the whole vivid, awful afternoon . . .

He went to Pond's desk and sat down heavily in the chair. "You take the left set of drawers, I'll take the right?" he said to Graham.

There was nothing much here, paper, an old inkwell, Corcoran and Sons stationery, an old newspaper (not the *Challenger* but the *Times*), another of Pond's pay stubs. But there was one thing that Lenox found that struck him—a short list of goods, seemingly all different varieties of fur from Canada, bound in on a steamer named *Fortitude*.

"Look at that, Graham," he said.

Graham studied it for a moment. "I cannot see anything remarkable, sir," he said.

"It's the handwriting."

Recognition dawned in the valet's eyes. "Of course," he said. "Identical, sir."

Lenox wasn't sure why it made his heart so heavy: yet here it was, a fact, that the handwriting on this list was identical to the handwriting of the first letter to the *Challenger*. Pond was their man.

Perhaps he would feel better when he could say who the victims were; perhaps in time he would care that they might have saved a life, one that Pond had planned to take sixteen days hence.

Was it cowardice or determination that made a man shoot himself rather than facing the consequences of his acts?

At last they bade goodbye to Jones and Carrington, still working by their low green-shaded lamps, and went home.

"I think that was the longest day of my life," Lenox said as he turned the key in the door.

Inside, it got slightly longer.

Mrs. Huggins, looking infinitely harassed, was trying with a desperate air to coax a great fleet of kittens, nine or ten of them, fifteen possibly, a hundred for all Lenox knew, back into a wicker basket.

She stood up, bright red, the first time she had been discomposed in their entire acquaintance. "They won't be any trouble, sir," she said.

Lenox burst into a laugh, and felt a huge release within. Life would go on; sooner or later. "It's quite all right, Mrs. Huggins—it's quite all right—here, I can catch the gray one. Graham, that orange one is just at your ankles, grab him up. . . ."

CHAPTER THIRTY-THREE

For the next three days, Lenox barely stirred out of his flat. He read the papers as soon as they arrived, and he and Graham caught up on several missed days of clipping; otherwise, the young detective spent most of his time sitting on the floor of his study, cross-legged, burning matches and dropping them into a glass.

He knew he ought to shake off this malaise, but found he couldn't.

More than once he thanked goodness for the two kittens they had kept out of the enormous litter Mrs. Huggins had rescued from whatever obscure alley in the East End. He didn't know where the rest were—he had drawn the line at two—though he had granted the housekeeper permission to keep them in the house until she had found them homes.

Lady Hamilton was taking one; it would be a kitchen cat, Mrs. Huggins reported with gravity and pride. Her harrowing fierceness had returned, and her attention to detail had been redoubled, as if to compensate for the humiliation of being caught using Lenox's flat as an ad hoc cat sanctuary, but fortunately her demands that *he* attend to detail had subsided, somewhat, in her distraction over the animals.

The cats they had kept were lovely little creatures, one black and white, the other an even sea-sky gray. The former was called Scout, the latter James.

Lenox had taken no part in the naming. "Cats didn't even have names where I grew up," he told Mrs. Huggins.

"They're more intelligent than dogs, sir."

"That is patently false."

She glanced at Graham, who wisely kept his silence. "The late Mr. Huggins said that the average cat was twice as smart as the average dog." She paused, then added, by way of concession, "But the smartest dogs are very smart, I will grant you."

"Mr. Huggins was fond of cats?" Lenox asked.

She almost smiled. "Passionately fond, sir. He grew up with them."

Lenox softened. "Well, name them whatever you like—only I shan't abide by the names, that's all. They'll be 'cat' to me, that's it."

"Just as you please, sir."

He immediately showed himself a liar—and in his three days sitting on his study floor spent most of his time calling out their names, enticing them with bits of string, watching them turn their stumbles into lithe rolls. They had alert little eyes, exploring paws. Their minds were so transparent at moments; such a secret at others. It was a pleasure to watch. A welcome distraction, too. They ate splendidly—Mrs. Huggins planned out their diets as carefully as if they were dignitaries visiting from an adversarial country.

In these three days, the evidence against Pond accumulated. It was Exeter who discovered in a second survey of the young clerk's flat a key that eventually proved to fit the trunk marked HMS GALLANT, G957.

After that, Lenox removed himself from the investigation of Pond. Instead, he sat in his study, striking matches, trying to piece together on his own the elements of a case that still felt unresolved to him, trying to join them together. But perhaps all cases felt this way, and he was only inexperienced. He could have used a mentor to tell him. That was the disadvantage of a profession one invented as one went along.

On the third day, he had a visitor. It was Edmund. There had been others (Hugh had been by twice, Lucia once; Elizabeth was in Paris, where her husband was on leave) but none so welcome.

He watched Lenox wave out a match, then said, "You're going to burn the whole building down."

"Ha, that's where you're wrong. They're those safety matches."

"Are they! Let me have a go."

For their entire lives, every soul in England had used lucifer matches, which struck with any friction—a great virtue and a great vice, since they could be carried loose and struck against a boot, a wall, anything really, in cold or in wet. That was convenient; until one caught fire in your jacket pocket, when it became very extremely inconvenient.

But now some ingenious person had invented the safety match, which came in a small box made of card and needed to be struck specifically against that box to be lit. The innovation had swept certain parts of society—the navy, which considered fire even more diabolical than France, outlawed lucifer matches immediately—and there was already a noticeable decline in the number of London house fires. And singed hair, more trivially, but not unpleasantly for people who had hair.

Soon Edmund (a devotee of the lucifer match, as befit his country preferences) was on the floor next to Lenox, legs stretched out in front of him and crossed, lighting matches himself.

"We'll have to send someone out for more," said Charles.

"I am willing to incur that risk," Edmund said, striking two at once and gazing at them with childlike joy.

"How were Mother and Father?"

Ed looked up. "Eh? Oh, fine. Actually, I stopped by to warn you. Father is coming to London this evening."

Lenox looked up from the match. "Is he? Why? Parliament?"

"No, he doesn't give a fig about Parliament. He's coming to see you."

"Why?"

Edmund shrugged. "That's all he told me."

Lenox pondered this in silence for some time. "What did you do, the two of you?"

"We rode every inch of the property together. I must say, it's very large."

"You were always clever."

Edmund grinned. "Shut up. Anyhow, I learned a great deal. I was taking notes the entire time—not that he told me to, but I couldn't keep up otherwise, and wouldn't you know it, at just the right moment, he happened to have a notebook and a piece of charcoal in his bag. A plum coincidence."

Lenox smiled. That was their father all over. "So what did you learn?"

"The name of every tree, every rock. He told me the stories of each tenant, going back to his boyhood. He took me right up to the line where Robinson's property begins and showed me the stone wall there—and told me about our great-great-great-grandfather building it himself, with the help of hired laborers. 1688, he said, and showed me a little scratching by some fellow called Jacob, who just decided to leave his name and the year there. That was a queer feeling, I can tell you. You could imagine his hand doing it. Probably nobody has spoken his name in a hundred and fifty years."

Lenox realized in that moment that his older brother was very young. He had never really thought of him like that before; or had, but not really, not truly. "You'll do a very, very good job, Ed," he said.

"I'll try anyhow."

"You will."

In a low voice, Edmund said, "He didn't mention—well, it, you know. Not at all. Except once. He said that we had to take care of Mother. And I said of course we would. And he said, no, I didn't understand—we had to take care of her. I didn't quite understand."

Charles hesitated, and then nodded. "There's time."

Edmund nodded, too. "Yes. Molly and I talked about it." He sighed. "Anyway, tell me about this case, would you? Even out in the country, there's nothing else anyone will talk of. And they all know you're involved, somehow."

They sat for a while. Edmund moved on from playing with the matches to playing with the kittens (a fair little encapsulation in twenty minutes of Lenox's previous three days) and they talked about the strange case. Charles described watching Pond die, and found that relating the story took away a little bit of its power over his imagination; he had been gazing into those eyes more often than he liked.

"My goodness," said Edmund.

"Worse things happen at sea."

"Not all *that* much worse," said Edmund.

"Yes, you have a point. I always wondered what they meant by that."

"People getting flogged and drowning and eaten by sharks, probably."

"That does sound worse," Lenox said. "Being eaten by a shark sounds just about as unlucky a go as you can have."

"I should add the shark people to my prayers at night."

"Who'll they replace?"

Edmund frowned. Both brothers had a strict one-in-one-out policy on their evening prayers, dating to the age of nine and six, when they had wanted to get through them as quickly as possible—it wasn't very Christian, their mother said, but Edmund and Charles had maintained over the years that it kept each conscious of the people for whom he was grateful or of whom he was particularly solicitous.

"Terrance acted as if I were an intruder all weekend. I think he really thought I might steal the silver. Two months' probation from my prayers wouldn't hurt him."

After Edmund had gone, Charles spent the rest of the afternoon dreading his father's arrival. He was sure it would be—what, some kind of plea? To find a more serious career. To keep his name out of the papers.

He thought with a kind of sickness in his stomach about their cousin Lord Billingsley's words at Lady Hamilton's ball.

To distract himself, he spent his time organizing his notes from the Pond case, including the clippings he had made from it. The petechiae still bothered him; the shoes; he wanted to know more, more. Something was still bothering him.

At six o'clock the bell rang. Graham answered, and ushered his father in. Lenox had dressed himself—his father, as always in London, was the last word in correct attire. He had often said to his sons that while in London, he was also every single person in Market-house, the ones he represented in Parliament; that was his duty. He dressed quite to his era, the perfectly tied cravat, the silk hat, the cane.

"Hullo, Father," said Lenox.

"There you are, Charles. Listen, are you free?"

"Free? For the evening?"

"For five days."

"For five days."

Edward Lenox took a folded sheet of paper from his inner breast pocket. "I'll tell you a secret. In my heart of hearts, I've always wanted to see Russia."

He smiled, and Charles felt about nine again, the immense, oceanic contentment one found in one's father's smile, one's father's love.

"Russia!" said Charles, his voice high pitched even to his own ears. "You mean, to travel there?"

"Only if you can spare the time."

"Spare the—I can of course spare the time, of course, Father."

"Good. I've booked us to leave by the ten o'clock train from Waterloo this evening. You'll be back by Saturday next, as if you'd never been gone." He looked down at his feet. "No doubt someone will be able to watch these cats."

CHAPTER THIRTY-FOUR

The express train to England's northeastern coast took four hours. Lenox's father had booked them sleepers across a slender red-carpeted aisle from each other, and he cheerfully and immediately turned in with an old copy of Gibbon, whose work he reread more or less continually. The fourth of his set's nine volumes, for their particular trip.

Charles, in his own small chamber, sat up at the little chair and table, legs and arms crossed. He watched the landscape pass. He was conscious of wanting to remember this very clearly. Villages whose names he would never know or speak, and a broad black sky, sparkling with stars.

At the start of the voyage, the steward gave him a very good supper—a cutlet of steak, mashed potatoes, crushed peas, a half bottle of hock, and then coffee, followed by a pipe. He read about Russia as he ate. (Graham had somehow packed all his books about the country, all his maps, into the neat little suitcase he had made up for Lenox a few hours before. The trip he had been planning was to have lasted roughly fifteen months. But five days would do.)

The hours passed. Finally, in the very last moments of the train journey, he took out a pen. He had been contemplating the letter the whole way, but nevertheless as he began to compose it, his heart raced, his hand trembled.

> *Dear Elizabeth,*
>
> *I love you. I know that nothing can come of this fact—of course. I would do anything before suggesting you leave England. I understand my position. But I don't want to die without telling you, and they say any of us can die at any moment, though it scarcely seems possible, does it.*
>
> *I won't mention it again. You have my word upon that. I had to do so once, however. Anyhow, please believe my sincerity when I say that you receive this letter with the very dear and constant love of,*
>
> *Charles Lenox*

Before he could second-guess himself, he jammed it into an envelope; handed it to the steward with a penny and a sixpence tip, asking him to post it as soon as he could; and before he knew what had happened, they were off the train, in a carriage, and on a boat.

And so Elizabeth would know.

The boat took them to Stockholm first. As dawn broke, Charles and his father shared a strong flask of tea—Lenox House tea, of course, packed specially for them by Crump—and watched penguins frolic among the rocks. Or were they great auks? After a flying stop at Stockholm to drop off cargo, not more than an hour, the ship proceeded on to Tallinn.

It was lovely to feel the air on deck, even as it grew more chill with each nautical mile they traveled. They were wayfaring in great comfort (a Member of Parliament and his son, after all), and Sir Edward spent much of the late morning in a small swinging chair that had been arranged near the bow of the boat for him, sometimes reading, more often watching the water furl behind the boat, large birds darting down to fetch a meal out of its wake, in such deep thought—or perhaps in such pure absence of his thought—that Charles was content merely to observe him from his own chair, a little ways off.

They had two Finnish porters who brought them a lunch of soft-boiled eggs, black bread with salted butter, tiny buttered potatoes, and salted fish. Lenox's father had brought a bottle of champagne, which they divided. During their luncheon, eaten upon an overturned crate, the father peppered his son with questions about Russia. Charles was hesitant at first, but eventually, after some coaxing, he began to describe in exuberant detail their destination, its immensely different culture, its people, the landmarks of St. Petersburg.

"My goodness," his father said, smiling, "you know a great deal. But you were always a very complete child."

"Complete?" said Charles.

The porters took away the leftover food, openly eating it themselves as they went, and then brought them a hard kind of biscuit for dessert. It wasn't bad if you dipped it in the wine.

Edward Lenox lit his pipe and leaned back against the dull blue metal siding of the ship. "I remember that before you had your first horse, you learned the name of every horse that had ever won our little race in Markethouse, back to, oh, 1770 at least. Your own horse was the descendant of several of them, it turned out."

Lenox smiled. "Yes, that's right. So was Edmund's."

"Yes. Before your time there was a farmer, Julian, who bred the fastest horses in our part of the country. That was when I was a child. He was quite mad for horses—let his farm go to seed in his passion for them. Anyhow, I think several of them must have been his. Died childless, though, and they sold off his horses, whatever nieces and nephews he must have had. Robinson bought the land."

This reminded Lenox of Edmund's tour of the grounds of Lenox House over the last week, and he said, "Our neighbor."

"Eh? Oh! Yes. A good neighbor, too, he's been over the years, Robinson. I hope I've been the same to him."

It was twenty-six hours after their departure—nearly to the

minute—that their swift little mailboat pulled in to the docks of St. Petersburg.

It felt as if it had been faster still. Lenox's father, who had been changing below deck into a suit and a fur-lined overcoat, came on deck, took in the sight of the city, and whistled.

"Gracious me," he said. His pipe was in his hand. Before them was an absolutely enormous dull-golden dome, which seemed even larger because of the busy stone bridge that passed underneath their view of it, peopled with miniature figures. "Keep your wits about you."

The ship's captain, a Finn with excellent English and Russian, personally arranged for them to hire a private carriage that would take them to the British consulate. There they were greeted very warmly, and offered small dishes of caviar and salted nuts, along with wine, by a minor diplomat, Aspern. He asked if they weren't very tired.

Charles looked at his father, who said that on the contrary, they would like nothing more than a little bit of the city—and some advice on where to stay. Well, then; they must go to the ballet. They could have the ambassador's box. He was out of town, fishing. As for where to stay, that was the least conceivable trouble. He would arrange it all himself.

"It's very kind of you," said Charles's father.

"Not in the slightest, sir. We are honored to have a Member of Parliament in the consulate."

They were off.

The next three days passed in a lovely flash, like one of those vivid countryside strokes of lightning that stays illuminated an unnaturally long while, more than a second, a second and a half, which feels an eternity even though it's still gone before you've begun to see it.

The hours were very full. They were met at the palace by Nicholas I, who had the most outlandish mustache Lenox had ever personally seen. (Its ends began at his lip and curled roughly up to eye level.) He was severe but gracious in his greeting. There was a spectacular ball, of the kind that Lenox had never imagined, much less seen. The least jewel there would have been the talk of Lady Hamilton's. They had a sense of magnificence, certainly, the Russians. It was borne on the backs of uncountable serfs, and in England you could find many people who would tell you that one day that bill would come due. Nevertheless, like the pyramids or an egret in flight, it was something to behold—something one would never forget.

But Lenox valued these moments less than the wanderings he made with his father through the city. In many respects—being the capital—it was like London. There were clerks and officials everywhere one looked. The guide the consulate had provided them, a very eager young Russian, took them through gardens full of enormous quilts of spring flowers; pointed out old women bundled under their wares, exotic creatures in the new, modern Russia; guided them through unmarked doors where they found small restaurants serving wonderfully fragrant stews.

Lenox's father had his usual durability, and he was in a superlative mood. Never would you have guessed he was living under a death sentence. Everything delighted him. The little Russian coins, their guide's interminable lectures, the ball. He didn't drink any vodka, and did decry the lack of beer. On the other hand, there was nowhere like Russia for champagne—the aristocracy spoke to each other exclusively in French, and thought nothing of putting away a dozen bottles of Jacquesson in a single sitting.

On their last evening, they were wandering through the Winter Palace. "I've never seen anything like it, I admit," Edward Lenox said.

Charles nodded. It faced the river, this building, constructed by Catherine the Great. Its beautiful, symmetrical frontage was a wintergreen color he had never seen in England—and ever so long, endless. "Do you think it's three times as long as Parliament, I wonder," he said.

"Yes, and a third as democratic," said Lenox's father stoutly. Then he smiled at his patriotism. "I never imagined I would see it in person. I must thank you for that, Charles. The etchings don't do it justice, do they?"

"No," said Lenox.

They decided to have supper in their suite of rooms at their hotel; their ship left at midnight. It was a merry meal. Charles didn't mention his father's health, but he did allow himself to ask a few questions about his boyhood, his father's own parents, and he found that Sir Edward, so often taciturn, was in an expansive mood. The wine, perhaps—it was a rich yellowish Hungarian wine—inclined him to reminisce.

There was a great deal awaiting Lenox in London: Elizabeth, who had never been gone from his mind; and Graham, whom Lenox had asked to take an initial look into Rupert Clarkson's little problem, their actual paying client.

But he found himself wishing this trip would last forever.

It didn't, of course. Soon enough they were in Tallinn; soon enough they were in Stockholm; soon enough they were approaching the English shore; soon enough Lenox would be not twenty-three, but seventy-three, and his father would have been gone for fifty years— and as he watched the older man in his little swing chair, reading Gibbon and smoking his pipe with great absorption, he felt overwhelmed with tenderness and sorrow, with loss, a desire to hold each moment.

As they were boarding the train, his father said, "Well, I wouldn't trade that."

"Nor would I."

It was a sleeper again—late in the English evening—and for the first time, Edward Lenox looked tired, old. It was only natural, probably. After summoning up something from inside, he said, "You were right about traveling, weren't you! Let no man say that I am immune to changing my mind, even at my old age. But—"

Charles looked at him curiously. "Yes?"

"I hope you will entertain the idea of other careers."

"Ah, that. I suppose I will."

"You're only twenty-three," his father said. He sighed. Lenox felt his heart sink horribly. "All right—I'd better sleep, I think. I'll see you at Waterloo."

They both slept heavily, waking up to a hurried cup of coffee and biscuit as they pulled in to the station. They parted there with an amicable handshake, Sir Edward changing trains to return to Sussex, Charles promising to come down to the country within the next week. It seemed too abrupt, too informal. He was tired and irritated in the hansom ride back to his flat. Already the trip was like a dream—with the peculiar estranged beauty of a dream, to be sure, but also with the pastness of a dream, the vanishedness of it.

Except that then, as he climbed the stairs, he found a little folded piece of paper in the pocket of his jacket.

Inside it there was a pound note, which was what his father had always given him when he left for school. He must have written it while his son was asleep, and placed it in his pocket as they were parting.

Charles,

What I would have said, had I not been quite so tired and so pompous, is that there is no conceivable life you could lead of which I wouldn't be proud—because you are yourself—and also, that you should be sure to swallow a little bismuth—very heavy food in Russia, very heavy—but then again, how glad I am we went. Until I see you next, know me to be both in this life, and in whatever life comes next,

Your loving father,
EL.

CHAPTER THIRTY-FIVE

The city to which Lenox returned after five days' absence was somehow more, not less, obsessed with Jonathan Pond. That surprised him.

The fashionable thing now was to say that he had been as good as his word: he had committed the perfect crime. This viewpoint rather breezed over his suicide, but was otherwise compelling.

"Randomness. That's the key to it. Kill someone completely random, and they'll spend perpetuity attempting to figure out what you did and why you did it. Rather brilliant, really."

That was Lord Markham speaking—the young, porcine toff who'd cut Lenox dead only three weeks before—at a very sparkly cocktail party in his broad-beamed house in Half Moon Street. Lenox's position had changed during his absence. It was known that he had been in on the kill, as it were—there at Pond's last breath. There was a certain prestige to this. You couldn't call him a *detective* quite, people were saying now. He was more of an adventurer. He didn't mind a bit of violence if it came his way. Indeed, wasn't it rather glamorous, what he did? So the word went around London.

Markham had written him personally twice, virtually begging him to come to this party. Now he gave his opinion on Pond. "Eh, Lenox?" he said.

They had all looked down on Markham at school for exactly this quality, being a know-it-all and a bore, but Charles, his mind only half there, said, "Oh, yes, I'm sure that's probably about right."

Markham nodded with deep self-satisfaction. "They'll be chasing their tails down at the Yard for a while, I guess."

Lenox had come because he'd been hoping that Elizabeth would be here. Most people were—most people in his London, his small London.

But not she. He knew she was in town. Lenox had called upon her twice (in the morning, at the appropriate hour), and she had been out on her own calls. Or perhaps—his fear—in, but "out." Either way he was miserable. Whenever he thought of the letter, he wanted to melt into a puddle of shame.

The only person in whom he confided this misery was his friend Hugh, whose forlornness in love was so constant that it amounted to a variety of good cheer in circumstances such as these.

"She's a brick," was Hugh's analysis. "She'll let it go. Or maybe she loves you, you know."

"No."

"You can never say. I've seen more lost causes pulled back from the brink than you would believe."

Lenox, heartsick, half-leapt at this idea. The trouble was that he didn't know what would be worse, though, reciprocation or rejection. He could never compromise her. He would rather eat crushed glass than say the word "divorce" to her face.

But in the last three or five weeks he had somehow begun to think of her so constantly, so deeply, other women had come to him to seem such diffident and insubstantial creatures, that the idea that she might love him was impossible to keep himself away from, though he would have thought better of himself if he could.

Two mornings after his return from St. Petersburg, he and Graham were sitting at the breakfast table. Graham had been very assiduous in his researches into their case—the Clarkson case—and come up with nothing, very exactly nothing. As he said, however, with a certain angry glimmer in his eye, he was still gathering information.

They sat in the quiet late spring light and clipped articles. More than half were about Pond. The media had tracked down his mother, who seemed slightly addled, and would admit only that she would miss the half pound he sent back to her each month, though she had wept copiously in front of the correspondent from the *Telegraph*. They'd found a few old friends to testify that he was a decent chap— but not very many, and certainly the image of him that emerged from his village was of a silent, rather reticent, queer person, studious and guarded.

One paper had discovered a young woman who had rejected his proposal, before he'd come to London; she had dark, wavy hair, and many saw this as a galvanizing incident to the young madman. Her name was Ella Beth Williams, however; not Susan. Otherwise, there were a huge number of articles with headlines like POND'S BLOOD-SOAKED JOURNALS, made up wholly, or, in more reputable papers, MURDERER'S MOTIVE REMAINS MURKY.

"That one's true enough," Lenox said with a sigh as he cut it out.

He turned it to Graham, who had looked up. "Ah. Yes, sir."

Lenox sat back, tossing his scissors onto the table with a clatter. "I have tried to stop thinking about it, to turn my mind slowly to what the identity of the two women may be, but I—"

He went into a long silence, staring at the branches as they dipped and rose in the breeze.

At very great length, Graham said, "Sir?"

Lenox started. "What's that?"

"You said you've tried, sir, to stop thinking about something?"

"Oh." Lenox shook the cobwebs out of his head and sat up. "I only meant that I've tried to let it all go. But there are—there are details that have been bothering me. Beyond the most obvious one, of wondering who the two women are."

"You think Pond guilty, though, sir?"

"Oh, certainly, that has been proved. It's only that I am trying to understand the exact dimensions of his guilt. For a wild moment, I even entertained the idea of an accomplice."

"What are the details that are bothering you, sir, if it is not impertinent to ask?"

Lenox smiled a melancholy smile. "You can ask me anything, Graham," he said.

There were three things that had bothered him through his trip to St. Petersburg, faint echoes in his mind at first, but more insistent as time passed, more and more insistent. He told them to Graham now.

The first was the nature of the second victim's death—Ophelia, as the press had named her. She had died of poisoning, he was nearly certain from consulting Courtenay, but there had been an attempt to make it look like strangulation.

"And the other two points?"

The second was Pond's spectacles. They seemed wrong to Lenox, somehow—that they had been crushed directly beneath the door that he must have carried down to the waterside. They had been on a chain, for one thing. Perhaps they had been in his pocket just at that moment, but even then he wondered how they would have ended up underneath the door.

"I have thought, myself, sir," said Graham, "that perhaps Pond intended to push the door into the water, and see how far it might float—like the trunk."

Lenox pursed his lips. "I've thought about that, too. It was such a staged, odd scene, that part of me thinks he wouldn't have wanted it overturned—the door, the body—but part of me wonders whether he wasn't interrupted, just as you suggest."

"What is the third detail, sir?"

"I am almost embarrassed to admit it, but—well—I have the strangest feeling that there is some face I saw twice."

Graham frowned. "A familiar face. Can you recall where, sir?"

"No."

"Perhaps at the warehouse? One of the clerks?"

Lenox paused, and then shook his head slightly. "I don't think so. No."

"Interesting, sir."

It was no more than a feeling along the back of his neck, a sense of recognition—misplaced recognition, like being sure he'd seen someone in a crowd that he recognized, only to tap their shoulder and find that he had been mistaken.

Graham watched him respectfully, despite the vagueness of this last point. Lenox sighed. It was very thin porridge, he knew, his three questions.

He shoved the papers to the side. One of the cats was down at his feet, and he gave it a distracted stroke. "Listen," he said. "Tell me everything there is to know about Clarkson. Pond is gone, but we still have our twenty pounds to earn. We might as well earn them."

CHAPTER THIRTY-SIX

Everything there was to know about Rupert Clarkson was not very much.

The only time Lenox had seen the elderly engineer, he had asked him to write, on a pad, his addresses in Dulwich and London, the names of all his household staff and his most frequent companions, along with any other information that might be of value.

Graham had looked into all of this thoroughly. The list of household staff consisted of a valet, two maids, a cook, and a boy, who was the valet's first cousin once removed. Except for the boy, none of them had been in Clarkson's service fewer than six years, and the boy, who was twelve, and whose annual salary was fifty pounds plus board, was hardly likely to have benefacted thirty pounds anonymously upon his employer, even had he not been working under the exacting supervision of his relative.

Lenox recalled that Clarkson had also mentioned a charwoman. "Did you find her?" he asked Graham.

"There was one in each location, sir," Graham answered, consulting a notepad, "but Mr. Clarkson rotated them out in the midst of this ongoing trouble, and had all his locks changed. It altered nothing.

The two new charwomen were hired out of the clear blue sky, after three envelopes had already been left, so they are beyond suspicion, of course, and the first therefore seem to be as well."

"I see," Lenox murmured, thinking. "Hard on them to lose their jobs. You have been to Dulwich?"

"Yes, sir."

"The servants' stories match Mr. Clarkson's?"

"They do, sir."

"I see." Lenox tapped his fingers on the breakfast table, and took a sip of tea. "Have there been any more envelopes?"

"None. Mr. Clarkson has remained in London, sir, with his whole staff. The new charwoman in Dulwich, a Miss Maria Horsepool, has wired Mr. Clarkson daily to inform him that nothing new has happened there."

"And what about his companions, his friends?"

"I've looked into them thoroughly, sir."

There were three men with whom Clarkson was fond of fishing, and perhaps a dozen with whom he dined in London. (Fishing and food: his dual passions, in semiretirement.) Graham had spoken to the three fishermen, and to a man they had been baffled. They were deeply fond of Clarkson, one of them going so far as to say how much he wished his friend might marry again, another that he looked upon him as a brother, if a slightly irascible one.

As for Clarkson's dining companions, they were a more varied lot, but Graham had looked closely and found nothing untoward. Many of them chaffed Clarkson for his lack of taste (he had an almost illogically stubborn aversion to wines of the Rhône valley) or his stinginess (he counted a supper bill closely), but all were affectionate. Nor were they in any way dramatic or interesting people, not a single one of them, no gamblers in their number, no adventurers. The steady burgher class, rather—the one quickly becoming the face of Victoria's England.

Lenox sat back, thinking. "What to do, then," he said at last.

"I am curious as to your thoughts on that subject, sir, as you can imagine," said Graham.

Lenox stood up and started to pace. "Four things are clear."

"Are they!"

Lenox laughed. "Anyway—seemingly clear. First, it is someone with access to the house, access that was not interrupted even by a change of locks. Second, it is someone who wishes to send Mr. Clarkson a message. Third, it is someone with a comfortable amount of money. Fourth, it is someone intimately acquainted with Mr. Clarkson's daily movements."

Graham nodded. "My thoughts, sir. And yet those with an intimate knowledge of his plans are his staff, and they are not rich. Nor can I imagine them wishing to send him a message."

"What was your impression of the servants?"

"They are a very dull, faithful lot, about averagely compensated, none in the least bitter or . . . intriguing, sir, I would have said."

Lenox frowned. "Interesting."

"Vexing, sir."

Lenox was still standing. He tapped his pipe against the table thoughtfully. Finally, he said, "I have a suspicion, Graham."

"Do you, sir?"

"What is your own guess?" The valet looked as if he were going to answer, but hesitated. "You can speak as freely as you like. Any idea at all."

Graham looked pained but said, "I have wondered whether perhaps he might have made it all up, sir."

Lenox nodded. "A lonely old man, not happy in retirement, intriguing against himself." He pondered this for a moment. "But he seemed too genuinely anxious, I think, for that to be our best guess."

"What is your suspicion, then, sir?" he said.

"Well—as to that." Lenox tapped his pipe one last decisive time. "The thing to do would be to set up a trap. But I think we can save ourselves the trouble of that. I'm going to Dulwich."

"Dulwich, sir."

"Please come if you like. The likelihood that his fishing companions are there is high, correct?"

"Overwhelmingly high, sir."

Lenox nodded. "Good enough."

"What do you propose to ask them, sir? It is a daily habit."

"We shall see. You may recall that when we first met Mr. Clarkson, I said there were two possible explanations I could imagine, one benign, one sinister. It is time to find out which it is. I have a suspicion, as I say."

They took an early afternoon train. There was a new kind of building going up all along this northbound rail line; made of dark red brick, turreted and dormered so that they looked like castles, in their odd way, but situated upon plots of land smaller than the average castle's stable.

"What do you think they call those?" Lenox asked Graham curiously.

"Houses, sir."

The young aristocrat rolled his eyes.

It was true that they were something new—they lay between the closeness of the city and the emptiness of the country, but they couldn't be said to belong to villages. Villages had always been there; that was what a village meant, at least to Lenox, who came of a village, in his own way.

As they neared Dulwich, the rural pastures of Lenox's father's childhood slowly took over the landscape, however, unmowed, dotted with modest yellow dandelions, edged with woodland. They passed a pond with children splashing in it. Lenox smiled, thinking of himself and Edmund and their friends at that age.

It was a short walk from the train station in Dulwich to the gentle incline by the town's river where Clarkson fished. Graham led the way. "They call it Lord's," he told Lenox. "A joke referring to the cricket ground."

It was certainly peaceful. Trees spread their quiet branches over the lazy stream, which was spotted with pools of gold light.

Two men were sitting in slatted wooden chairs there. "It's Mr. Graham," one said when they were near.

"Hello, gentlemen," Graham said. "This is the employer I mentioned to you—Mr. Charles Lenox."

The two men were both of Clarkson's age. Neither stood. "How are you?" Lenox asked.

"Passable," one answered.

He was a leathery old chap, short. Ex-military, Lenox would have bet. The other was a bit softer in the middle. Both were carelessly expert in the way they cast their flies. "Did you need something else, Mr. Graham?" the second fellow asked curiously.

Lenox patted the thin leather case over his shoulder. "Actually, I proposed the trip. I thought I should hear it all from you, though it seems as if there's not much to hear. To be honest, fishing didn't sound a bad way to pass the afternoon."

"You'll have to settle for the grass," said the first fellow. "I'm Joshua King. My friend here—Rupert's friend, too—is Jack Stuart. Cast away!"

Lenox did. Graham (as they had agreed) went into town to order lunch from the public house there, leaving them with two bottles of a very fair Sauternes that had been packed in London, chilled and delicious. The conversation drifted by like the river, slow and pleasant; Stuart proved easily the best fisherman of the three.

"This is England," said Lenox, sighing happily.

"It's not Brazil," said King.

Two hours passed, when finally Lenox, who was thoroughly enjoying himself, at last set down his rod. He stood, stretched his arms high—his shirtsleeves were up, his jacket long abandoned, the remnants of a meal of cold chicken and brown bread nearby—and said, "Well, gentlemen, I wish you would tell me something, if you please."

"What's that?" said Stuart.

"Why are you leaving these five-pound notes for Mr. Clarkson? The sport has gotten out of hand."

King—the military man—remained impassive, eyes on the river, but Stuart started, and turned to Lenox, wide eyed, lulled, through the drowsy afternoon, into thinking he was no figure of suspicion.

In that moment, Lenox had them—and it was an exhilarating little victory, exactly what he had imagined being a detective might be like.

An hour later, when he and Graham boarded the train to return to Waterloo, they had their answer, or at least enough of it to be going on with. They discussed Clarkson's case on the return trip, teasing out the details.

Lenox's intention was to go straight to see his client, but at home, where the cats greeted him, there was a note that immediately commanded his whole attention.

Charles,
   Come to the Marchmains', would you? I shall be there
between six and nine o'clock—they will give you supper, I'm
sure, if you've not eaten and have no plans.

                                                            Elizabeth

CHAPTER THIRTY-SEVEN

Lenox put on his favorite suit, a light gray twill which was appropriate enough on a late May evening. He felt pure terror, standing in the mirror and tying his tie. It wouldn't do to get there at six o'clock; it also would be impossible to get there later than 6:05.

At 6:04 he stood on the steps of a wide terraced house, bright with lamplight inside, which made the evening, pink and still not close to dark, feel unnaturally still, almost lonely.

He knocked on the door and was brought in. The Duchess of Marchmain greeted him. "Charles! How welcome you are. Elizabeth said she had mentioned that you ought to come—having been all over Russia, and catching murderers, and generally becoming infamous."

He smiled. "You're sure I'm not troubling you?"

"Quite the reverse. There's a mountain of cabbage salad that only you can make a dent in."

"I say, what an enticement."

She laughed and led him inside. She was a woman of thirty-three, cheeks highly colored, pretty and very cheerful and affectionate, friend to several of Lenox's closest friends, though they had never been more than acquaintances.

It was a newer dukedom—but a dukedom nonetheless, and the front hall was very grand, with a Van Dyck portrait of Charles II over a table dominated by a huge bowl of brilliant purple and white flowers.

Just as Lenox was about to ask the duchess how she had been, there was the clatter of a door, and a little boy came sprinting across the black-and-white checkerboard tiles, running hell-for-leather. He wore a suit jacket, a tie, short pants, and brown shoes with white socks. He had very knobbly knees, much bruised and cut.

With a swift, effortlessly athletic motion—she was a mother to four—the duchess caught him in a strong arm.

Suddenly a harassed-looking governess emerged from the same door, breathing heavily. "I'm very sorry, Your Grace."

The duchess was scowling at her son. "John Dallington, what were you doing? Can't you see we have guests? Say hello to Mr. Lenox."

The little boy, bright faced, probably about four, looked at Lenox directly and said, "No, thank you."

"John," said his mother threateningly, and the little boy, sensing he had gone too far, said a sullen hello to Lenox.

"Pleasure to make your acquaintance," Lenox said, smiling.

"What was he running for, Susan?"

"He stole a tin of biscuits, Your Grace."

It took only a quick search to find and confiscate this contraband, and within less than a minute, the prisoner was being led upstairs toward bed, badly out of countenance.

"Never have children," the duchess told Charles as she took him into her sitting room, where she entertained most evenings.

"I see no immediate prospect of it."

She smiled. "Oh, you'll be caught soon enough."

Lenox followed her into the room, expecting a small gathering. To his surprise, only Elizabeth was there, sitting upon a pink sofa, a book in her hand. She looked up and laid the book down in her lap.

"Oh, hello, Lenox! I had hoped you would come by. We are desperate to hear about this murder."

"Wait," said the duchess. "Don't start. I'm going to run into the kitchen and tell them to bring in more food—and I want to say goodnight to poor Lord John. He had been hatching plans to steal those biscuits for days."

"You're a soft touch," Lenox said.

"I am, it's true. The duke should be home any moment, too—at any rate, wait five minutes, and then you will sing for your—well, for your cabbage salad, because really it is priced to go—absolutely mad amount to have made—"

And the duchess left them alone, Elizabeth laughing.

When Lenox turned back to her, however, her face had changed entirely.

She was sitting straight upright, and staring at him intensely. They were alone.

He felt his heart begin to go faster. "Elizabeth—"

"Listen to me," she said in a quick voice, "for we may only have a moment. By every law of marriage to which I swore, I ought to send your letter directly to James. That is the truth."

"But—"

"I don't plan to do so. He would tell me never to see you again, and he would be quite right. But I care for you as a friend, Charles."

This was all said so quickly that Lenox barely had time to absorb it. "I—"

"We shall of course not be alone together again. Not now. I am happy to meet you, whether it be at dinner, or a ball. But we cannot be alone together anymore. We cannot even be in a group as small as three or four."

In his worst imaginings, it had not been quite this bad. "Very well," he said.

"I love my husband," she said.

"I know—I knew that when I wrote."

She looked at him searchingly, and then, with an air of release, leaned back into the soft cushions of the sofa. "I cannot begin to imagine what you were thinking."

"No," he said. "I apologize."

"I have imagined something of your feelings, but our friendship—I cannot conceive what your motivation was, except to hurt me."

"Never that," he said miserably.

"Then what?"

Now he leaned forward on the sofa. "I think you are being very hard, Elizabeth," he said quietly. "I am—I am beyond sorry, if there were a word stronger than the word 'sorry,' I would speak it, you know I would. But I think you are being very hard."

"Hard!"

"Well—yes," he said.

She sat up again, too, and looked at him, eye to eye. "Hard, you say! Think for a moment in your simple life what it means to be a woman, Charles."

"I know that, it's only—"

"No—stop, and please, think of it for a moment. Use your brain. You would have to *murder* a man to suffer the same damage to your reputation that would occur to mine if I were to kiss one."

He paused. "I know that."

Her voice had fallen to a low hiss. "A single whisper of a romance between us, and my name would be gone forever. It is also all I have. Nothing is my own. When I married, every penny that was ever mine passed to James. And I made that bargain willingly! I love him. But do not speak to me of hardness—please, don't, when my life will be so irredeemably worse without your friendship, and when I am bound for the great empty countryside in five months, and when—when—"

He saw that she was near crying, and with his whole being he wanted to reach out and take her hand. Instead he leaned even farther forward and said, in an insistent voice, "You are right, and I am wrong. That is all there is to it. I have been hideously thoughtless. I hope you will forgive me."

"I forgive you, you fool," she said.

In that moment, he could almost have sworn that she loved him.

She stood up and went to the sideboard, where for fifteen or twenty seconds she busied herself with something. Then she turned back. Her face was a mask. "Lucia Chatham has been talking about you virtually without stopping, you know."

"Has she?"

"She's very beautiful."

"Indeed she is," Lenox said. He had never been unhappier. "Indeed she is."

CHAPTER THIRTY-EIGHT

Three days passed. The only joy Lenox had in this time came from rowing down the river, the exercise emptying his mind.

On the third morning, unable to help himself, he rowed all the way down to Walnut Island. It was just barely light by the time he got there—he had taken to setting out earlier and earlier in the day, well before dawn, since his sleep was restless—and after pulling the scull to, he watched the sun rise slowly over London's eastern edge. He had brought a sandwich wrapped in a cloth napkin and a bottle of water, and he gulped down both.

When he was finished, he turned the scull and pulled more evenly, though still with effort, the roughly half hour it took to get to Bankside.

Here it was already busy, large men hauling cargo in and out of the various anonymous warehouses, including that of Corcoran and Sons, where evidently business carried on.

Lenox wondered if its title partner had returned from Scotland upon hearing of Jonathan Pond's death. He must have. Daughters married badly every day.

When he had been standing there for fifteen or twenty minutes, perhaps even longer, a fat little boy passed. There had been maybe fifteen or twenty similar boys, but he was the first who was juggling four eggs as he walked, easy as you please. Lenox smiled.

"I say, are those hard-boiled?" he asked.

The boy turned. He was perhaps thirteen, with an angelic mischievous round face. "Not yet. Why?"

"They'll break if you drop them."

"Don't mean to drop them."

Lenox laughed, and the boy started to juggle again, standing there, showing off a bit. He had a battered rucksack made from coarse cloth. In large faded black letters, it said HMS MATILDA and in smaller faded black ones, underneath it, MCEWAN.

"I'll give you a shilling if you can do a fifth," Lenox said.

"Haven't got the egg," the boy replied, eyes on the four that were flying in the air. "Could I have the shilling for this?"

"Can you do it on one foot?" In response, the boy, who was almost uncannily graceful given his bulk, first stood and then began to hop on one foot. Finally Lenox laughed, passed him the coin, and said, "Here you are, then. What do you do on the *Matilda?*"

"Rope maker's mate." The boy looked at him suspiciously, flipping the shilling across his knuckles to check it was real. "Why?"

"Just curious. You'll be shipping off soon, I expect." Lenox gestured at the bag. "The *Matilda.*"

"Us? No, we just arrived in London last night, thank the cross. She'll be going up into dry dock for six weeks. We've been away eighteen months. Plenty of ropes to remake, but it'll be nice to have a bit o' London. My mother and father's here. Going to see them now."

"But—"

"Shore leave," the boy added importantly.

Lenox looked at him strangely. "Last night?" he said.

The boy pointed upriver two docks. "You can see her there. Not a lick of paint left on her hull. Hard weather down the cape."

Lenox's mind was rushing. "You're entirely certain of this. That the *Matilda* arrived in London last night."

The boy looked at him as if he were mad. "Yes," he said.

Lenox was already racing back to his scull. "Thank you," he said. "Thank you, thank you, thank you."

The boy, standing on the pebbly shore, shouted after him. "Why?"

"It doesn't matter!"

The boy watched as Lenox pushed off. "Well, so long, then," he called. "Thanks for the shilling."

"I owe you another!" Lenox shouted back.

The boy answered, but Lenox had already pulled hard into the river, and he couldn't hear the reply—would never see the boy again, in this life or the next, but he thanked the Lord he had called out to him.

He rowed as hard as he could across the river, and then, having handed off the scull, sprinted home, arriving breathless.

"Mr. Lenox," Mrs. Huggins said sternly, "in Lady Hamilton's—"

Was this how little time the blasted cats had purchased them? "Not . . . not right now," he panted. "Food and tea. To take with me. Five minutes. Graham too. Get Graham."

"I've never—"

He didn't wait to see what Mrs. Huggins had never, but darted back to his room. There was a standing bowl of water, and he splashed himself as clean as he reasonably could in fifteen seconds, soaped his arms and his face, rinsed himself, and shoved himself not very carefully into a suit.

He ran back out into the front hall. Mrs. Huggins—whatever her faults, she was a marvel of a housekeeper—was waiting with a little metal holdall. "Soft-boiled eggs, toast, beans, coffee, sir," she said.

"Thank you. Graham?"

"Out, sir. I can—"

"He'll find me at the Yard or they'll tell him where I am. For God's sake, though, urge him to hurry."

Finally her employer's seriousness seemed to have penetrated

Mrs. Huggins's disapprobation, and she looked concerned. "Are you quite all right, sir?"

"Yes—only a damned fool, a blind fool. You'll tell him?"

"I shall, of course, sir."

Lenox hailed a taxi and ordered it to Scotland Yard. It took an infuriatingly long time to get there; his mind was too busy to formulate ideas; the omnibus ahead of them wouldn't move; his heart raced.

When he had become a detective, he had often imagined moments like this, the great resolution, the clues at last slotting together.

But then why did he feel ill?

Why did he wish he were anywhere else?

He arrived at the Yard and sprinted past the porter, Sherman, who called an indignant word after him. He ran up to Mayne's office, and here, too, ignored the protocol of the building and flung the door open without asking.

Mayne was sitting there with Exeter. He looked at his visitor— who was no doubt slightly mad looking—and said curiously, "Lenox?"

"I believe I know who the victims are."

"How could you possibly know that?" Exeter said.

Lenox looked at him angrily. "Perhaps it's because I'm a detective."

"Who are they, then?" Mayne asked him.

"Will you come to Corcoran and Sons with me?" he asked.

Mayne looked dismayed. Lenox saw the calculation in his mind: the case was closed, nobody had come forward to protest the anonymity of the women, and he, the commissioner, was too important to spend his mornings running down false trails.

On the other hand, Lenox was his responsibility.

"Exeter can go with you," he said.

Lenox looked at the large inspector warily. Suddenly there was the sound of the door behind them. It was Field, the Yard's most famous inspector; evidently he had come on another matter, but he looked at them curiously.

"What's this quorum for, then, gents?" he said. "We're only missing Sinex, it would appear."

That word—"gents"—was very pointedly a derogation of Mayne and Lenox. Lenox ignored it. "I know who the women in the water were," he said.

"Who?"

"I'm going to Corcoran and Sons to find out."

"I'll come," Field said mildly.

Lenox looked at Mayne. "Do you remember the arrest the Yard made on the morning of the Ophelia murder?"

"Nathaniel Butler? We let him go, the poor sod. I hope he's gotten his job back."

"Not Butler."

Exeter looked at Lenox curiously. "Johanssen? The Swede?"

Lenox nodded. "Of the *Matilda*." Internally he cursed himself for his lazy little act of showmanship in getting them to release the sailor. "Scruffy beard. Tall. A bit worse for his night out?"

"What on earth does this have to do with the victims?" asked Mayne.

"The *Matilda* arrived in London last night," Lenox said. "She had been abroad for eighteen months before that."

There was a silence in the room.

"Pond had a conspirator," said Field.

Mayne stood up. There was no question of his staying behind now. His face was black with anger. "Wilkinson," he shouted to the outer office, "order my carriage ready!"

CHAPTER THIRTY-NINE

Blackstone, the foreman of the warehouse at Corcoran and Sons, was busy supervising the transfer of a set of enormous teak boxes from Ceylon into crates to be shipped around England.

They hailed him, and he came over, touching his hat. "Did these arrive on the *Matilda*?" Lenox asked.

"They did, as a matter of fact." Blackstone looked at him curiously. "Black tea. Teak keeps it from moldering. How'd you know?"

There were dozens of people around, and Lenox scanned their faces. He was looking for the one he had seen twice: the ghost, as he thought of the fellow, whose blurred image he still couldn't quite distinguish in his mind.

On the way over, he had described to Mayne, Exeter, and Field the young rope maker's mate, newly arrived back in London.

"I got it right, then," Exeter had said in the carriage.

"Eh?" Lenox had replied.

"I had him. I arrested Johanssen."

Lenox tried to keep a straight face. But really. Gotten it right! It was true—but for every wrong reason, through blindest luck!

Yet Exeter had a point, and Lenox was a fair-minded person. "Yes," he said. "You had your hands on him."

In the warehouse now, Lenox had just one question to ask. The others had pressed him to tell them who the victims were, but he would tell them only that he had a suspicion.

He could feel the ropes tightening, the steps of his logic perfect, as locked into each other as the workings of a clock, if he could just get the correct answer to the question he had.

"You have worked here quite awhile?" he said to Blackstone.

"Nineteen years."

"Did you ever see Eliza Corcoran?"

The burly steward looked at him oddly. "Not more than five hundred times."

"She was here often enough, then."

"Yes. Why? Has Mr. Corcoran drug her home yet?"

"What does she look like, Miss Corcoran?"

"Mrs. Leckie now, you mean," said the burly steward. "She's a woman like most others, I suppose. Dark hair, curly. A young woman that looks like a young woman."

"Was she overweight?"

"What kind of question is that?"

"Answer it, please," said Mayne.

"No, not overweight. Slimmer than most girls her age, I would have said."

Lenox felt a wash of despair.

They had gotten everything wrong.

Lenox glanced at Mayne to see if this had registered with him yet, but he didn't think it had.

Suddenly he noticed that Exeter wasn't among them. Mayne had been just to Lenox's left, and Field and Exeter behind them. "Where did Exeter go?" Lenox asked Field.

"To inquire with Mr. Cairn whether Mr. Johanssen had been seen lurking about the place," Field said. "The senior manager here, apparently. Thought it would be good to get a head start."

Lenox felt the blood drain out of his face. Somewhere in the distant back part of his mind he marveled at that; he hadn't known it was more than an expression.

"Oh," he said. "He didn't. Tell me he didn't. The bloody fool."

He turned and sprinted toward the back right corner of the warehouse, where the stairwell to the upstairs offices was.

Behind him, after a moment, he heard Mayne and Field give chase. He looked back and saw Blackstone staring after them—in his mind, Lenox could already hear him telling his mates in the public house, that evening, how inexplicable it had all been.

Little did he even know.

"Lenox!" called Mayne. "Stop!"

"There's no time," Lenox called. He was taking the steps two by two.

"Exeter and Cairn will find Johanssen if he's here," Mayne called.

Lenox stopped for just an instant, looked back with despair, and said, "Cairn *is* Johanssen, Sir Richard. He killed Eliza Corcoran. He killed Jonathan Pond. And he killed another woman—Exeter may be the reason we never know her name."

He turned, ignoring the astonished faces of Field and Mayne, and sprinted up the steps.

"*Cairn?*" Mayne called incredulously toward Lenox's back.

Cairn.

In bearing, entirely different from Johanssen, the sailor. But take away the polished hair, the distracting eyeglasses, the fussy manners, the pedantic voice; add in three days of beard, a few bruises and scrapes, a Swedish accent; and what did you have?

Both were well above average height. Both had white-blond hair, scruffy in one case, slick in the other.

One of them had been present at the death of their Ophelia, Johanssen.

One of them had been present at the death of Jonathan Pond, Cairn.

And the most damning detail of all: he had lied, lied directly, about

Eliza Corcoran's appearance, calling her overweight and fair, when she was shader and dark.

As he flew into the large clerks' room of Corcoran and Sons, it was all coming together in Lenox's mind. Cairn's performance with Pond had been masterly. He must have shot him and then staggered back toward Mayne and Lenox, the picture of shock and distress, before pretending to faint.

The gun had been found a foot or two to the right of Pond's body. Lenox hadn't noticed that right away, and wondered, now, if Cairn had tossed it down the hallway of the records room after shooting him, or had concealed it upon his person and used the ensuing commotion to place it.

Either way, Pond—Pond had known. Lenox could see his eyes now, innocent.

He stopped in the center of the clerks' room. "Where is Cairn?" he called loudly.

Fifteen faces looked up at him. Pond replaced already. He heard Mayne and Field enter behind him. "He just stepped out," one voice piped up. It belonged to a reedy fellow who looked as if he were in his father's suit. "Not a minute or two ago."

"With anyone?"

"Alone."

Lenox whirled around, as if Cairn might attack him.

What he couldn't figure out was *why*, why Cairn had become a murderer. Why he had written the letters. Why he had staged the elaborate scene on Bankside.

And who, too; who the second woman was, if Eliza Corcoran was the first—which she had to be. The timing, the description, they fit Walnut Island too well.

He went to Cairn's office door, which was closed. He took the handle, then dropped it as if it were hot and took a step back.

He swore an oath under his breath. What if Cairn was still in there, holding his revolver?

"You're sure it was Cairn who left?" he hissed at the clerks. "Not a police inspector?"

They all nodded.

Lenox threw open the door and stepped back, half expecting the blast of a gun.

Instead he saw a sight that, in other times, he might have found comic: Exeter was gagged and bound, sitting in a chair, red from all but screaming his head off. Apparently the gag had muffled his hollering, however.

Lenox, Mayne, and Field came into the office, and they immediately began to undo the complex knots binding their colleague. (Not for nothing had Cairn been in the shipping business for two decades. Though he'd had less than a minute, he'd done an expert job. *Was this one called a Turk's head knot?* Lenox tried to recall.)

The clerks crowded in around them. "Blimey," one said.

That about summed up Lenox's own feelings on the matter. He met Exeter's eye—and Lenox saw, for a second time, that he had an enemy in the inspector.

When they had finally worked loose Exeter's gag—no easy task—Exeter spat and swore, then spat again.

He was irate. "Why didn't he shoot me, the coward?"

"The noise," Lenox murmured. He turned back to the clerks. "Has Mr. Cairn taken any vacation recently?"

"His annual trip to the seaside with his cousins," one volunteered. "He goes every spring."

"When was that?" Lenox asked.

They looked between them. "A few weeks ago, perhaps?"

Just when Johanssen had appeared. Lenox understood now that Cairn had taken that time to get into character, grow out his beard, get into a pub fight—become a Swedish sailor rather than a proper English clerk. It was another deception, like his imitation trunk from the *Gallant,* yet another altered appearance.

Brilliant, in its way. No two figures could be more different than Cairn and Johanssen.

Mayne shut the door. "Wait there. Don't move," he told the clerks. He turned to Exeter. "What in the devil happened?" he asked.

Exeter looked caught between anger and sullenness. "I came in and told Cairn about Johanssen being the guilty party. He asked who had cottoned on."

"What did you tell him?" Lenox asked.

"I said we all knew it. I suppose I said that you'd been asking Blackstone about Eliza Corcoran's appearance." The fool. "Then, quicker than you can say jackrabbit, his gun is on me, I'm in this chair, and he's gone."

"What a foul-up," Mayne said, brushing his hair back. "Did he say anything else?"

Exeter shook his head. "No." Then he took it back. "Wait—yes. He said to tell Lenox something, once I mentioned that you were the one who had figured out about Johanssen, and was speaking to Blackstone."

"What?"

"He said he had been tracking us for his own protection and that he knew about—was it—Elizabeth—I believe? That was the name he said, I think."

CHAPTER FORTY

Elizabeth.

It was like this in novels, the desperate chase. Only he hadn't known that it would feel like the worst thing in the world.

Elizabeth lived in Mayfair, and Lenox would have given everything he had, down to his last farthing, his last scrap of clothing, his own life, to be able to cinch the whole of London up for just a brief moment and step, take a single step, to wherever she might be.

There were carriages flying to three addresses at that moment, one (with Exeter, Field, and two constables) to Cairn's, one (with Mayne) to the Yard to muster up constables to search both for Lenox's friend and for the murderer, and one (his own) to Elizabeth's house.

There was also a whistle relay from one constable to the next, which would indicate—seven longs, two shorts, three longs, one short, in this case—whose beat had trouble afoot. But there would be innumerable houses and people on that beat, and no way faster than Lenox's carriage of conveying who exactly, which house exactly, was in trouble.

Lenox had heard his first tales of crime during his schooldays. Back then they were as far from his own experiences as Earth was from Neptune. He came by the stories, which captured him from the start, at the costermonger's. Every Tuesday, the butcher (who could read, which made him a learned fellow by the Markethouse standards of 1837) would sit in front of the costermonger's huge slatted bins of apples and pears and read aloud from the new penny blood. (Why Tuesday? He couldn't recall.) The butcher's fee was a cup of strong tea, which he said helped soothe his reading voice. He would also usually take an apple on his way out, taking triumphant leave of his little crowd of twelve or fourteen, who remained behind discussing whatever they had just heard in a state of chilled credulity.

A costard was what had once, long before, been the name of an apple, after all—still was in some parts—and so it seemed a fair salary from the costermonger.

But Lenox had known in his heart, even then, that he was hearing something only tangentially related to real life.

Whereas now, thirteen years later, nothing could have been so dull, so awful—or so lifelike.

Lord, he hadn't known how sheer physical space—the streets outside his carriage, the crossings, the horses, the people—could seem an enemy, the relentless seconds passing by.

"Can you go any faster?" he shouted up to the cabdriver through the open window. "Knock people out of the way. I don't care. I'll double your fare—double it again—if we get there with haste."

The cabman grunted. "Right."

There was a grievously minute increase in their pace.

He forced himself to think about Cairn. He pulled out his soft leather notebook. He jotted a few words very nearly at random, trying not to look out the window; it was too close to torture.

He wrote down the name, *Cairn*. Then he crossed a letter out. *Cain*.

What a strange mind he found himself in battle against. Clearly those letters to the *Challenger* had been a disguise—the "perfect crime" business was perfect to pin to Jonathan Pond, the quirky, quiet, friendless, "literary" clerk, as easy for a detective's imagination to sketch in as you could please.

And yet it was funny, Lenox sensed even more strongly Cairn's own personality in the letter. They would discover his motive for murdering Eliza Corcoran, but this second play on a name (*pond*erous, *Cairn*) made Lenox feel sure that in part the letters were *true*—that he did want to commit the perfect murder.

What had set him off after decades of scrupulous work? He must have been very bright to ascend to his position at Corcoran and Sons; the letters seemed to Lenox to contain some distillation of all that effort, a will to be seen, to be admired. He was a man who felt underappreciated. He had drawn and erased those straight lines himself.

If the first victim was Eliza Corcoran . . . perhaps the motivation was love? Money? She was her father's heir, after all.

But then who was this adventurer, Mr. Leckie, then? How did he come into it?

It was all so extremely confusing, and he was trying to be calm, and if she were harmed, if she were harmed . . .

"Hurry, hurry," he muttered, looking through the window.

They crossed the bridge. He thought about hopping out here and running. It would have taken him eighteen minutes, probably, perhaps twenty. But he knew that the carriage, glacially slow as it might seem, would take only seven or eight.

He forced himself to look at his notepad.

It was the second body that remained puzzling. He read over his notes twice, three times.

1) **Why so many flowers?**
2) **Why the shilling?**
3) **The shoes**
4) **Leckie? Corcoran? Gretna Green?**
5) **Why the door, rather than another trunk?**
6) **Cairn/Johanssen at the scene.**

He studied this until he thought he would go cross-eyed.

But then, suddenly, in one of those strange moments of London traffic, the way before them cleared, and the horse pulling the cab broke out into a brisk trot, its driver, conscious of his imminent pay-day, whipping the beast along.

At the end of Elizabeth's block, Lenox leapt from the carriage. He threw a pound note at the driver—infinities beyond the fare—and took tearing up the street.

He arrived at her door and banged it as hard as he could, terrified of what he would find.

Their young butler, portly and dignified, answered the door. He knew Lenox well, and greeted him without any apparent surprise. "Hello, sir."

"Is she here? Lady Elizabeth?"

"No, sir. Her Ladyship is out upon a social call, and will be through lunch."

"Where? Has anyone been here?"

The butler looked puzzled. "Been here, sir?"

Lenox could have wept. "Yes, been here! Been by! Asked where she was!"

"There was a telegram for her, sir. I directed the messenger on to the duchess's, being as it is so cl—"

But Lenox was already flying down the steps three at a time.

The duchess's house was two blocks over. He had never run harder. Somewhere in a far, far part of his mind, he knew that his fate hung in the balance during this run. It would last a minute or so; it would be the last minute in which he didn't know whether Elizabeth, the woman he loved, would be the third woman in the water. If she died: no, it was impossible to think about.

But impossible not to imagine, too, as he ran up the crowded pavement along Bond Street, attracting looks from everyone he passed, skipping nimbly among them.

Whether she died or lived, he would never marry. That he knew.

If she died—a lifelong grief, a life only of atonement to her. He didn't know (he turned the corner to the duchess's) whether that would mean giving up detection, or dedicating himself to it completely.

And then, as he came within forty paces of the duchess's wide, amiable town house, two things happened.

The first was that he suddenly knew—his brain working behind his back—who Cairn's second victim was. His list had told him.

The second was that he knew—knew—that Elizabeth was dead.

He stopped at the door. There was a great welling in his chest, which would be there forever now. He thought of his father—how much his father loved Elizabeth, how disappointed he would be in Charles—and thought of her, herself, her soft brown hair, her slim waist, her long fingers, and felt filled with a despair unlike any he had ever known.

He would murder Cairn.

He took the steps two at a time and banged this door now.

A housekeeper answered. "Yes, sir?" she said.

"Is she—here?" he gasped.

"Her Grace, sir?"

"No, no. Lady Elizabeth."

And then,

a miracle,

there she was. Herself.

She emerged into the hallway with a look of curiosity in her eyes. "Charles?" she said.

He was still breathing heavily, and could barely get the words out. "Elizabeth. Good Christ."

She looked alarmed. "Charles, what is it?"

"Go inside, go inside." He shoved his way in, closing the door behind him. "Go."

"Charles, what's happened?" she asked. But he was in such a state—bewildered, relieved—that all he could do was stare at her. He took her hands tightly in his own. "Charles, that hurts."

"I thought you might be—might be harmed," he said.

"Harmed?"

And then he laughed, giddily, released from himself. Well; none of it mattered now. She was safe. And inadvertently, before he knew it, he called her the name that she had used throughout their childhood together. "Jane," he said. "My goodness. You're safe."

He expected a rebuke, but he didn't care. In Lord James Gray's family, their pride in their royal ancestor was such that the name Elizabeth was sacred, and when they had learned that it was Jane's middle name, that had been her betrothed's one request, that she might adopt it.

But instead of reprimanding him, she smiled, faintly worried but with her sense of humor there, present as it almost always was—a part of why he loved her.

"Lady Jane, you mean," she said, and switched their hands so that hers were holding his. "Not Jane anymore, Charles, but Lady Jane, if you will not call me Lady Elizabeth."

CHAPTER FORTY-ONE

I t was around noon the next day, and Mayne was staring at Lenox as if he had two heads. After a long moment, he said, "Repeat that once more."

"I—"

"No. Wait. Wilkinson!"

This bark brought forth Sir Richard's secretary, as dapper as ever in a suit of lawn. "Sir?"

"Where would we have the Ophelia's body?"

Lenox observed that even Sir Richard, in this moment of extremity, had resorted to using the press's nickname. "In Heathgate, sir. There is quite a backlog of corpses."

"Was it not put forward to the front of the queue?" said Sir Richard angrily. "I asked that it be."

Wilkinson looked pained. "The coroners have quite a latitude, as you know, sir, and there are—"

"Asinine. Completely asinine. Never mind. It will take fifteen seconds to prove or disprove Mr. Lenox's theory. Tell them in no uncertain terms to pull the body out. We will send someone along very shortly."

Here he gave Lenox an irritated look. Youth, Lenox knew, was a state of being perpetually embarrassed; he had thought that perhaps he had grown past it, but for the moment he sat as if under his headmaster's gaze.

Wilkinson nodded crisply and left, and Mayne asked Lenox, again, to repeat his theory.

Inspectors Sinex and Field were currently at the apartments of Eliza Corcoran and of Theobald Cairn, respectively, to see what they could discover. Cairn himself was still on the loose. As for Lady Elizabeth Gray—Lady Jane, as Lenox had briefly received reprieve to call her— she was under heavy guard on a floor of the Savoy Hotel. She was the daughter of an earl, the daughter-in-law of another, and the wife of a future third; there were constables lining the halls. It was only a miracle that the Queen hadn't dedicated a regiment.

Similar notice—and similar, if lesser, protection—had been extended to the families of all those who had investigated Cairn, since he had proved that he had investigated the vulnerabilities of the men investigating him. Would it be a surprise if he went after Field's family?

Lenox did wonder if Cairn had actually intended Elizabeth harm, or if he had merely been buying time, sending Lenox, at the least, off on a chase. The telegram to Elizabeth had merely said FRIENDS WILL BE WATCHING YOU, hideously. Sent in at Waterloo, the train station closest to Corcoran and Sons.

Which in no way meant that Cairn had boarded a train. The return address might be merely another sleight of hand, from a murderer who had shown himself adept at them over and over, disciplined, ingenious, and elusive.

The Ophelia's disguise, if Lenox's hypothesis proved correct, would be Cairn's most unusual of all.

"My theory is simple, I suppose," said Lenox in the level lie of a voice that he had used during his most nerve-racking tutorials at Balliol. "Five or six weeks ago, Cairn learned some piece of information to his disadvantage, involving the firm. Who knows if he had been of a violent temperament before then? It would not surprise me.

Nor would it surprise me if the madness was always there, but has only cracked open now.

"His first victim was Eliza Corcoran. That seems very clear to me from his lie in describing her looks and from the timing of her disappearance. I don't know if there is a fellow called Leckie, or if he was another of Cairn's inventions. What I do think I know is that she was the woman in the trunk marked G957 that washed up on Walnut Island, and which Cairn designed to look as if it had belonged to the HMS *Gallant*.

"His second deception was the letter." Lenox paused and took a deep breath. "And here we come onto the shores of speculation, sir."

"Yes, I should say we do," Mayne retorted, not happily.

"Under my theory of the matter, the second woman was, as I have said, Eliza's father. George Corcoran."

There was a long silence.

This was the fifteen-second test to which Mayne had referred. "There were perhaps a dozen of us who examined her."

"And because of the letter, all of us were anticipating a woman— a woman, Sir Richard. The letter was very clear upon that point."

"She had long dark hair."

"Did you examine it *closely*?" Lenox asked. "I acknowledge that I did not."

"No," Sir Richard admitted. He looked tired. He had the whole constabulary under his supervision, a dozen other irons in a dozen distant fires.

"Moreover," Lenox said, "the body was bedecked in flowers— absolutely covered, head to toe."

"At the time you thought this was a poetic gesture."

"Yes, indeed. But it served a practical purpose. It covered the corpse's body entirely—superfluously, layer upon layer of flower. We all remarked upon that."

Mayne was looking away from Lenox, through the window at

Whitehall. "The face did have very heavy white makeup on it, didn't it," he murmured at last.

Lenox nodded, encouraged. "An inch thick. The brilliance of it from Cairn's perspective—well, he is fiendishly brilliant, I think, sir. The second murder was brilliant in three ways. In the first place, the disappearances of a twenty-year-old daughter and a fifty-year-old father would be very different from the investigation of two women of indeterminate age.

"In the second, his use of the river in the first murder meant that he could place the body within a stone's throw of Corcoran and Sons, and we would assume that it might have come from anywhere along the river at all."

Mayne nodded. "You were always agitated about the dryness of the body and the bier."

"And third," Lenox said, "Cairn, as the firm's senior manager, controlled the outflow and inflow of all information about the Corcorans. He could have placed them in Scotland for the next six weeks without any trouble, as far as the employees and suppliers and traders were concerned. He had been at the firm for ages. His work was beyond reproach."

There was a knock at the door. It was Inspector Field, buttoned up to his beard as usual, looking grim. "Come in," Mayne said.

Field was holding a bundle of papers. "We were deceived. Jonathan Pond did not live with Mrs. Hutchinson."

"What?"

"We have discovered that it was Cairn himself who rented that room. Every last shred of evidence in it, the whole case against Pond, was planted there by him. Pond's real rooms are in Vauxhall."

"The landlady said that he rented the room only a month ago," Lenox murmured. "And that she barely saw him."

Field nodded. "We found the address at Cairn's. Two of my constables immediately went to Vauxhall and discovered a great deal of correspondence with Eliza Corcoran. She and Pond have been secretly engaged for some time. In the second-to-last letter he received, she expressed some fear about her father's reaction, but her last letter is overjoyed. Her father was delighted and had promised that the whole business would be Pond's."

"He was the third victim, then," Mayne said. "The letters did promise a third murder."

Lenox nodded shortly. He had not forgotten looking into Pond's eyes as the young clerk died. "Yes."

"Field, come in. You may as well hear this theory."

Field looked as if there were few things on earth he wanted less than to hear a twenty-three-year-old cub's theory about a murder, the focus of decades of his attention. But he came in and sat down.

To his credit, he believed it much more quickly than Mayne. "Makes sense. You'll recall that the elder Corcoran was described to us as very slight and thin, under five feet six inches. A wig would do for the hair. We never questioned that it would be a woman.

"Meanwhile, there were enough clues that if we *did* associate the murder with Corcoran and Sons, we would immediately find Pond. The spectacles. The letters in his desk. The rented room, obviously. Cairn must have been able to mimic his handwriting."

"All these clerks are fairly able in that respect. Wilkinson does my own hand to a fineness." Mayne sighed. "But what if we had never found Pond? Eventually the Corcorans would have been missed."

"Easy," said Field. "Pond kills himself and leaves a note in his own hand—in his rented room."

Mayne nodded slowly. "Now the question is how to find the bastard, I suppose."

Field winced. He was known to be very religious. Mayne put up a hand, apologizing. "Anyhow," said Field, "Lenox, you must be congratulated."

Lenox felt himself flush. "Thank you, sir."

His skepticism had fallen gratifyingly away. "I think it's the fourth finest piece of detection I've seen."

"What are the first three?" Mayne asked Field.

"Oh, those are mine," Field said mildly. "But the boy is only twenty. And he started out with the disadvantage of going to Oxford. In time he'll overcome it. Hang on to him, Sir Richard."

CHAPTER FORTY-TWO

Lenox and Graham were up very late that night. It wasn't for any particularly exigent reason; they were merely untangling Cairn's methods and motivations to their satisfaction, going over the same facts again and again.

"Think of his deceptions. Not one of them was bad."

It was around midnight. Graham—who had spoken these words—had dropped the "sir" from the end of his sentences an hour or two before, and even loosened his tie.

"No." Lenox ticked them off with his fingers. "The stencil for the *Gallant*. The letters—giving us the date of the second murder, telling us that it would be a woman, ensuring that we thought his motive merely vainglorious, not practical. The flowers, the shilling, the white makeup, the rented room full of proof against Pond—proof just subtle enough, such as the flowers in the Bible, to make the investigators proud of their discovery."

"The performance as Johanssen. It was quite brilliant to take a vacation and become another person, briefly."

"The performance as Cairn!" Lenox remarked. "Never would I have suspected that rough-and-tumble sailor, just out of a drunken brawl, as living within seven post codes of the fussy and well-dressed senior manager at Corcoran and Sons. Merely as an *actor* he did so well."

Mrs. Huggins, who, to her credit, had stayed stolidly up with them, came into the room. One of the cats trailed her. "Would you like me to freshen your tea?" she asked.

"Oh, heavens," said Lenox, standing. "I'm so terribly sorry, Mrs. Huggins. No, it's still warm—no, please, retire for the night. Take the morning off. We've only lost track of time. Unforgivable to keep you up so late."

"Not at all, sir," she said.

"Are the cats—they've had milk, and all that kind of thing?"

She looked at him as if this were a risible question, but said, "Yes, sir, they have been fed."

"Oh, good. Good."

"If that will be all, sir?"

"That will be all."

It was not close to all for Graham and Lenox, however, and not much later it was Lenox who went to the kitchen to boil more water for their tea leaves.

He was in an old school sweater full of holes. A part of him was still vibrating with the joy of Field's compliment of him in Mayne's office; another part still, residually, anxious about Elizabeth, though he knew logically that she was safe; and in still another he was thinking only of his father.

"What about the strangulation, sir?" Graham asked when Lenox was back. His formality had returned during Lenox's brief absence. "Why feign it?"

"To make it seem like a crime of passion? Wouldn't you think? To match the letter."

Graham frowned. "Yet in the Walnut Island case, it really was strangulation."

"A young woman," Lenox said. He winced. "Perhaps Cairn didn't fancy the risks of a confrontation with Corcoran, and resorted to poison, but wanted the methods of murder to match."

"Possibly," said Graham.

Lenox frowned. "He must have been days in making the plan, though, because he had the clothing of a sailor, and the beard, too. His hair was all fallen about."

Graham nodded slowly. "If Corcoran really did hire a private investigator—"

"Another skillful deception!" said Lenox. "This whole Leckie business."

"But what would he have said when the investigator returned?"

Lenox shook his head. "It doesn't matter. He helped Corcoran hire the investigator."

Graham nodded wonderingly. "Good Lord, the effort and expense."

"He was well paid for many decades, and a bachelor. He evidently staked everything on these murders. The question is *why*," Lenox said. "That is what I still don't understand."

"What I still don't understand," said Graham, "is how someone so methodical could have mentioned the *Matilda*!"

"It was his only error. Listen—I've no doubt it was a jarring morning for him. He had adopted the character, but it must have been a near miss with Nathaniel Butler, if Cairn was discovered close by enough to be detained. For all we know, he actually intended to push the body on the board into the water and was more or less caught in the act.

"Anyhow, he would have had the *Matilda* in the back of his mind, given that she was expected soon with a shipment of their wares. He was caught, and he blurted it out."

"Mm."

"And I let him right off the hook, didn't I," said Lenox bitterly. "What I have learned, above all, is to examine every body carefully when one has the chance. At least I shall take that knowledge forward."

In the next hours, they went on discussing the case. Graham speculated that perhaps Cairn had some reason to believe that if Pond and Miss Eliza Corcoran never married, he stood some chance of taking over the business himself.

Long service, after all.

But could a man's character remain hidden for so long? Thirty long years of work—and then the sudden, brutal outburst of violence, as calm as a bank deposit, as carefully plotted as a trip to Asia.

The next morning, as the search for Cairn continued all over London, Lenox went to see Lady Jane—Elizabeth, as he knew he must call her—at the Savoy.

She had friends surrounding her. One of them was her husband's cousin Mrs. Edward Taylor, a young lady of sturdy appearance, whom Lenox had met many times. "Well, here is the hero of the hour," she said.

Her tone was not kind. "How do you do, Mrs. Taylor?" said Lenox.

"Would you care for a cup of tea?" Elizabeth asked him, far more solicitously.

He rubbed his eyes. "Indeed I would, if you could spare it. I was up very late, and up very early."

"The price is your story," Elizabeth said, rising to fetch a teacup from the sideboard of the hotel room herself. "All the papers will say is that the London police are in hot pursuit of an anonymous senior shipping manager named—what was it, Cousin?"

"Theobald Cairn," said Mrs. Edward Taylor without hesitation.

Lenox raised his eyebrows. "There are details of the story that I'm not entirely sure are quite right to repeat in mixed company."

He had been to the Yard that morning: the second victim, the Ophelia, had indeed been male.

If there was a single sentence designed to elicit Mrs. Edward Tay-

lor's sympathetic interest, it was this one, however, and soon Lenox
was telling them the entire tale, beginning to end.

"Good heavens, Charles," Elizabeth said when he had finished. "I
must say, I think you're brilliant."

"I've always thought so."

She smiled. "Stop that."

He smiled in return. He was grateful to Cairn in this one respect,
perhaps—that the events of yesterday had returned his relationship
with his childhood friend to its normal footing. "Only joking, of
course."

"What a glorious beginning to your career."

Lenox shook his head. "I don't know that I shall continue as a
detective, as it happens."

"No?" said Mrs. Edward Taylor.

He thought about Pond's face, and the brutal infinite twenty minutes when he had thought Elizabeth dead, and the ugly reality of seeing
a body, a corpse, and shook his head once more. "No. I think my first
case will be my last. There is a good deal of traveling I would like to
do. Perhaps when I return I will have some idea of how I might most
profitably use my days."

"You won't go immediately?" said Elizabeth.

"Oh! No. No, not until—not for some while." She looked at him,
understanding as well as he did what he had been going to say, or
what he meant, anyway, about his father. "Anyhow, I tell a lie. I have
another case, and there is a certain Mr. Rupert Clarkson whom I
intend to call upon this morning."

"Who is he?" asked Mrs. Edward Taylor, frowning. "Do I know
that name?"

"I doubt your circles overlap, ma'am," Lenox said, taking a sip of
his tea. "An unrelated matter."

"You will have to postpone your travels until this Cairn villain is
caught," said Elizabeth's cousin.

"The Yard have that well in hand." Indeed, they had been all through Cairn's rooms, and were interviewing his sister this morning. All the ports were alerted to his appearance. "My own utility is at its end."

"That can never be true of a capable man," said Mrs. Edward Taylor very finally, with the pomposity of a person for whom cliché is the only real wisdom.

"No," said Elizabeth stoutly. "That is true."

She was so young—nineteen!—and yet Lenox, several years her elder, and until the fall before having, out of habit, thought of her as of very nearly belonging to a different generation, looked at the wisdom and the intelligence in her face, and renewed his word to himself. He could not marry her;

well, he would not marry;

and he would not be a detective;

the price was too high, this feeling too sickened for all its exhilaration;

and he would go to Lenox House and spend as much time with his father as he could;

and he would write down every minute detail he could remember about their trip to Russia;

and then he would travel;

except that now, before all that began, before he could begin not marrying and not detecting and writing down and traveling the far reaches of the earth and being a person, a real live adult, he would go and see about Rupert Clarkson.

CHAPTER FORTY-THREE

A letter arrived at the *Challenger* that afternoon and was published that evening. The hue and cry went up all across London, and Lenox first learned about it as he passed a newsstand, going home from seeing Clarkson.

The letter was different in tone from the previous two, though it bore a similarity to them, too.

31 May, 1850

Sirs,

Few people know the world's shipping passages more intimately than I do, despite never having ventured outside of England myself. Now, it would appear, is the moment to take advantage of that knowledge; by the time this letter reaches you, I shall already be far from these shores.

Nevertheless, I wish to convey three small truths.

1) Since the game is up, I may as well tell you that my aim— and nobody could have come closer!—was to take possession of the firm of Corcoran and Sons. I wrote George Corcoran's will myself, knowing his hand as well as my own; I was to be vested as 51 percent owner in the event that his daughter was deceased at the time of his own death, with various family members receiving the remainder. (To aspiring criminals reading this: Be just avaricious enough, and no more.) It was the least reward I had earned through twenty-eight years of scrupulous service. Scrupulous acting, I may add. Pond's suicide (attributable, as I envisioned it, to the madness of having Eliza reject him in favor of her father, which would have accounted for his anger at both of them) would have been the ideal coup de grâce. Alas—the world loses a work of art, in losing my crime.

2) *In that light, it is some comfort that the crimes remain, if I say so myself, perfect. My previous crimes, which you will never discover, were perfect, too—but they were less challenging, since they did not involve my own acquaintances.*

3) *Any attempt to trace my whereabouts will result in a direct attack on my pursuers and their families. This I take as my personal insurance policy against the absurd society which would put a mind as brilliant as mine to such inadequate use.*

Yours very sincerely,
Theobald Cairn

Graham, who had come along to see Clarkson, also had a paper. He and Lenox finished reading at the same time. "That is our man," Lenox said. "What do you make of it?"

"I think he is a very brilliant and a very mad person, sir."

"As do I." Lenox stood, ruminating, on the corner. It was early evening, the trade in the street quiet and amiable. "That phrase—'my previous crimes'—gives me a chill. I wonder which bodies are buried where."

Graham nodded, unsettled as Lenox rarely saw him. "Yes, sir."

"If this is our introduction to the profession, I suppose we had better see the ugly parts of it right at the outset."

"I suppose so, sir."

Their walk home took them across the river. Around the curve was Bankside; to the west, a ways, Walnut Island.

How sordid it all seemed.

There had been bridges across the Thames for two thousand years or so. The first one had been built by the Romans, who had asked themselves what they should call it, and replied, very sensibly if perhaps not with the keenest sense of creativity, London Bridge.

It had been rebuilt and half-rebuilt fifty times since then. Its towering two-tiered presence was visible off to their right. Beneath them were various small craft, traveling the river; a fishing boat with its nets out, a junk collector, a shallow little flat-bottomed skiff upon which two boys were entertaining themselves. The water was dark, both always still and always moving.

Lenox struggled to step back from the case, to assess his role in it. Was this it? Was Cairn to go unpunished? He felt disgusted with himself. The torment of it was that Exeter was quite right—if not for Lenox's arrogant little on-the-spot scraps of detection, they might have hauled Johanssen in.

As if reading his mind, Graham said, about three-quarters of the way across the bridge, "It occurs to me, sir, that the police would have been unlikely anyhow to hold Johanssen—Cairn—at Newgate for very long."

"How's that?"

"In the first place, I suspect he might have told them that he saw Nathaniel Butler, the clerk who discovered the body, committing the murder, sir."

"But the *Matilda*."

"Yes. I was getting to that, sir. He was playing the inebriate, at the time, and at that very moment a ship called the *Mariah* was docked nearby. She was due to depart that day on a one-month voyage."

"The *Mariah*."

"I looked through the old naval gazettes this morning. There are two able seamen upon her lists named Johanssen. Brothers, no doubt."

Lenox stopped. "My goodness."

"Yes, sir."

"He meant the *Mariah*. He only misspoke."

"Precisely, sir. No doubt the *Matilda* had been on his mind."

"If he had merely said the *Mariah*, we might never have caught him at all."

"Indeed, sir. Or if you had not gone for that row, or if you had not spotted the juggling boy."

They walked on in silence for some time, and then, after they had taken the four steps off the old wooden bridge and into the streets of North London again, Lenox said, "He really was so close to getting away with it, wasn't he."

The thought made him feel ill. "No, sir," said Graham, shaking his head and frowning. "We would have found him."

"Perhaps. You are better at this than I am, you know. You would have found him, I reckon."

Lenox felt a strange absolution in this moment, for whatever reason. It made little sense. Though perhaps it had to do with how far off Field's investigation had been, not to mention Exeter's and Sinex's. (He had suspected Sinex himself, in fact, briefly.) They had at least cleared Jonathan Pond's name.

What a few weeks it had been! Two cases; two resolutions; neither party satisfied.

For Clarkson, whom they had just visited, had cut up pretty rough.

Lenox and Graham had gotten to his rooms in the Strand at around half noon, just as Clarkson was beginning his lunch. He invited them to sit, though not to join him in the meal.

It was a densely packed old place, not musty but accumulative, with old books in Moroccan leather piled high in the shelves (*Quarterly Review of Midlands Engineers* was a typical title), big, dark, heavy furniture, rock samples under glass, compasses, astrolabes.

"How do you find yourself, Mr. Clarkson?" Lenox asked as they sat.

He scowled. "Very unhappy, sir," he said. His facial expression, his close-shaved white hair, and his spectacles gave him the look of a banker in that moment, an Ebenezer Scrooge. "I have not been to Dulwich these three weeks. I find myself quite paralyzed. And by something so trivial!"

"Yes, as five pounds," said Lenox.

"As five pounds!" Clarkson banged a fist upon the table.

Lenox glanced at Graham. "I wonder if you might tell me how you came to live in London," Lenox said. "Did your family set you up in business as an engineer?"

"My family! Ha. No, it was not my family."

"How then did you begin?" Lenox asked again lightly. "It must have been a challenge—and you have ascended very high."

He gestured around him, and Clarkson actually followed his gesture, looking at the spacious room, the expensive paintings on the walls, the footman waiting faithfully nearby to clear his filet of salmon.

"It was a challenge, to be sure," he said. A subtle change came over his face—nostalgia, pride, though both remained contained within his usual curtness. "It was many years ago now."

"Fifty?"

"More. It is funny that you should mention the sum of five pounds, in fact," he said. He chuckled. "That is precisely the sum with which I came to London initially, believe it or not.

"From a very early age, I had a mechanical aptitude, you see. I could have been a farmer, like my father. But even at six, at seven, I could fix the equipment on the farm better than he or any of his hands could. For some time, I went to school in the mornings and worked in the afternoons. But I stopped at twelve. That was when he allowed me to hire myself out to other farms to mend their equipment."

"What was your wage?"

Clarkson laughed, delighted at the question. "Pennies an hour," he said. "It seemed fair enough at the time. We were deep in the country, of course.

"I was always a frugal lad. I had nine elder brothers and sisters—one among them still alive, and she has visited me in Dulwich—and I certainly learned to look after myself. At fifteen, I had saved five pounds. I was determined that I should come to the city. How I even had heard of the city, I am not quite sure—but I was determined."

"Five pounds, was it indeed," Lenox said in a mild voice.

But Clarkson was already in the midst of his reminiscences—and, ignoring this gently pointed interjection, went on with his story, which in the fluency of its telling seemed like one he had told many, many times before.

CHAPTER FORTY-FOUR

I lost a pound almost instantly," Clarkson said. He motioned for his plate to be taken away. "One of the usual deceptions they play—a flashy smart-mouth fellow renting a room that isn't his to rent, disappeared when you return with your things. I may tell you that I wept bitterly over that pound. I had never regretted the loss of a sum of money so much, nor have I since.

"Finally I found a room in a respectable coaching inn. It was ten shillings for six months. A single room. It included breakfast and tea. The landlady, Mrs. Cooley, was one of the dearest people ever to draw breath. The old Chequers, it's gone now, but then everyone in London knew it, had an arcade, and my room let out straight onto a balcony. There were many days when breakfast and tea were all I had to eat, for I was very stringent with myself, but Mrs. Cooley seemed to have a sixth sense when too much time had passed, and would slip me the remains of an eel pie, or a rind of cheese."

"A generous person."

Clarkson nodded. "Surpassingly. At any rate. That was one and a half pounds gone. I hired a suit for five shillings, and some shirts and trousers for another two. Those were mine for a year, with a one-shilling deposit. Then there was the basic expense of keeping alive.

No matter how prudent I attempted to be, the pennies would make their way out of my purse. They kept only two hundred forty to the pound in those days, then as now.

"I wore out my shoes at the engineering firms in town—thruppence, that was, having them resoled, in case you thought I was using a figure of speech—but nobody wanted to hire me. There was one place above all that I longed to work, under a Mr. Carroll Cary. His reputation was the highest, both for the quality of his work and the fairness of his terms to his apprentices.

"Needless to say, he was also the most difficult to gain an apprenticeship under. I aimed my sights much lower—cheap engineering firms. I would have worked anywhere. I had several very close calls, moments when I was nearly hired. I regretted their loss almost as much as I regretted that pound."

Clarkson settled back into his chair as a beefsteak with potatoes came before him. He had a glass of wine, and he swirled it, thinking. Lenox could have stopped him here, but he was curious about the story that had started Clarkson's troubles—his benign troubles—and whether he had found employment under Mr. Carroll Cary.

"Finally I had only eighteen shillings left. I was a month away from the end of my rent, and whatever Mrs. Cooley's generosity, it would not have extended to free board. Understandably! We all have to make our way in this world, gentlemen.

"It was almost the New Year," he went on, "and I don't mind saying that it was hard, very hard, to see the families together, smell the gooses roasting . . . and then, suddenly, I had an idea. I trembled at the very thought of it. I knew I couldn't do it. And at the same moment, I knew I must.

"Old Cary had a granddaughter of whom he was very fond. It was well known—even I, who had no job and had been in London for only five months, knew it. She would play under his desk at work, he took her to the theater—doted upon her.

"I took fourteen of my eighteen shillings to a shop and bought the best materials I could. Solid, gleaming brass. Coils, springs, screws. Then I spent the next nine days in my room, barely leaving. It was freezing—I had no money for coal or firewood—and I worked in my gloves.

"At the end, what I had made fit in the palm of my hand.

"It was a small brass frog. When you turned its lever, it jumped over its own head. It had—oh, I would say seventy pieces or so. When I finished it, I knew I had constructed a masterpiece.

"I left it at Cary's office with a note: 'A gift for your granddaughter on the occasion of Christmas, as well as a sample of my work. If I am not hired soon, I shall return to my father's farm—but I will not regret having made this frog for her. Many happy returns of the season.' And with it, my name and address."

"You got the job," Lenox said.

Clarkson sat back, gazing happily into the past, ignoring his food. "I got the job. Mind you, it wasn't easy—not at all. The wages were fair, but not high, and the hours were endless, nineteen hours a day, sometimes seven days a week. Usually seven days a week, I daresay. Then again, we knew what hard work was, back then."

"And all from only five pounds," Lenox said.

There was a just perceptible roll to Graham's eye, and Lenox had to stifle a smile. "Well, yes," said Clarkson. "Why?"

"Have you told your friends this remarkable story of your origins before?" asked Lenox.

"One or two of them, perhaps," Clarkson said.

One or two of them a day for the past ten years, perhaps. That was the truth.

What Lenox had discovered in Dulwich was that Clarkson's two sets of friends—on the one hand the fishermen of Dulwich, on the other the diners and oenophiles of London—had begun to worry about the old widower since his retirement.

He was old, rich, alone, and in each of these traits had begun to show some genuine eccentricity. Several had asked him independently to serve upon some charitable board or other and been met with a surprisingly violent rebuke that such things were all swindles. He was growing stingier and stingier, too, disputing small bills with friends who had considerably less money than he did.

On the other hand, he had the habit, especially in his cups, of retelling again and again the story of his first tenuous months in London.

"We thought perhaps we would give him a gentle push," one of the gentlemen upon the banks at Dulwich had told Lenox—Joshua King. "A chance to look into his own conscience. We thought it might alarm him just a bit. But then perhaps he needed to be alarmed! None of us need a farthing from him. At our age, though, one of the joys of life is passing down what one has earned. Clarkson has been cutting himself off more and more. Why, he fell out with us here over a lost lure just last week—demanded his penny from me. I didn't have it on me. He left in a fury."

"Evidently he didn't understand the message," Lenox said.

King, the former military man, had looked at him smoothly. "I suppose that you find it in your hands to deliver, in that case."

The conspiracy extended to four or five friends (there was some overlap in the groups) and one insider—though here Lenox refused to press. He was no informer.

At the conclusion of Clarkson's tale, Lenox had sat for a moment, and then said, "I think that perhaps the story of your five pounds has made as strong an impression upon your friends as it has upon me, Mr. Clarkson."

Instantly the engineer looked suspicious. "How's that, then?"

"What I have gathered in my researches is that these—acts of mischief, you might deem them, belong to one of your friends. He wonders if you are perhaps becoming too stingy, too close, in your retirement, and hopes that you will remember how much five pounds once did for you, and what it could do for others."

Clarkson had risen out of his chair before this statement was done.

He was crimson with fury. "Who!" he cried. "Was it Dinkins, that interfering fool?"

"I do not know that name."

"Then who!"

Lenox shook his head very slightly. "That is not my place to say."

"Not your place to say! You took my money!"

Lenox took the two ten-pound notes from the inner pocket of his jacket. He held them up. "I am handing one of these to Mr. Graham, who did most of the work on the case, and whom I would not deprive on account of my own scruples. The other I shall leave here. Please take it in the spirit as your friend's own emoluments. A man of your means and lack of encumbrances could do an immense amount of good with it."

Clarkson was furious—still standing, one hand balled. "You're in league with them," he said.

"I am not."

"Is it King? Lewis? Wassner?"

"Good day, Mr. Clarkson," Lenox said quietly. "There won't be any further envelopes. You may return to Dulwich at your leisure."

As they departed, Clarkson continued to call names after them—insults, too, and Lenox suspected that his client (his final client, perhaps!) would remember him as a bounder.

It couldn't be helped.

Was this what a long, unmarried life meant? He wondered; but the feeling had returned to him throughout the day, recurring again and again more strongly: Elizabeth would only ever be his friend; from this day forward, he would think of her only in those terms; and he would not marry.

It was very easy to make vows at twenty-three, he knew. Still, he intended to keep this one.

As they returned home from Clarkson's, each with the *Challenger* underarm, Lenox and Graham discussed their busy day. Lenox was due to have supper out. They passed an old man wearing a Waterloo medal, the first battle for which all participants received a medal of commemoration. His was no doubt still earning him glasses of ale—perhaps too many of them, judging by the broken veins spreading out from his nose onto his cheeks—and it was impossible not to notice that he lifted one leg as if it were heavier than the other, and to wonder about the noble acts of that ancient day; or if a donkey had run over it two weeks before; and to feel guilty for wondering.

He returned home to find Hugh waiting for him, drinking black tea and reading a newspaper, tie elegantly loosened. "Hullo, old fellow," he said. "Heavens, you've been busy."

"Why are you looking at me as if I had leprosy?" Lenox asked suspiciously.

Hugh grimaced. "It's the newspaper." He tossed a copy of the *Daily Star* onto the coffee table.

Lenox took in the headline as a whole before its words individuated themselves: SON OF SIR EDWARD LENOX LET OPHELIA MURDERER SLIP AWAY, then the subhead, INSPECTOR EXETER HAD COLLARED SUSPICIOUS SWEDE BEFORE INTERFERENCE.

"Interesting," murmured Lenox.

"They're fools. Still I thought I would bring it by—best to hear it from a friend."

Lenox stared at it for a moment and then laughed. "Well! Do you fancy a drink before we go to Lady Wilkes's? I'm going to have a Scotch."

Hugh looked as if there might be a catch coming, but then, hands in pockets, simply shrugged. "Go on, then, whisky and soda as usual." He sighed. "This and the princess returning to Paris in a fortnight—barely aware I'm alive. What a world, Charles. *Lacrimae rerum*, and all that. Not so much soda—yes—top it up with brandy—I suppose we're young yet, we may as well play out the string."

CHAPTER FORTY-FIVE

Lenox's father had an eccentricity, which was that he truly loved to paint fences.

There was a common English belief that every landowner had one such eccentricity. Lenox's friend Bartley was the son of an earl in Nottinghamshire who shaved his lawns—their many, many acres—with a pair of scissors. Just across the county here was a baronet named Bessenger who pleased himself by holding formal wedding ceremonies for his canaries. That was perhaps taking it too far, of course, though in every other respect he was a normal fellow; served in Parliament.

When Lenox arrived home two mornings later, his father was near the gatehouse of Lenox House, no doubt making old Carter, with his stone flask of tea and his morning newspaper, extremely uneasy. Sir Edward had on a smock and was painting the pure black of the wrought iron with delicate precision. Charles saw him first, and noticed the smile of inner happiness on his father's face.

Nearby was a ladder. "Do you need a ladder-holder?" he called out to his father. He had walked from the station. "I offer myself for the post."

"Charles! Yes, by all means. Do you want a paintbrush?"

"Oh, no, I'll leave that to you."

"Yes," said Sir Edward with satisfaction, "I flatter myself I've got it down near a science."

They stayed out until around lunchtime. They reminisced a great deal about their trip to St. Petersburg, which was fresh in both their minds. Lenox's mother, sensing by some maternal magic that he was home—for he had only said he would get a train sometime that day—traipsed down the long avenue after a short while, bringing with her a footman who had three folding canvas chairs and a pitcher of iced lemon. It was a warm day.

"There you are, Charles!" she said. "How is London?"

"Still standing, I believe."

The past few evenings hadn't been entirely pleasant. Lenox could tell from the social gatherings he had attended that the shine was gone off him; he was only a detective, and a failed one at that.

"Elizabeth is at Houghton House, you know," Sir Edward said.

"She mentioned that her father wanted her home until all of this had blown over."

"Yes, I hear he was very firm." The Earl of Houghton was their close neighbor, Elizabeth's—Jane's—father, and one of Sir Edward's close confidants, though their politics were virtually diametric in every respect. "We ought to invite her to dine."

"Naturally," said Lenox.

"Yes, naturally."

His father reached to apply his paintbrush to a high corner—it was a very slender paintbrush, and the black paint superbly glossy; he was particular about his tools—and winced, holding his chest. After only an instant he regained his composure.

That was one of two or three moments of weakness he saw in his father that week. For the most part, Sir Edward was in very good spirits. His mother was, too. It was a truly lovely summer, and people dropped in to play lawn tennis and have tea every afternoon. There were three or four times, when he wasn't expecting it, that his mother embraced him and didn't let go for forty or fifty seconds, laying her head against his shoulder. He felt very wise and old in those moments. Or perhaps it was that he felt very young and very afraid? The difference was so narrow.

When he had been in his old childhood room for five nights, his father told him, at breakfast one morning, that he had received a long letter from Sir Richard Mayne.

"Have you?" said Lenox. "Make him take you to court before you pay anything."

Sir Edward laughed. They were both eating heaping bowls of oatmeal with healthy piles of brown sugar and cinnamon atop their undulating peaks. "He says you are gifted."

"Does he?"

Lenox had been thinking a very great deal about his career all week. "Yes. He laid out the whole sequence of events in the clearest terms." There was a pause. "He mentioned that you have taken a salary, too."

"That is false," Lenox said stoutly. The morning after Cairn's final letter to the *Challenger,* he had gone into the Yard and retired.

"Is it?"

"I was forced to take half a pound a week from them. But I made it clear that I was not willing to continue the practice—and should remain a strict amateur." He shrugged. "Anyhow, I doubt I shall continue in the profession."

"Do you?" asked Sir Edward. "Oh, I don't know. You sound from the letter to have a genius for it. I myself have never had a mind inclined to see hidden patterns. Nor has Edmund, I think."

"Mother has."

"Yes, she is good at puzzles. So is my father, your grandfather," Sir Edward said, smiling. "He was a fearsome chess player."

"I never knew that."

"I don't believe I ever beat him. In fact, I'm sure that I did not, though I have been playing these many years." He smiled at the memory. "Anyhow, Mayne says that there have been developments in the—case, you call it, I believe? He asks me to invite you to call upon him should you wish."

"Perhaps I'll go up for the night, then."

His father frowned. "You still have time for a ride, though? I had thought I might take you to Willingham Wood. I don't think you and I have ridden there together. The view of the country is very beautiful, very beautiful."

Charles's heart leapt with a child's happiness. "Oh no—as to that, I have all the time in the world," he replied casually. "I could even leave it until tomorrow."

Lenox and Graham did take the evening train back to London, however. The next morning, they presented themselves at Mayne's office. A reading of the papers on the way—there were fewer in the country, which had been surprisingly pleasant—showed that Theo-bald Cairn, the perfects, Walnut Island, the Ophelia, Corcoran, all of it remained very much in the news. NOT RECOMMENDED FOR FE-MALE READERS, blared one headline, Lenox presumed because of the discovery that the second woman in. the water had been—a man.

Sir Richard greeted them with solemnity. "How do you do, Charles?" he said.

"I hope you don't think I'm reluctant to show my face," Lenox said. It had been preying on his mind. "I take full responsibility for let-ting Johanssen go."

"I do not blame you. You were the youngest man there by some years and the least experienced by even more." Sir Richard glanced at the door. "Inspector Exeter's limitations are known to me."

Lenox didn't quite know how to reply to that—if he had started, he could have elaborated upon those limitations for a while. Instead, he said, "What new information do you have?"

"Ah! Yes. Well, three pieces, really. First: there was never a Peter

Leckie. He was an invention of Cairn's, it would appear, as we suspected. Cairn must have taken the night train to and from Scotland several times to keep the ruse going.

"Second, Corcoran's will, found in his desk, did indeed name Cairn as his heir. Rather a bright stroke, in fact—let me see—yes, here is the line, 'It is not out of any particular affection that I bear for Mr. Cairn, loyal that he has been, but because the business has been a second child to me, and Mr. Cairn alone knows the strength of will it takes to run.' Rather plausible, in its way."

Lenox nodded gravely. "Just so."

Mayne sighed and looked down at his paper. "We have been looking into his history, his rooms. It all seems rather mild on the surface. But I'm not sure it was. He came to London from his hometown under some cloud—apparently a neighbor's livestock was mutilated, someone Cairn was known to bear a grudge against. Not just killed, mind you, but butchered. Threats written in blood."

"Good gracious." Lenox paused. "Has there been any sighting of him?"

Mayne shook his head. "Here is the circular that is going to every British port."

Lenox looked at the paper, which bore a very good likeness of Cairn, and a description of his disguise as Johanssen. The eyes that looked at him were lifeless—not because they were printed in black and white, but because they were so accurate—and in that moment, he vowed to himself that whether or not he remained a detective, he would find Theobald Cairn. He didn't care if it took twenty years. His first case couldn't end in this irresolution—nor his last. Either way, he was honor-bound. And even as Mayne went on, in his mind, Lenox began to formulate his plan. . . .

"Then there is the third matter. It is a job offer," he heard Sir Richard say.

Lenox stiffened. "I had hoped that I made my feelings clear on—"

"Oh! No, no. I'm sorry. Mr. Graham, the offer is to you. I would like you to come aboard as an inspector as soon as possible. My vision of the department demands men of just your energy and skill."

Graham looked surprised. For some time, he did not speak. "I am deeply conscious of the honor your offer does me," he said.

"I have never been happier to make such a one."

"I must decline, however."

Mayne laughed. The step from service to the position of inspector at Scotland Yard was so profound that he assumed Graham was joking. Then his laughter subsided and he looked uneasy. "Excuse me?"

Lenox looked at Graham, alarmed. "Well, Graham—don't—take time to think about it."

"Yes, you may take your time," said Sir Richard in a slow voice.

Graham shook his head firmly. "I can tell you again that I have rarely been more honored in my life—but my answer is definite. I must decline."

Now Mayne looked baffled. "I see."

"Thank you, sir."

After they had departed, they walked back to Lenox's rooms. Most of the walk consisted of Lenox's reproaches to Graham.

At last they arrived at the door. Mrs. Huggins greeted them. "Mr. Lenox! How pleased I am to see you. There is a list of trifling matters, not more than twenty-three on my list, referring in most cases to the practices of Lady Hamilton's house. I know for a fact that you are not scheduled to do anything this morning."

Lenox looked around wildly for an excuse, until he saw that he had been caught, at long last. He could not decline Mrs. Huggins's demand again.

He followed her toward the admittedly welcome scent of tea and toast. "Now I see it," he muttered to Graham, "how could you have given up all this grandeur?"

CHAPTER FORTY-SIX

London forgets a great many murders, but it did not forget the murder of the Corcorans and Jonathan Pond. This was due in part to the press, and in greater part to Tussauds.

This minor museum had begun several decades before as a waxworks, featuring a modest sampling of historical, literary, and political figures. Only when it opened its Chamber of Horrors had it become the most popular attraction in London. (The madame herself had died earlier in the year, having lived long enough to grow very rich.) Now it contained waxworks of "Cairn," upright clerk, and of "Johanssen," wild-eyed, bearded madman, with blood dripping from his hands and feathers strung—inaccurately—around his neck.

But the showstopper was the re-creation of the Ophelia, laid out upon her board.

"Tell me, how many times have you been?" Lady Elizabeth said.

They were at Houghton House for supper. It was just July. Lenox's father, who had been growing fatigued easily recently, had remained home, and Charles and Elizabeth had a great deal of time to converse.

"Only once."

"Too good for the hippopotamus, but not for this gaudiness," she said, with faux displeasure.

"I didn't have a hand in creating the hippopotamus," Lenox pointed out.

"It would be deeply disturbing if you had." A beat passed, and she burst into laughter. "You should see how wide your eyes just became, Charles!"

"Make your jokes now, because I don't think they will find favor with Lady Deere when you move there in the fall."

She sighed. "You're too right. What a pity. I do love my little house in London."

"Worse things happen at sea," Lenox said.

"I've always wondered what those were."

"Whole ships going down with all hands aboard, Jane, goodness me. And getting eaten by sharks. That sort of thing."

"Oh, yes." She ruminated on this for a moment. "I suppose I had imagined they meant quarrels and running out of water and everything."

"Perhaps you shouldn't join the navy."

"I may not be ready," she agreed. "Elizabeth, by the way, please."

He reddened. "Of course. I'm very sorry."

Down the table, there was a roar of laughter at something her father had said. "Speaking of my house," she said, "there's one for sale next to it. We should be cheek by jowl. How nice that would be."

His heart beat painfully. "On Hampden Lane?"

"Yes, indeed. Finer than ours, in some way. And since we will only be in town for the season, your neighbors would be eligibly quiet."

"I'll come round and look."

"Yes, do." She glanced around to be sure they weren't overheard, and then said, "Tell me, if it's not too intrusive a question, how your father fares."

"Not too badly, taken all in all. He is nearly done with the fence around the sheep pen. A very pretty white."

She smiled. "He painted that last year, I recall. It was quite a comic sight, him in his smock."

This passing statement stilled Lenox's heart. For of course, his father generally painted the fences every three years, and he had painted them all the summer before.

But in two summers he wouldn't be here.

In that moment it hit Lenox with awful force that one day, not too long from now, his father would *not be alive*.

How stupid the thought was. And yet how strong and immediate and vivid in his mind, as if he had missed it before somehow. And yet it was true! How real his father seemed, and soon he would not exist any longer!

Lady Elizabeth noticed the change in his face. She asked if everything was all right.

"Oh! Yes, yes. I was just thinking about all that must happen at sea." He shook his head. "If I do intend to travel, I hope I'm not—well, eaten by a whale, or anything of the kind."

She laughed. "I hope the same for you."

He returned home very late that night, head heavy with champagne. His brother was due at midday. He woke up at around nine o'clock, fuzzy and in a disagreeable mood.

He called for Graham, who came instantly, bless his heart, with coffee, toast, eggs, and a glass of iced water. Lenox took a long sip of water. "A letter, sir."

"A letter?" He took it off the silver tray. Its return address was from a Solomon Amberson. He tore it open and read it through. "I say, Graham, what do you think of this?"

Graham, who had been retreating to the door with the tray, turned back and took and scanned the letter. "An opportunity for employment, sir."

"Yes, it would appear. But did you catch the postscript?"

Amberson was a barrister at Gray's Inn. He had a problem: his housekeeper's son had gone missing. The Yard would not look at the case.

> *Young men run off, they tell us, usually to the army, but I can attest to the young man's steadiness of character and the unlikelihood that he would make such a plan without consulting his mother. He was in training to go into service himself. His mother, who has been in my employ for many years, is frantic with anxiety. I wish to alleviate her worst fears, at a minimum.*

Graham turned the paper over and saw what Lenox had—he was writing, he said, on the advice of his friend Mr. Rupert Clarkson.

He looked at Lenox. "Are you committed to your retirement, sir?"

Lenox thought of the wires he had sent, crisscrossing various nations, in pursuit of Cairn. "Fairly."

"I observe that we have continued our practice of clipping the newspapers, sir."

Lenox frowned. "Don't browbeat me, Graham."

"I apologize, sir."

"Fellow can't have three minutes of peace." He lay back on his pillow, looking up at the alabaster ceiling. "Still, I suppose you could go to London this morning and collect one or two details from Amberson, if you wanted to. Or would that put you out of your schedule?"

Graham looked at his pocket watch. "I could catch the nine fifty, with luck."

Lenox paused. "I suppose you'd better do it."

Graham smiled. "Very good, sir."

"It's not your retirement, after all—it's mine."

"Just so, sir. Would you like the kitchen to send anything else up, sir?"

"Yes, fourteen more plates of food."

Charles finally emerged from his room at a little past ten. His father was in the drawing room, reading the *Times*. "Charles! Long evening?"

"Only averagely long."

"You're in a mood, I see."

He denied this. He was, though—consulting his feelings, he traced it back to the realization that his father was painting those fences for seasons he would never see. It wasn't the kind of thing to know when you had a stomach full of wine; scarcely even the kind of thing one wanted to contemplate sober.

But his father was evidently having one of his good days, for he was very keen to go out riding. Lenox would have preferred not to, feeling tired and heavy. Nevertheless, he consented.

And the exercise actually improved his morning head, that and a great deal of water and sunshine. They rode very hard over the soft summer grass, not speaking for more than an hour. At last they stopped at a different point in the same brook that wended throughout the Lenox land.

"My gracious," said Sir Edward when they had both rinsed off and watered their horses. "What a lovely day. And I think with luck we may miss the rain on our way back, if we move quickly."

"Rain? I don't see a cloud."

"No, but it's coming." Sir Edward looked over at him. "Crump says that Graham has gone up to the city?"

"There's a case he's looking into."

"Not you?"

"I'm retired."

"Ah, of course." He squinted up through the trees toward the sun, his gray hair tidy despite the beads of water in it. He chuckled. "When I was your age, I believed, oh, mightily in the government, I recall."

"Do you not now?"

"I do! I do. I only mean that the young tend to believe very pure things. Nor am I sure they're wrong. The old tend to think they re-member the feeling of being each age, but I doubt they really do."

"Mm."

Lenox's father looked him directly in the eye. "The hardest part of losing a person, Charles, is that grief is only an absence. There is nowhere to go to touch it."

In later years, Lenox would wish that he could have that moment back. But he supposed, too, that at least he remembered his father's words with perfect clarity. That was something.

"You seem very well at the moment," he said.

His father smiled. "Oh! I, yes I'm fit as a fiddle. Race you back, in fact. A shilling on it? Your mother is eager for you to start gambling."

His father had been correct: It began to rain when they were about three-quarters of the way. It was pelting down, kicking up the dirt at the edge of the woods like gunfire. Lenox felt the water stream down his face, though it was still somehow also very warm, the heat lingering in the day.

The freshness of the rain at this time of year was remarkable, wip-ing clean something that was already close to immaculate; a scent, a silvery half-catchable scent, the smell of the living world returning to its full summer greenness, to its memory of itself, of what it had re-become every summer forever, this little green patch renewing itself back year on year through all the infinity of time.

Edmund Lenox, who would soon be its steward, arrived at home just in time to see his father and brother storming up the heath. They rode very closely side by side, father and son, and though it was too far to see their faces, even at this distance, Edmund smiled to see the pure physical joy in both their two bodies; the way that in the most intense moments of being alive, it was possible, lost in living, to forget that one was even alive at all.

TURN THE PAGE FOR A SNEAK PEEK AT
CHARLES FINCH'S NEXT NOVEL

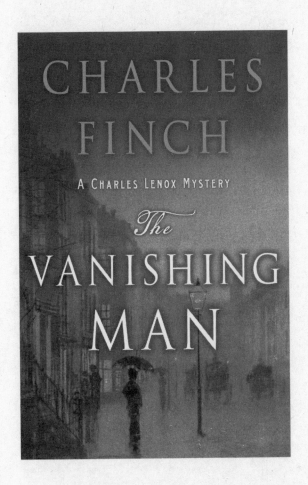

CHARLES
FINCH

A CHARLES LENOX MYSTERY

The
VANISHING
MAN

AVAILABLE FEBRUARY 2019

CHAPTER ONE

Once a month or so, just to keep his hand in the game, Charles Lenox liked to go shopping with his friend Lady Jane Grey.

On this occasion it was a warm, beautiful, windy day in early June of 1853, quiet, the hour of late morning before the clerks filled the streets on their way to take lunch. The two friends were next-door neighbors on a small street called Hampden Lane, and he was waiting on her steps at precisely ten o'clock. At five past, she came out, smiling and apologizing.

They turned up Brook Street together and walked past the little string of streets that ran parallel to their own, talking.

"Why are you checking your watch every fifteen seconds?" she asked after they had gone about halfway.

"Oh! My apologies," said Lenox. "I've an appointment at noon."

"I hope it's with someone you've hired to teach you better manners."

"The joke's on you, because it's with a duke."

"The worst-mannered wretch I ever met was a duke," Lady Jane said thoughtfully. As they crossed Binney Street, Lenox's eyes stayed for an extra moment on a man painting an iron fence with a fresh coat of black paint, whistling happily to himself. "Which one is it?" she asked.

"Out of discretion I cannot say."

"I call that disagreeable."

Lenox smiled. "It's a case."

She turned her gaze on him. It had been a long drought since his last case—more than a month. "Is it? I see."

Though both considered themselves tenured veterans of London now, anyone observing them would have seen two very young people, as young and resilient as the summer day. Lenox was a tall, slender, straight-backed young bachelor of twenty-six, bearing a gentlemanly appearance, and with, whatever Lady Jane said, a courteous manner. He was dressed in a dark suit, hands often behind his back, with hazel eyes and a short hazel beard. There was something measuring and curious in his face. As for Lady Jane, she was five years his junior, a plain, pretty woman of twenty-one, but she had been married for fully a tenth of those living days, which gave her some shadowy right to matronly self-regard. It told in her posture, perhaps. She had soft dark curling hair, a light blue dress, and boots of a tan color just visible beneath its hem.

They had grown up in the same part of the countryside, though until he had moved to London, he had never considered her part of his own generation. By the time he'd noticed that she was, Lady Jane was already engaged.

They neared New Bond Street, where the shops began, as the church clocks chimed the quarter hour.

In truth it was not altogether customary that *she* went shopping quite so often as she did—in most households like Lady Jane's, the task would have fallen to a maid—but it was one of the things that she liked, and Lenox liked it for that reason.

The meeting at noon was continually on his mind, even as they walked and spoke. Lenox was a private—well, what word had he settled on! Investigator? Detective? It was still a new endeavor.

Three years could count as new, when the field was one of your own rough-and-ready invention, and when success had been tantalizingly close at moments but remained mostly elusive.

A duke might well bring it close enough to hold with two hands.

This intersection was vastly busier than their peaceful street. She stopped at the corner and looked at a list.

After she had been studying for a moment, he asked, "What do you need today?"

"Are you going to bother me with questions the whole time?" she said, trying to decipher, he could tell from many years of knowing her, her own handwriting.

"Yes."

She looked at him and smiled. She pointed to the window next to which they were standing. It was a barber's. "Shall we buy you some moustache grease?"

"Oh no," he said, looking at the sign that had inspired the question. "I make my own."

"How economical."

"Yes. Though it puts you in the way of quite a lot of bear hunting."

"Very amusing, Charles. Let's go to the greengrocer's first."

He bowed. "Just as you please, my lady."

They made their way carefully down New Bond Street. They stopped in at every third or fourth shop. Jane was very canny, while Lenox shopped almost at random—at the confectioner, as she was remonstrating with Mr. Pearson over the price of an order of six dozen marzipan cakes she wanted for a garden party she was having, Lenox decided with little prompting to order a cake to be sent to Lady Wenborn, who had invited him to the country for August.

"That reminds me," Jane said to the baker. "I have an odd request to make. Could I have an eggless cake from you? Vanilla. It's for my husband's aunt. I wrote down the recipe she gave me. She's lord-terrified of eggs, I'm afraid."

"Why on earth?" said the baker, so moved by this horrible information that he forgot himself.

"Can you think I have asked her, Mr. Pearson?"

"Blimey," he said. Then amended himself to say, "Blimey, my lady."

She raised her eyebrows. "I know. Imagine being married to her."

"I couldn't," said Pearson fervently, which was true for several different reasons.

Lenox was just about to interject that he knew the lady in question, a larger person, and that he would stand on his head if she had ever refused a dessert in her life. But as he was about to speak, Jane shot him a look and he knew to keep mum.

In the street again, after they'd gone, she explained that she had read a recipe for an eggless cake from Germany and wanted to try it, but didn't dare insult the baker.

"You could have made it at home."

"No—no. He has the lightest hand in London, Mr. Pearson," she said with reverence. "Speaking of tact, how is Lancelot?"

He made an irritated face at her, and she laughed. Lancelot was a young cousin of his, who was on half-term from Eton, and was in the city for two weeks of what his family had optimistically called *seasoning*. "I would prefer not to discuss it."

"Does he still want to come with you on a case?"

"Ha! Desperately."

"Has he gotten you with the peashooter again?"

"I'm busy looking at cheese, please give me some peace."

They ordered their cheese and left, proceeding past the cobblers, then the book stall—*Back in stock, exclusively in all of London, Uncle Tom's Cabin!* a sign declared excitedly—before arriving at the dressmaker. Here Lady Jane went inside alone to have a word, as Lenox skulked outside, feeling like a schoolboy and meditating on the upcoming meeting.

The Duke of Dorset!

He thought of the title with a tightening in his stomach, and then of the letter that contained the entirety of his knowledge of the case thus far: "His Grace has discovered that a possession upon which he places high value is missing. He would appreciate your advice upon its potential recovery."

He checked his watch and saw that it was 11:10. They were near the end of their ramble, and he felt a quick flicker of melancholy. When he was with Lady Jane, he could forget himself. Just at the moment this was a welcome oblivion.

If Lenox's first year in London after moving down from Oxford had been characterized by his tenacious, mostly fruitless search for work as a detective, a profession that didn't really exist, the subsequent eighteen months had been more complex and difficult. In part it was still to do with work—the scorn his profession drew from his peers, as they steadily advanced in their fields—and in part it was to do with the lonely feeling that all around him his friends were marrying, having children even, while he was still by himself.

But most of all, of course, it was to do with the death of his father. At first he had borne up under this misfortune well, he thought— fathers were *supposed* to die before their children, after all, and he knew any number of friends who had been orphaned long ago. But recently, especially in the last six months, his grief had shown itself in odd, unexpected ways. He found himself losing minutes at a time on train platforms and in gardens, thinking; he found himself dreaming of his childhood.

Perhaps it had to do with the fact that they had never been especially close. He had loved and revered his father, Lenox, but his truer friendship had always been with his mother. Had he assumed there would be time, later on in life, for their relationship to grow? His father had been only sixty at the time he died; and for his second son, it had been, surprisingly, not as if some venerable building in London disappeared, which was what he had always imagined, Parliament for instance—but as if London itself had disappeared.

This past year he felt the loss more keenly with each month, not less, and he was sure that was unnatural. For the first time in his life, he woke each morning with a sense of dejection—a sense that, well, here was another day to be gotten through—rather than happiness. He was not sure he could endure it much longer.

CHAPTER TWO

Of all people, Lady Jane perhaps sensed her friend's state of mind most perceptively. When she came out of the dressmaker's, a look that was difficult to read passed across her face, as if she could read his thoughts.

"Everything acceptable?" he said cheerfully.

"Yes, they're still making dresses."

He smiled at the joke, and they resumed their stroll.

A few shops down the long boulevard, they passed the optician. "I really would like a barometer above anything," Lenox said longingly, pausing before a beautiful brass one in the optician's window. "Ah, well."

"What a waste of money it would be," she said.

"They say it is good to have friends who support one's interests," Lenox murmured, studying the barometer.

"You are dead in the center of the largest city on earth. When was the last time you even saw a ship?"

"Ha, there you're going to feel foolish, because I see them nearly every day on the Thames."

"From a cab." She pulled his arm. "Let's go, you can't be late to your duke."

They proceeded down New Bond, talking of this and that. It seemed Lady Jane had a kind word for every person they passed, and it occurred to Lenox that just as he had been struggling to find his feet in his profession, she had perhaps felt something like an impostor in her first years in London—in the very earliest days of her grand marriage, to an earl's first son. Perhaps this was why she shopped for herself, if it gave her a sense of intimacy with their leafy, occasionally intimidating London neighborhood, making of it a community.

Like him, she belonged, from first, to a small place, a village. Now she had made a small place here, in the biggest place. A village of its own.

They spent some discussing the duke. A duke, after all! The whole of the United Kingdom, in its population of thirty million, possessed just twenty-eight such creatures. The least of them was a figure of overpowering consequence. Yet even among them there were finer gradients, and the man Lenox was shortly to see held one of the three or four greatest dukedoms.

It went so, with the nobility:

In the highest rank were the dukes, first in the land beneath the royal family. Not only that, but in their innermost souls not a few dukes and duchesses would have pointed to their lineage (the title of "duke" had come into existence in 1337) and claimed a greater stake in the leadership of Britain than the come-lately family currently chattering around the throne in German accents.

Next came the marquesses, thirty-five of these, their wives marchionesses. Then earls—and there it became complicated, because the title of earl was nearly oldest of all, had originated as long ago as the year 600, historians said, when each shire of England had a *jarl* (Norse for *noble warrior*), which was the reason that in England each earl was still entitled to a small crown; a coronet.

Many earls in England (including Lady Jane's father, Lord Houghton) would not have admitted for a second to being beneath a duke.

In practical terms, too, there were old earldoms of immensely greater importance, to those who parsed these things, than the newer dukedoms.

On top of all that their wives were called countesses, because nobody had ever thought to name them earlesses—which had struck many schoolboys learning these facts as very stupid indeed.

Thereafter it got greatly simpler. Viscounts were next, nearly a hundred of these, common as church mice the poor devils, and some of them just as poor. Finally came barons, last rank in the peerage.

"And there you'll be, at the very top of the heap," said Jane.

"I doubt he'll make me a duke there on the spot," Lenox said.

"Probably just a baron or something."

"I do wonder what he wants. *A possession upon which he places high value.* I only hope it's not his lucky kilt, or something equally stupid."

Lady Jane laughed. "And the laundress has lost it, yes. I could see that being the calamity, I'm afraid."

Lenox himself held none of these titles. Just to confuse things, there was still one title left, and it was here where he did enter the picture; baronets were called "sir," as Lenox's older brother, Sir Edmund, had now been in the eighteen months since their father's death.

A knight was also called sir, but his children couldn't inherit the title. It belonged to a sole person and died with him, a great writer, say, or artist, or dear intimate of the Queen's ninth favorite cousin.

All of these gentry taken together with their families numbered not more than ten thousand, but Lenox, as the second son even of a very old, landed, and honored baronetcy, was as far down the slopes of the mountain of aristocracy from the Duke of Dorset as the thirty millionth Briton, drunk in a ditch, was from Lenox himself.

It was an absurd system—almost nobody believed in it as more than a matter of chance, except for the very old aunts and uncles who kept the genealogies. Yet all of them also, somehow, believed in it implicitly. Strange to be an Englishman.

At last they reached the turn of New Bond Street, where they saw the most dignified shop in the whole row, housed inside a handsome stone building with purple wisteria climbing its face. This was the leecher's—the best leecher in town, people generally agreed, where they boxed the living leeches in white boxes bound with blue ribbon, as if they were marzipan cakes themselves.

Despite this enticement, they passed over the leecher's in favor of their own favorite shop, which was just around the corner, behind a short porch made of plain unsanded boards. Over the door it said nothing but BERGSON in plain white stenciled lettering.

They pushed the door open and saw Bergson himself in a chair behind a broad counter, looking infernally grumpy, and making absolutely no movement to rise and greet them. A duke or an earl or a murderer or anyone on God's green earth could walk in and his reaction would have been exactly the same.

He was a silent old Swede, Bergson, who had spent most of his life in America and then, for reasons known only to himself, come to London and set up an exact replica of the shop he had once owned in the Wisconsin territory.

An exact replica, truly exact, which meant that there were items of no conceivable use to a Londoner, like two-hundred-pound bags of cornmeal (enough to last a long cabin winter, but in lesser demand here) mixed with those of delightful novelty and tireless fascination.

"Look!" said Jane, handling a necklace with a large polished turquoise at the end of two rubbed-leather ropes. "These are the fashion right now."

Lenox looked at it doubtfully, then at the stone-faced Bergson. Some people said he had lost his whole family to a fever, others that he had left America when Wisconsin became a state five years ago, because he had murdered another man over a plot of land once and could not survive a land with laws.

Lenox suspected him simply of being shrewd; it was one of the most popular shops in London, stock replenished just often enough to be endlessly fascinating.

Bergson was not telling—he barely deigned to speak to his customers—but he did half-heartedly sell Charles and Jane a variety of items: bars of pine soap, bags of sifted brown sugar, rough lumps of silver, a woven fishing creel that Lenox thought he would give his brother, Edmund. Lady Jane bought a handsome leather cap for her husband, who was due back from India with his troops in August. Lenox considered a tinderbox before buying Lancelot an arrowhead, silvered with mica.

"See, you do like having Lancelot," said Lady Jane, as they left.

"In fact I do not, but I love Eustacia very dearly." This was Lancelot's mother, Lenox's first cousin. "As for Lancelot, he'll slit my neck with this arrowhead tonight."

She mulled this over. "Better than the tinderbox, then, all things considered, since our houses are side by side. Look, it's eleven-forty, Charles. You had better go and see about your duke."

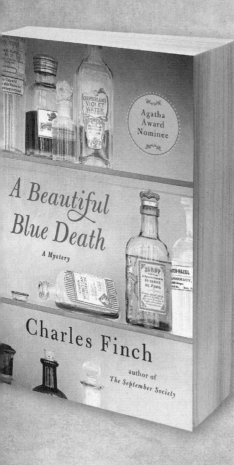